I0678360

PSYCHIC

INFERNO

Page Turner

Psychic Inferno

Psychic State Book 2

Published By: Braided Studios, LLC

https://braided.studio

ISBN: 978-1-947296-08-4

A special thanks to my Patreons

Elan

Alex

Andrea

Annabelle

Hillary

Jason

Kit

Nada

William

Allyson	Katrina
Andrew	Larissa
Anna	Marion
Bionyx	Maureen
Brendan	Nicki
Endre	Pour
Gregg	Rae
Jenny	Riki

For everyone who's been to Hell and back

"If you're going through Hell, keep going."

-often attributed to Winston Churchill, true source unknown

"Okay, Kip," Detective Penelope Dreadful said, "I'm ready to know. Who am I? Who am I, really?" She said the words with as much conviction as she could muster, but her old friend Kip didn't respond for a while. Instead, he sat silently underneath the desert willow and peered up through its branches.

Penny caught her breath, recovering from the sprint that had led her here to Skinner's Public Gardens, the botanical jewel of the Psychic City. A dizzying variety of flora surrounded her, coaxed into improbable life by the machinations of psychic gardeners who willed things to grow where they shouldn't.

As she waited for Kip to answer her question, Penny found herself thinking that she intuitively understood the botanical transplants that surrounded her. She was a transplant herself, after all, with a life she inhabited that felt more like a costume than anything else, something she'd slipped into and maintained. But she had become more and more aware recently that where she lived was not where she had come from. Not where she would normally be. She was a transplant. That much she knew... but from where?

Finally, Kip lowered his head and met her gaze.

"I think that you should sit down, little one," he said resolutely. His tone left no room for question. No room for doubt. Penny did as he said, sitting next to him, close enough that her skin brushed against his. She felt the familiar coldness of his touch. In her experiences as a spirit medium,

Penny had tangled with many undead, but she couldn't remember another who had assumed a form so corporeal as Kip's. He was solid, if lacking the standard body heat one tended to expect from living beings.

Penny wondered again, as she had many times, how many years had passed since his heart had last pumped. Long enough that he probably didn't remember what it was like, she imagined, since he tended to avoid the question, warning her that she didn't want to know the answer.

In general, this was enough to deter her. Kip had never led her astray, after all.

But now here she was, asking a different question he'd warned her against asking. And this time she wasn't about to be deterred.

Kip turned towards her and studied her face. "You've made your mind up, haven't you?" he asked.

Penny nodded.

"There is no unknowing, little one." He seemed to consider this and then corrected himself. "Well, there won't be another one."

"Another unknowing?" Penny asked.

"You knew once. You knew it all. Who you were, where you came from. Once upon a time, it was obvious to you. It was all burned into your memory like the address of the first house you ever lived in. Your parents' names. Your phone number. The kind of information that parents make their children remember in case they're ever separated from them." He shook his head slowly. "But you forgot it all, everything that came before. You wiped the slate clean. You started over."

"I did?" Penny asked.

Kip nodded. "No one has ever been able to stop you, Penny. Not once you set your mind on something."

Penny found herself smiling at this idea, but then she wondered if what he had said were actually some kind of veiled insult. A dig. She frowned as she studied Kip's face for answers, but his expression revealed nothing. In the ambiguity, her own face evened out and she neither smiled nor frowned.

"It is the best thing about you," Kip remarked, "and the worst."

Sighing, Penny realized he had meant it as both compliment and insult.

"I'm surprised you're not calling me Rhea Stygius," Penny said.

Kip let out a cry of alarm. "Where did you hear that name?"

"People keep calling me that," Penny explained. "That weird shapeshifter Change and the head lady at the Warrens of Persephone." She lowered her eyes.

Kip said nothing.

"That was my name, wasn't it?" Penny said. "Before I forgot."

Kip didn't answer.

"You said a long time ago that if I wanted to know something that all I had to do was ask," Penny pressed Kip. "Well, I'm asking you now, and you're not answering."

"That's because it's hard to go back on a promise," Kip explained.

"Go back on a promise?"

He nodded.

"I'm not asking you to go back on a promise," Penny said.

Kip laughed. "You said you'd say that."

She cocked her head at him.

"When you made me promise not to tell you, you told me that you'd give me an out. That you'd say that I wasn't breaking a promise. That you'd find a way to frame it as acting out of loyalty to you." Kip shook his head. "I'm a little surprised how accurate you were back then. Especially since you're not a precog. You're not supposed to be able to see the future, little one. Not even possible ones. But here we are."

"Back then?" Penny asked. "How long ago?"

Kip stared off into the distance. "All of these questions, they all lead to the same place. To a place that you told me never to take you again."

"So I'm *really* the one who told you never to tell me?"

He nodded. "You forgot on purpose. You said you never wanted to remember."

Penny considered this. "Never is an awfully long time."

Kip laughed. "Indeed, little one. I've had a small slice of never, and it's been more than enough for me."

"Oh Kip," she said. The sadness in his voice was almost too much to bear.

"Oh, don't worry about me, little one," Kip reassured her. "I always get by. I always have, and I always will." He smiled. "And so will you."

"Whether I know where I came from or not?"

He nodded. "It's a curious thing you're asking me to do."

"What's that? What am I asking you to do?"

"Basically, I get to be a debate judge. Your past self and your present self are pitted against one another. Both versions of you want diametrically opposed outcomes. Your past self wants to keep the door closed, to keep your former life behind you, your history, your family, your first home. All of it locked behind a door." He paused for effect, letting the words sink in.

"And your present self, who sits next to me now," he continued, "wants to open that door, step through, and see everything that's on the other side."

He looked up through the branches of the desert willow again, watching the moonlight play against the bunches of blossoms, causing them to shimmer like will-o'-the-wisps.

"Obviously, my present self wins," Penny said.

"Of course that's what present self would say," Kip shot back, smirking.

"Well," Penny said. "If you don't show up for a debate, don't you forfeit the bout?"

Kip erupted in laughter. "Very clever, little one," he replied. "I'm impressed."

"I'm good at finding loopholes," Penny said proudly.

"You are," Kip said. "You always have been."

"How long is 'always?'" Penny asked him.

He studied her. "Are you asking me how old you are?"

She nodded.

"I lose track of things like that," he replied.

"That's a non-answer," Penny said.

"A true one."

"Well," Penny tried again. "My Psychic State identification lists my age as 27. Is that correct?'

Kip hesitated, before replying, "No."

"Is it close?" Penny prompted him.

Kip shook his head.

Penny nodded slowly. "I'm older than that, aren't I?"

Kip sighed. He nodded.

"How much older?" Penny asked him.

"I told you," Kip said again. "I lose track of things like that."

Penny chewed her lip. "I'm a lot older than that, aren't I?"

Kip's entire body seemed to tense and then relax. "Yes," he said finally.

"I'm not older than you, am I?" she asked.

He laughed. "No."

"There's one thing I can't get."

Kip waited for her to continue.

"Why would I ask you to never answer these questions?" Penny said.

"Oh, that's easy to answer," Kip replied. "You wanted to forget. It was your idea to forget."

"Really?" Penny said.

Kip nodded.

"Why would I do that? Why would I want to forget?"

"It's how you were able to come here," Kip said.

"It was how I was able to come here?" Penny said.

"Well, that's not exactly right. It's how you were able to *stay* here."

"And if I remember," Penny said, "what happens?"

"Then you go home," Kip replied.

"I go home," Penny replied. In an instant, all the strange messages that had been finding their way to her over the last several weeks flashed through her mind. *Come home*, they'd all said. *Come home.*

Perhaps there was a reason why she was being asked to come home. There usually was, wasn't there?

And perhaps the reason that it had all been necessary would become clear upon her return.

In any event, the question had been raised. And the more that Penny was learning from Kip, however reluctantly he offered the information, the more her curiosity was piqued.

It was becoming harder moment by moment to walk away from this mystery. She felt herself merely circling the issue. She knew that eventually all would be revealed, and she would return home.

It was just a matter of time. And of method.

So she asked the next logical question. "If I go home, will I be able to return here again?"

"I don't know," Kip said.

"Kip," she admonished him. "Don't play coy with me. I need to know. It's important."

"I'm not playing coy," he insisted. "I really don't know. It's never been done before."

"It's never been done?"

"Penny," he said gently. "People generally do not leave…" He caught himself before he said the name of the place or revealed too many other details and possibly set things into motion that he still wasn't sure he wanted to unleash. "Where you're from, people do not leave," he rephrased. "Not voluntarily."

"But I left?" Penny asked.

"Yes," Kip replied. "And you took me with you."

"Oh," Penny said. "So you're stranded, aren't you?"

"Well," Kip said. "I suppose that's one way of putting it. Not the way I would put it. But you're correct. I am unable to return home while you're away from home, yes. Regardless of my feelings on the matter, one way or the other."

"Oh Kip," Penny said. "I'm sorry."

"It's fine," Kip said. "It's all a matter of duty. A duty I'm happy to perform. And I knew the job when I signed up for it."

"The job?" Penny asked.

He didn't reply. This, too, was behind the locked door, the one that he was still eyeing mentally and straining over, trying to work out whether it should be opened, now or ever.

"All of these years, I thought you were my friend," Penny said. "But you're my employee."

"I *am* your friend, little one," Kip replied. "Regardless of whatever business arrangements are in place, that much is true. I greatly enjoy your company. And this duty has been my pleasure." He paused before adding, "Anyway, I can tell you, truthfully, that I'm not your employee."

"But you were hired to be with me," Penny pressed.

Kip hesitated and nodded. "I became your friend though," he added.

"How did we become friends?"

"Settle in, little one," he said. "Because *that* is a story I would be quite willing to tell you."

Penny leaned her head against Kip's shoulder and closed her eyes.

Later that morning, Karen and Viv woke up at the same time. The birds were singing outside their bedroom window. They sang the same songs as any other morning but perhaps a bit more quietly, as though they were further away than normal.

The light coming through their bedroom window also seemed dimmer than normal, not as bright or piercing.

"Penny's gone," Karen told Viv.

Viv frowned, not sure what to say. They descended the stairs together, holding hands.

On the kitchen table, there was a note in Penny's handwriting, scribbled on the back of a blank florist's card:

> *I've gone on a trip. Not sure when I'll be back. Give Martin my best.*

Viv read the card first, stared at it for a few moments, shook it back and forth vigorously as though she were developing a Polaroid picture, and read it again.

It was of course the same message. Disappointingly enough. Viv sighed and handed the card to Karen.

Karen's eyes widened as she took in the message.

"Before you ask," Viv said, "no, I don't want to talk about it."

"I know," Karen replied. "I can feel it."

"Because she's not here," Viv confirmed.

Karen nodded. Her empathic powers were usually held at bay by the presence of both Viv and Penny. She had never figured out exactly why, but so long as both of her partners were nearby, no more than about a football field away, her emotional inner life functioned mostly like she was a normal, a non-psychic person. Somehow being with the two of them created interference that made it possible for her to function in a way that otherwise eluded her.

Now with Penny gone, it was like the treatment she'd come to rely on had abruptly stopped working.

Karen had weathered periods in the past when she'd been separated from either Viv or Penny – and sometimes both. In fact, that was how she primarily did her specialist work on their team. She could only do a "feel," in which she channeled a witness's emotions, if Viv and Penny weren't immediately nearby.

But she'd also been taking more and more walks alone outside of their home, trying to build up a natural tolerance to the stream of emotive multi-consciousness that hit her every time she was out and among the public.

She found that she could tolerate such a din for short lengths of time but that if she went too far she always regretted it. The longer Penny or Viv was gone, the more intense her empathic powers seemed to become.

It was strange, really. Penny had only been gone for a handful of hours, but Karen was already a having much more intense reaction to her absence than she should have been.

Viv's emotions were screaming at her, and Karen felt bombarded by other miscellaneous emotions that were coming from somewhere outside of the house. She turned and looked out the front window, trying to pinpoint the source.

Passing cars, neighbors, work crews repairing a sidewalk. She could feel it all emanating. She closed her eyes and took a few deep breaths.

When she reopened them, she saw something new. Shambling amorphous vaguely humanoid-shaped masses lumbered outside. They were at a distance now, down the street at the intersection of Blitz and Bell, the street she lived on. They had a way to go, but they were moving steadily towards the house.

The figures reminded Karen of black candles that had been partially burned and snuffed out but before the wax had time to fully cool. Their forms were misshapen and dripping.

"Viv, come here. What the heck are those?" Karen said.

When Viv didn't answer, Karen turned and noted that Viv wasn't there anymore. Where had she gone? Had Viv excused herself from the room and Karen had just missed it because her exit was drowned out by the atmospheric din of so many ambient emotions?

I should go see if she's okay, Karen thought. After all, Viv always struggled with poor health, these days mostly side effects from the medications she took to keep her migraines and seizures in check. And Viv had been in especially bad shape lately, ever since their last case ended. Finding out Penny had run off somewhere like a stray cat again probably wasn't helping matters.

The right thing would normally be to go up and join Viv, gently check in with her, and see if she were okay.

But this was a special circumstance. They had very strange unwelcome visitors, ones that were rapidly encroaching upon the house. Karen cast another worried glance out the window. No, there wasn't time to do the right thing. Those monstrosities – whatever they were – they were getting closer.

"Hey Viv," Karen called up the stairs. There was no reply.

"Viv!" Karen said again, trying her best to project.

Silence.

"I'm sorry, Viv," Karen muttered to herself. "But if we don't do something about that mess out there, there will be no helping any of us."

Shaking her head, Karen scooped up Viv's cell phone from the coffee table. It was an older model, a device that would have been considered obsolete by most of the non-psychic population, but to Viv it was a lifeline, a source of pride. Most intuitives went without. It was a big deal that their family had a cell phone, even if they had to share and it wasn't the latest and greatest.

Karen felt a jolt of her own anxiety over the thumping that was already underway in her chest. She couldn't remember ever holding Viv's phone in her hand before. Viv was so protective of the device that she generally didn't want anyone else to touch it, let alone use it.

Well, she can kill me later, Karen thought. Because she had a feeling that without the phone, whatever those things were outside would probably kill her first.

Her heart pounding, Karen stepped out onto the porch, down the stairs, and onto the lawn. Her hands shook. There was better reception out here in the open air, important with their low-powered phone. It was theoretically capable of interfacing with modern mobile network technology – but it did so grudgingly as if even the phone were scandalized that someone was using it, assuming that most other owners would have thrown it away by now or donated it to a charity store. Any sensible proprietors would have discarded the phone once the person dropping it off was out of sight.

The strange visitors were getting closer. Karen stared at the phone. For an outdated model, it was still fairly complex. It had been ages since she'd used any phone she realized, having led a largely itinerant life for the past decade, shuffling between hospitals. Sure, things had been stable the last few years living with Penny and Viv, but it dawned on her that as much as being with Penny and Viv had meant she'd had stability that relying on them had meant that she also hadn't been forced to pick up normal life skills that other people took for granted.

She didn't know how to use the damn phone. Shit.

She looked up at the hordes descending upon her. Coming from every direction. Their collective moans blended together, reminding her of the sound of a big rig truck passing – except in this case the truck never stopped passing. Never stopped shaking the front porch.

As they neared, she could better discern their faces. It was her usual visitors. The emotions that came to see her from time to time in human form. Anger. Fear. Sadness. Grief. Boredom. Disgust. Loathing. Contempt. Guilt. Awe. Surprise.

Even Joy.

Really? Karen thought. What was Joy doing getting wrapped up in this? She had never seen Joy be menacing before. This was quite out of character for her.

Joy typically paid a visit when Karen felt guilty about good things happening in her life. Karen tended to have trouble when she got something she knew someone else wanted, even if she had worked hard for it.

At those moments, Joy would visit and tell her to knock it off and remind her of the hard work she'd done to get there.

To see her descending upon the house in such a menacing way was quite disconcerting.

Joy normally didn't participate in threatening behavior. None of them did, really. Her emotional visitors mostly came to see her when Karen should be feeling something but wasn't letting herself feel it for some reason. And recognizing their faces in other people's emotions was how her empathy powers worked. Sometimes they were obviously there; other times the emotions were a lot more subtle, and at those times, finding their faces when feeling a subject out could be akin to finding human figures in a psychological inkblot projective test.

Why are they all visiting me now? Karen wondered. They'd never done that before. Sometimes they arrived in pairs, but it was much more common for them to visit her alone. She'd certainly never had them visit her all at once like this.

They usually come when I'm not feeling something, Karen thought. *Not when I'm feeling* everything. *Why now?*

The phone she was holding in her hand rang. Karen whipped it up to her ear.

"Hello, hello?" she said.

The phone continued to ring.

Oh right, there was a damn button somewhere. She looked for the biggest one she could find. There were two of the same size, one green, one red.

"Red means stop, so that's probably not it," she said.

The phone rang back as if to reply to her.

Karen pressed the green button. "Hello, hello?" she tried again.

A voice came to her, but it was scrambled like it was underwater.

Amarynth. Her coworker. The Connections Agent for her team at PsyOps. Karen strained to make out what Amarynth was saying, but the sound kept cutting in and out.

"Amarynth, if you can hear me, please get here as soon as you can. Bring backup. Something terrible is happening at the house," Karen said.

The only sound that came back was garbled, the words unintelligible. Karen had no idea whether Amarynth could hear her.

She held the phone to her ear and repeated what she'd just said over and over again. Several times. She knew it was silly even as she was doing it – just like when a person is talking to someone who doesn't quite understand their language and decides if they just talk more slowly and loudly that the other person's vocabulary will somehow improve – but she wasn't sure what else to do.

As the hordes neared, she noted another curiosity. There wasn't one Anger in the crowd but several, interspersed throughout the mob, her knifelike bearing and posture punctuating the pack of beings like thin-spread fence posts. There were also multiple Fears, each one frozen in a half scream with their eyes bulging open. It was the same with all the emotions. They were like a mob made up of computer-generated extras. And not a clever one that depended on some complex algorithm to fool a discerning human eye. But a sloppy copy-paste version.

Karen continued to repeat the same few sentences into the phone over and over again until the clone army was upon her. She knew she should probably run, but she felt herself freeze in place.

Why can't I be a fight or flight person? No, I have to have a freeze response to danger, she thought miserably as Anger raised her fist and thumped her soundly on the head.

Karen crumpled to the ground. She dropped the phone as other emotions crouched and pummeled her.

A whorl of synesthesia swept her away. She saw blood and tasted light.

Then everything went dark.

"What are you doing sleeping on the lawn?" Viv said.

Karen started. She noted that several hours had passed. The last thing she knew, it had been morning. It was now after dark.

Somehow an entire day had disappeared.

"I..." Karen looked around her. "I'm not sure." She glanced at the lawn next to her. "Oh shit, I think I lost your phone."

Viv frowned. "What are you talking about?" she said. "I have it right here." She held her phone up.

"Oh," Karen said.

Viv shook her head. *Penny'd better hurry back*, she thought. *I'm in no state to babysit Karen if she's gonna act like this.*

But then she noticed the distressed look on Karen's face. "Are you okay?" Viv said. The question came out sharper than she'd intended it to.

"I'm fine," Karen lied.

Viv scrutinized her face. "Karen, it's okay if you're not," she offered.

"Maybe to you," Karen replied.

Viv cocked her head.

"I think I'm going crazy," Karen admitted.

"Oh, all the good people are a little crazy," Viv replied.

Karen shook her head. "Not like that. I don't mean it that way." She frowned. "I think… I think I was hallucinating."

"What did you see?" Viv asked her.

Karen recounted the ordeal of that afternoon. "I thought it was weird at the time, that parts of it made sense, though not all of it… but it seemed real. I thought it was actually happening. I heard them. I saw them. When they hit me, I felt the pain."

"Well, if that really happened, then I slept through it," Viv said. "Stranger things have happened. I am a heavy sleeper, after all."

Karen laughed. "Yeah, but you had your phone with you the entire time, didn't you?"

Viv nodded. "It was up with me in the bedroom."

"If the phone wasn't real," Karen said, "then the rest of it definitely wasn't."

Viv yawned. "We can talk about this in the morning. I'm going back to bed."

Karen sighed. That was Viv lately. It seemed like all Viv wanted to do these days was sleep. Viv was undoubtedly going through a depressive episode, but knowing why her partner was having difficulty didn't make it any easier for Karen to watch her go through it. Explanations were like that. They didn't change the situation, and they didn't fix problems or right wrongs. Explanations just organized the relevant information logically so you could talk about it more directly. The other person had to be willing to discuss it, however, and even more implausibly, they had to be willing to do something about it.

"Fine, go back to bed. I hope you stay there," Karen suddenly wanted to spit at her because she wasn't sure how she'd face the night on her own, especially not without Penny here as a mediating force. But that was a nasty thing to say.

So instead Karen said, "Sleep well."

Once Viv had gone back inside, Karen looked up at the stars. She found herself wishing she knew the names of them and of the constellations.

If Penny were here...

Karen caught herself. It wasn't a productive train of thought, but she couldn't help herself. Penny knew a lot about mythology, having majored in classics in college. Her astrophysics was a little spotty, but Penny knew the positions, shapes, and backstories of all the constellations from Greek mythology.

If Penny were here, she'd tell me what those are and the stories behind them, she finished. Productive thought or not, it was true.

Penny was like that in general. She had a way of anchoring her, orienting her.

Viv, too, of course. But it wasn't the same when Penny wasn't there.

And now I'm floating, Karen thought. *With no idea of where I am.*

She looked back at their house, the sweet little two-story colonial that stuck out as an anachronism among the other houses on their street, which were mostly ranches and glorified trailers packed with intuitives sleeping sometimes as many as twelve to a single room. Their house was different than that, a luxury most intuitives never enjoyed. It was a comforting sight. It had become home.

She could easily go inside, crawl under the covers next to Viv, and try to sleep.

But she wasn't tired, not as far as sleep went anyway. Emotionally, she was exhausted. Even now, a sharp feeling of unrest whistled through her chest – probably someone in one of the nearby houses was having a stressful dream.

As she thought about the night ahead of her, she was hit with a feeling of dread that she recognized not as atmospheric but her own. She could picture the night ahead of her. She would be staring at the ceiling lost in her thoughts, at the mercy of wandering emotions, wide awake while Viv slept.

That's if she didn't crack again and do something dangerous this time.

She frowned. It was beyond demoralizing after all the work she'd done on her mental health over the years to still be this vulnerable to changes in fortune.

"Have I mistaken a good love life for sanity?" she said aloud to no one.

No one answered. Thankfully. The last thing she needed was a repeat from earlier.

Sighing, she hoisted herself up onto her feet, feeling pins and needles rush through her limbs as she did so. She shook her legs aggressively one at a time and winced at the sensation.

Finally, feeling fully returned, and she walked towards the house.

After a few steps, she almost tripped, slipping on something tangled in the grass. Bending over, she retrieved the offending item. It was a piece of paper.

Wide-eyed, she unfolded it and walked over to the radius of the porch light to read it.

Viv woke the next afternoon, surprised at how long she'd slept.

Usually Karen would have gotten me up by now, she thought. If not waking her directly, then indirectly, by making enough noise by doing things like using the bathroom, cooking a meal, or taking a shower that Viv's brain would spring to life.

That was a really deep sleep, Viv thought. There were countless dreams, although she was having trouble remembering what they were when she went to try.

Might as well be in hibernation, Viv thought, as she hit the bathroom before walking down the stairs. *Strange to hibernate in the middle of summer. It's usually a winter thing, but I guess I've always been different.*

"Oh for fuck's sake," Viv said. The florist card Penny had left the day before was turned over onto its other side, the front this time. A short note was scribbled on it in pen. This handwritten text had been crammed in awkwardly around the business logo and name of the florist shop. Viv recognized the spiky penmanship instantly.

> *There's something I need to go do. I'm not well. I will be back when I'm better.*
>
> *-Karen*

Not again.

Sighing, Viv walked to the shower. She felt like absolute crap, but in light of recent events, vacation was officially over.

"Time to get back to work," she told herself as she started the water running and stripped down. "Someone has to. This house isn't going to pay for itself."

She tried to focus on the good things she still had left. The house was still here. She had a good job to go to. And both of her partners would be back whenever they finished… well, whatever it was they were doing.

There was no reason to be upset or overwhelmed, she reminded herself.

But as the warm water hit her back, she cried.

"The story of how we became friends?" Penny said to Kip. "Is it a good story?"

"Only one way to find out, little one," Kip replied. "Would you like me to begin?"

He waited for her to nod her permission. Once she did, he gathered his thoughts and began.

Kip's Inferno

"Pay a man enough and he'll walk barefoot into Hell."

-Xanatos, Gargoyles

It was never supposed to be a permanent gig. Just a few weeks of hard work, of scraping crumbs off the tablecloth with a blade, suggesting the best possible wine to go with dinner, and he'd be set.

That was how it worked. If you could get an upper echelon gig and hold it, even for a fortnight, you could live for decades on your wages down in the slums, where even a thin rusty coin could sustain you for weeks, provided you knew the right people.

And Kipper Dante knew all the right people.

It was all the same to Kip where he lived. Hell was the same no matter which circle you lived in. Sure, the upper echelons came with their perks, certain amenities – but there was no way to escape the tedious parts.

Or so he thought.

He'd come to realize later that he'd been a little bit hasty in considering Hell to be eternal or an inevitability.

However, that hadn't yet come to pass.

For now, he was answering a Help Wanted ad – and quite successfully, too. He'd expected more competition going in. In Hell there could be seemingly endless bureaucracy, especially when the person in charge had something you really wanted.

But this manservant gig had practically fallen in his lap. It had been a simple three interviews with the same man before he was told, "You've got the job. You start tomorrow."

The interviewer was Harry Stygius, the lord of the manor, and the lord of *everything* underground. The man at the top of the heap of the pile of lost souls inhabiting Hell. Or, as a lot of people called him, the victor of victors. Rumor had it that Stygius had once been a big cheese up in Heaven, but that was ages ago.

Probably a silly rumor, Kip thought. But he'd watch his language just in case, he'd decided when reporting for his interviews. If you lived in Heaven, there were probably things that stuck with you. He'd never been to Heaven himself, but he'd heard a lot of rumors about what it was like, from people who claimed to have been there. And a biggie was that there was no profanity in Heaven. The rumor was that everyone there spoke with proper grammar, too.

Well, that was probably a lost cause, Kip decided. He'd never been much for arbitrary rules, for regulations that were prescriptive for the sake of prescription. Proper grammar seemed to be full of that stuff. Given a chance, he'd take improper grammar any day, so long as people understood him and he could get by.

But profanity he could avoid. It seemed like a happy medium for approaching the interview process.

This approach went over well. His suspicions had been correct, Kip realized, once he met the man. Mr. Stygius spoke casually and without pretension, but he didn't swear. Unusual in Hell, where spicy language was its own dialect.

It made Mr. Stygius seem otherworldly, like he viewed himself as an outsider in Hell, even as he ruled it. Perhaps the rumors about him were true then.

The job was "domestic duties." As Kip left the final interview, it occurred to him that he'd never clarified with his new boss exactly what this entailed.

He had noted as he arrived at the manor on the day of each successive interview that the esteemed Mr. and Mrs. Stygius already had a butler and a very capable one at that. There also seemed to be several maids.

Kip hadn't dined with Mr. Stygius yet, and maybe there was a reason for that.

I bet I'm a waiter, Kip thought. *He probably needs someone to set the table, bring out food, that sort of thing. Scrape breadcrumbs off the tablecloth.*

It couldn't be anything terribly skilled or specialized anyway, Kip decided. For instance, he couldn't be the family chef as Mr. Stygius had never once asked him about his cooking skills.

In fact, the set of interviews had focused solely on Kip's personality, his temperament, and his interests.

Or at least that's what it seemed like to Kip. For much of their meeting time, Mr. Stygius wasn't even assessing his fit for a particular job description. The lord of the manor was instead simply chatting with him and trying to get a feel of who Kip really was and would be outside of work.

It's probably lonely at the top. I imagine that's one of the ways you suffer in this layer of Hell.

Probably a smart strategy. Besides, Kip resolved, that's the best way to know if people will be personable and polite to guests. Chat with them long enough to get their guard down, make them feel like you're their friend, and see who they are when they relax. You couldn't get to know a person when they were stuck in Job Interview Mode, could you?

Anyway, he had heard of personal assistant gigs where you were basically being paid to be someone's friend. Perhaps that's what Mr. Stygius needed, someone who understood him – or was paid to pretend to.

A confidant could be hard to find in Hell. As best as he could tell, the Stygius marriage was strong – particularly for Hell, where the divorce rate was astronomical and wandering eyes were common. If pressed, Kip couldn't think of a single relationship – romantic or not – where he didn't feel like the person on the other end of it was constantly sizing up their options, and if they found someone better – to befriend, to love, to fuck – they wouldn't hesitate to discard what they had and move on to the next conquest.

The only thing more valuable than water in Hell was loyalty. It was certainly rarer.

In that way, Stephanie Stygius stood apart from the other victors' wives. She lacked the insatiable greed and ambition that seemed requisite to be part of the Hellish nobility. Surrounded by luxury, she nonetheless seemed to care little for it. She dressed well, make no mistake, but with an economy and restraint that made her stand out in stark relief among the social circles she frequented.

Stephanie Stygius was beautiful but largely unadorned. Other victors' wives would attend the formal balls with gowns that swept out for several feet around them on all sides, stitched with platinum threads and studded with chiseled crystals of obscure rarefied elements, bombastic getups that caught the light and required staff to help the wearer maneuver through the social event. Their faces would take hours to paint. Their help would be subjected to complex processes that took an entire salon of experts to execute.

Stephanie would instead put on a simple cocktail dress and a few swipes of mascara, smile, and leave the house.

And yet, all eyes would travel to her. Some of them were the adoring gazes of men who thought she would be a rare creature among the Hellish nobility – a lovely wife who was also easy to please. Low maintenance. These observers regarded her as another precious jewel coveted by their never-ending greed and ambition. But many other eyes regarded her with scowls. These came mostly from jealous victors' wives who wondered who the Hell Stephanie Stygius thought she was attending the party half-naked and... well, plain.

It was hideous and disrespectful. Low class. What was she doing? Why did Harry Stygius allow such lowbrow behavior from his wife?

But Stephanie didn't seem to mind the disdain that came her way. If she saw it, she didn't bow to the social pressure. She wore her pink ruffles and sunny yellow prints, even though those colors stood out sharply amongst the formal neutrals and flame reds that were all the rage in Hell. During cocktail hour, she stuck to white wine, even though it raised eyebrows. She didn't care that tannic red that made your jaw ache was in vogue in Hell – the bloodier the better.

And she was polite and said "thank you" anytime anyone did anything nice for her.

Basically, by Hellish standards, she was a total weirdo.

And yet… there was something so compelling about her. Kip could remember springtime if he strained his memory, although it had been an awfully long time since he'd experienced anything other than an oppressively hot summer.

The closest thing to springtime he'd seen in Hell was Stephanie Stygius. Spring seemed to follow her, like an aura. It was evident in the strange frilly vegetables that Stephanie grew on the grounds of the Stygius Estate. There wasn't an awful lot of water in Hell of course. Enough to drink but only just. Certainly not a lot left over for such abominations as an Earthbound suburban lawn with its endless square yards of thirsty grass.

Not that Hellish homes were entirely without plant life. A few cacti and succulents found their way onto the estates of the Hellish nobility, even so, drinking whatever ambient moisture they could snatch from sizzling air.

But Stephanie Stygius had a proper garden. It was landscaped beautifully, held in check by a barrier of cobblestones that prevented it from spilling out into the public street or overtaking adjacent properties. Her garden grew vegetables with stems that opened into colorful blooms.

Stephanie had laughed the first time Kip had pointed them out and asked her what she cooked with them, these colorful blooming vegetables.

"You don't cook with these," Stephanie had said. "These are *flowers*."

"Flowers?" Kip said. And then the old memory creaked forward, buried deep within his subconscious, from his former life, his life before immigrating here to Hell. He could remember flowers. Vaguely. "Oh, now that you mention it, I seem to recall something like that."

Stephanie had smiled. "I knew you would. That you could."

Kip had smiled back.

"You're capable of a lot more than you know, Kip," Stephanie had said. "You will do great things, of that I am sure."

"But of course," Kip had replied. "When I'm in the company of such great people, it's inevitable, isn't it?"

And she'd laughed and laughed at this. "I'm just a simple girl," Stephanie had said. "Harry is something else though, isn't he?" she added.

"Yes," Kip agreed. "Harry's a great man."

"One day we'll have a family," Stephanie had said. "And you'll be part of it, Kip."

"Me?" Kip asked.

Stephanie nodded.

Kip had been nervous at this thought. Like a lot of people who were used to being outsiders, he wasn't sure if fitting in somewhere would be a good thing. If it would feel more like a security blanket or a prison. Kip had never really felt at home in his own family. How would he manage to fit into someone else's?

And when Stephanie had gotten pregnant – not hard to accomplish in Hell's fertile atmosphere, which seemed to bring forth new life easily even without active physical consummation – Kip had become extremely nervous.

He had felt as though he were pregnant himself, gaining weight, becoming sick in the mornings just as Stephanie did.

Even as she laughed at his anxiety and reassured him that he would do fine after she gave birth, Kip still had his doubts.

How would he cope with a new child in the home? He had no experience with babies that he could recall – not in this Hellish existence or any before it, as hard as he could push the creaking wheels of memory to spin up faint images of the past.

A baby. This would change everything. What would his employers expect of him? Would he be asked to tend the nursery? Feed the child? Change diapers?

Finally, the big day came when Stephanie gave birth to not one – but two girls, identical in every way. She named one Rhea, after her beloved grandmother whom she missed terribly, and the other Dem, after her mother Demeter who missed *her* terribly.

"Absence makes the heart grow fonder," Stephanie had explained, "and they are my dearest heart."

That didn't make much sense to Kip, but he assumed that Stephanie was still heavily under the influence of the drugs she had been given to facilitate painless labor, so he nodded sagely and held her hand until Harry could tear himself away from Hellish courtly duty to be by his wife's side.

Kip noted with great surprise how tender Harry was with the newborns and how attentive he was to his new wife. It wasn't every day that a father doted so on their Hellspawn.

"You will be their tender," Harry told Kip then.

"But… I don't know the first thing about babies," Kip had admitted.

"You don't have to," Harry had replied. "Not beyond the basics. And anyone can learn that. How to change diapers. How to prepare a bottle and feed an infant."

Kip frowned.

"Not that you'll have to do that," Harry continued. "That's not why we hired you."

"No?" Kip said.

Harry shook his head. "We have a nursemaid who is coming in to help Stephanie with all of that. The Third Circle's finest, matter of fact. She comes very highly recommended."

"Then what am I supposed to be doing?" Kip asked.

"You will be their tutor," Harry replied.

"But I'm not an expert on anything," Kip replied.

"You don't have to be."

"But how will I…?" Kip let the question trail off.

"Teach them?" Harry finished.

Kip nodded.

"I think you'll find, Mr. Dante, that my children are perfectly capable of teaching themselves. You will mostly be there to encourage them and support them," Harry said.

Kip thought of asking Mr. Stygius how he knew this, but it wasn't his place to question such authority, was it? Instead, he frowned. "If you say so, my lord."

"I do," Harry replied. "You'll soon see that I'm right. I trust my source."

Dem was the older of the twin girls, having emerged into the underworld a mere four minutes before Rhea. Four minutes is a blink of the eye on Earth, but in Hell, where time doesn't march onward but instead crawls along on its belly at an agonizingly slow clip, four minutes amounts to even less, a rounding error.

That didn't stop Dem from holding it over her "younger" sister Rhea's head that she was the older, and ostensibly wiser, twin.

And a mere delay of four minutes didn't stop the rules of succession from differentiating between the two young Stygius children. On the distant day that Harry Stygius were no longer able to rule, whisked off to some other plane to pursue a different existence, it would be Dem Stygius who would preside over Hell, not Rhea.

It was as the River Styx commanded. There was no straying from this edict.

The other victors protested. Why would a daughter be chosen to reign over Hell and not a son?

After all, a long line of greater demon rulers extending back into the formation of the plane had all been male.

The Styx had the answer. It said that Stephanie Stygius – or Persephone in much of the tatty tabloid coverage that finally found its way to Earth as myth – would only bear female children.

And after eons of blazing, stifling, oppressive summer that seemed never-ending, it was finally a slightly colder time in Hell.

Spring was here. One cycle was ending, another beginning. It would take thousands of years yet, with everything moving at glacial speed, but Hell was entering an ice age, one that would be ushered in by the daughters of spring itself.

The way the word is used in other planes, Hellspawn are depicted as vicious monsters. Many would expect that a child born in Hell would be vicious, a natural villain.

Like much reporting about Hell that reaches neighboring planes, this is in fact far from the truth.

It's true that Hellspawn are strong-willed and can be quite defiant when their opinions are contradicted or their aims are blocked.

However, they are not as evil as one would expect; in fact, a good many Hellspawn are sweet and possess a good, benevolent nature. They are just incredibly independent and self-guided, at an age that predates typical child development on other planes.

Part of their precociousness and depth of will simply stems from the fact that it takes so much longer to grow up in Hell. The natural hazards are greater, which exerts additional pressure upon a Hellspawn to become savvy and headstrong. Even the most diligent helicopter parent could not successfully protect their offspring from every threat that Hell has to offer. Offspring need to learn to protect themselves as quickly as possible.

Some of these children do grow up to be quite manipulative and cynical; others are simply skeptical. And there are a few who manage to maintain an optimistic outlook – even if it's tempered by a sense of realism about uncertainty and how transactional others can be, not only in Hell but across the entire vast array of planes that make up the universe.

Both of Stephanie Stygius's daughters would fall into that last category. They would become women who were as realistic as they were optimistic.

The Styx whispered to Harry Stygius that Dem and Rhea would live long productive lives, on this plane of Hell and others, and would by the time they were called on to their next permanent planar assignment be renown as independent by those who interacted with them many, many times.

All Hellspawn were so. But Dem and Rhea were blessed with a strength of will that didn't hinge around shunning all others – but instead was defined from by a strong sense of knowing where they ended and others began.

They were controlled by no bond, not even the one they shared as identical twins. Well, mostly, Kip noted.

There was a little more sway there, a little more give – particularly on Dem's side of the relationship. Despite her incessant lording over her slightly younger sister Rhea that she was the one fated to be the future ruler of Hell, Dem often seemed troubled and lost when Rhea wasn't by her side.

Dem would protest vehemently that she didn't care what Rhea did, but her behaviors told a different story. Whenever Rhea wandered out into the lower circles of Hell on her own, usually fairly un-cleverly disguised in garments scrounged from the manor servants, Dem would become despondent and listless. She wouldn't eat or sleep until Rhea returned home.

And that was why it was so difficult for the young heiress apparent on the afternoon that little Rhea Stygius ran away from home.

Kip's heart caught in his throat when he spotted her there on the bank of the Styx. She looked more like a refuse pile than a small child, but then the pile moved, and no critters or imps scrambled out.

The coat Rhea had nicked this time was massive, black, and shiny. It shimmered in the heat of the three oppressive Hellish suns that hung in the sky. The other three were down at the moment, but he imagined at least one of them would be up shortly. Then the day would really heat up.

The black coat twitched again. As Kip came nearer, he noted that Rhea's shoulders were shaking. The little girl was sobbing.

"Rhea, dear," Kip said.

She jerked her head around, before cursing at him in three distinct dialects of Hellish. Kip only understood two of them, but he could follow the gist: It was a request for him to do something anatomically impossible as hard as he could.

"Why do you keep doing this?" Kip asked.

"I don't know," Rhea snapped. "Why do you keep coming after me?"

"Because I care about you, little one," Kip said.

Rhea scoffed. "You just care about getting paid."

"Is that what you think?" Kip asked her.

Rhea nodded.

He lowered himself down slowly next to her. "It's true that I came to your father because I needed a job. I'm not going to disrespect you by pretending anything different."

Rhea sniffled. She edged towards him so they were sitting closer together.

"That's how it started," Kip admitted. "But well… once I met you, little one, it was love at first sight."

"Ewww, that's gross," Rhea said, scrunching up her nose.

Kip smiled. "I don't mean it that way," he said. "It's a brotherly love. I don't exactly think we're suited for that other kind of love. We're from different worlds. I wasn't even born here, not in Hell."

"And you're a boy," Rhea offered.

Kip nodded. "And I'm a boy. I know you don't like boys that way." He stared at the Styx for a moment, watching it churn. "The Styx told your father you never will. Not boys. Not men."

"The Styx is smart," Rhea agreed. "Dem's different though. She's already boy crazy. It's so gross. I can't understand it."

"There are many different ways to be, little one," Kip said.

"If you say so," Rhea replied.

"I do," Kip said. "And I'm also saying that I care about you. I didn't think I would care so much to be honest. I never did have much experience with children before I came to work for your father. What little experience I did have wasn't positive."

"Then why did you take the job?" Rhea asked.

"I didn't know at first that was what would be asked of me," Kip admitted.

"But once you did," Rhea pressed, "why didn't you quit then?"

"Because of you. And your sister, yes. But mostly because of you," Kip said.

"Ewww," Rhea said.

"Like I said, it's not a marital bond. Nothing physical. It's nothing like that, little one. I just knew when I met you that we belonged together."

"That is so gross," Rhea said.

Kip laughed. "Maybe you'll understand when you're a little older."

"I doubt it," Rhea said.

"Anyway, that's why I keep coming after you. You asked. It's because you're my closest friend," Kip said.

"Well, that's a little weird, seeing as you're a grown man who has lived on multiple planes and I'm just a little kid from Hell," Rhea observed.

Kip shrugged his shoulders. "Maybe I'm just really immature."

Rhea laughed at this.

"C'mon," Kip said. "We've gotta get home before the fourth sun comes up. We don't want to be out after Tetrasol rises. There will be too many beasts."

Rhea shook her head. Crossed her arms. "You know what'd be nice, Kip?"

Kip frowned at her resistance. "What's that?" he said, feeling his patience strain as he humored her.

"It'd be nice if we could get a break from the suns," Rhea said.

"A break from the suns?" Kip asked.

"Yeah, a time when no sun is out. When the sky is dark. When it's a little cooler out."

"That, little one," Kip said, "is known on other planes as 'night.'"

"Like the plane you're from?" Rhea said.

Kip nodded.

"Hell is so dumb," Rhea said. "I'm glad I'm not going to rule over this stupid place."

"You don't mean that," Kip said. But even as he said it, he could tell that she did.

"I do," Rhea said. "Hell is dumb. The people here are all obsessed with what everyone else thinks of them. It's hot. The traffic is terrible."

"There are places like that on other planes, too," Kip challenged her.

"Well, maybe," Rhea said. "But not the whole plane. Not all the time. Not like this. I'm sure anywhere would be better than Hell. Hell is the worst."

Kip closed his eyes and shook his head slowly. "That is not true, little one. It's not for everyone, but Hell is not a bad place."

"Well, it's a bad place for me, Kip!" she exploded, before covering her face with both hands.

Kip regarded her then, as she stayed in that defensive posture. And as he mentally calculated the window of safety they had, the seconds, minutes, and hours to Tetrasol-rise which would bring beasts emboldened and unleashed by the presence of the fourth sun (as well as the dreaded beasts that would arrive with the brief presence of the fifth sun), he saw her for the first time not as just a child he was charged with watching over but as a fully-fledged person.

A person who might know what was best for herself, even if it sounded wrong to other people.

And a person who, because of draconian notions of autonomy found across many planes, was not being allowed to make important decisions for herself.

He also realized, watching her authentic grief and noting how much she looked like a trapped animal, that so long as she lived, which would be a very long time indeed according to the Styx, Rhea Stygius would never stop running away. She would never stop pining for more.

And every moment she spent stuck in Hell against her will would in fact be a form of great suffering for her.

An idea struck him then. "Do you really want to see what life is like outside of Hell?" Kip asked her.

"Yes," Rhea replied. "More than anything."

"It's not an easy journey," Kip said. "I know someone who can get us there. It will cost most of what we have to get across the Styx and back to the plane where I used to live. But I know the way."

Rhea smiled a grin as oversized as the giant stolen coat she wore and grabbed his hand with her small one. "Lead the way," she said.

VIV'S INFERNO

Burn It to the Ground

"Arson duty?" Viv groaned.

Her eyes were flashing through several shades in quick succession as she did. Martin had learned over the time he'd known Viv that this meant she was supremely agitated. Viv swore the color of her ever-changing irises had nothing to do with her own mood and was more likely linked to the mood of the observer, but Martin had his doubts. Still, he knew better than to ever challenge her on it. Viv was like that – she liked to fight and as a result got into way too many battles. If you cared about her, you learned to pick her battles for her because she seemed incapable of doing it on her own.

"Yes, arson duty," Martin replied. "You're lucky to have a job at all after everything that's happened."

Viv knew her boss was right, but that didn't help the truth sting any less. The past couple of months had been beyond rough. At times, they were practically unbearable, as her body had attacked her at every opportunity. In the early days after they solved their last case, she'd been racked with seizures. Even after those were controlled, she'd slogged through a postictal haze for longer than she could remember. Her medication regimen had to be readjusted.

Weeks later, it still wasn't quite right. She found it much harder to rise in the morning. Much harder to shake the grogginess.

Unfortunately, it wasn't easier to sleep, not in an otherwise empty bed that was sized to fit three people. But with Penny and Karen gone…

Viv sighed.

"What?" Martin said.

"Nothing," Viv replied.

"Sometimes I wish I were a telepath," Martin admitted. "Then I'd know how much bullshit you feed me."

"Maybe," Viv said, "although telepaths often miss context. They're really specific about details but screw up the bigger picture." She paused. "Empaths are better at the big picture."

It was something that her partner Karen had tried hard to impress upon Viv, that empaths had different strengths than telepaths. That empaths were better at the big picture, even if their powers could be more ambiguous and required more interpretation. Viv felt a pang of guilt for not properly appreciating that about Karen while she was still around, guilt for second-guessing her partner's empathic work when she shouldn't have. And now Karen was gone, off who knew where.

"You miss her, don't you?" Martin said.

Viv nodded. "I do. I miss both of them. As much crap as I liked to give Karen and Penny, I don't know how I'm going to work without them," she admitted.

"Well, luckily, you don't have to," Martin said.

Viv cocked her head. "I'm getting a new partner?" She steeled herself. This could be a huge hassle, getting used to working with someone new. The Department of Psychic Operations, or PsyOps, housed all manner of different intuitives. Some were grounded, down to earth, easy to work with. Others were pretty darn full of themselves. Telepathic boy wunderkind Ryan Roscoe sprang immediately to mind, with his mysterious family connections and suspiciously expensive clothes, typically inaccessible on a PsyOps detective's paycheck. He was cocksure, arrogant, and off-putting.

Viv wanted to work with anyone but Roscoe.

"Yes," Martin said. "It's someone you've worked with before."

Oh no. That was a short list. One that terrifyingly included Roscoe.

Please not Roscoe, anyone but Roscoe, please not Roscoe, Viv chanted over and over again in her head, with the added pleasure of knowing that Roscoe's telepathy would mean that he'd hear those thoughts if he were waiting in the wings.

A figure emerged. But it was not Roscoe. Viv knew as much the moment she spotted the spooky expression and wild mass of crimped frizzy hair that grew out of her new partner's head like a topiary that hadn't been trimmed in months.

"Hey Viv," Amarynth said.

Viv glared at the wall. The universe had a way of playing cruel tricks, she mused. This was indeed anyone other than Roscoe, technically speaking.

This was arguably worse than Roscoe, however. Amarynth and Viv had clashed many times over the years that Am had worked as the team's Connections Agent, tasked with weaving together the various clues on open cases and generating new investigative leads, angles that they could try to get at the truth.

Amarynth Watson – "no relation to *those* Watsons" – was arguably the most gifted Connections Agent who worked at PsyOps, but her talents were lopsided. She inevitably spotted the most tenuous links well before anyone ever would, but she was simultaneously condemned to be unable to explain what she knew convincingly to others.

This made it very difficult for Viv to trust her. And now here they were. Partners.

Viv rolled her eyes.

"I'm not exactly thrilled about this either," Amarynth said.

"Then why are you going along with it?" Viv asked.

"Well, if you hadn't noticed, Martin happens to be our boss," Amarynth said.

"Thank you, Am," Martin said.

Amarynth beamed. Viv felt like she was going to throw up in her mouth.

"Seriously, Viv, I think this will be good for you," Martin said.

Viv frowned. "Why do you say that?"

"You're a great agent, one of the best I've ever had working for me, but you don't believe it. You don't know how good you are. And that limits you," Martin said.

"Whatever," Viv said.

"No," Martin said. "No whatever. Cut that out."

Viv stared at the ceiling.

"Honestly, sometimes I wonder if I wouldn't be better off teaching elementary school, especially when you act like that," Martin said.

Viv said nothing.

"It's been a long time since you've worked without Karen. And you've *never* done detective work without Penny. This is your chance to know what you can do without either of them in the picture," Martin said.

Viv didn't want to agree with Martin, but she had to admit he had a point. She nodded slowly, understanding.

"Anyway, I thought with all the rumors flying around about you that you'd be eager for the chance to prove yourself as a professional," Martin said.

Viv cringed at the word "rumors." That was another uncomfortable truth. The last big case she'd worked had been a little too close to home. Viv had learned that people really do judge you by your family, even when you're estranged and your relatives have little to nothing in common with you. When you have a relative behind bars, people find it easy to take a second look at you and wonder if you've committed crimes they haven't seen – or if you are about to.

It wasn't fair in the slightest, but people did it.

It was an uncomfortable position for a psychic detective to be in. Psychophobes were everywhere, eager to warn anyone within earshot of the danger of intuitive powers. Being an intuitive had already been one easy strike against her. A relative behind bars made things even worse.

"You don't have to remind me about the gossip, Martin," Viv said. "I'm not stupid. I know what people here at PsyOps are saying about me. I've heard them talking shit when they don't know I can hear them, and rooms have a way of going silent when I walk into them these days."

Martin cringed, not sure what to say.

"I suspect I've had it coming for a while," Viv said.

"You think?" said Martin.

Viv nodded. "People have been looking for an excuse to trash me. I'm an easy target. Sure, they *say* it's inappropriate that my work partners are also romantic ones, but they're just jealous."

"Well," said Amarynth, "they do have a point when it comes to bias interference."

Viv glared at her, irritated that Amarynth had raised an uncomfortable truth. Everyone knew how susceptible psychic powers were to bias, and in many eyes, psychic detective work tainted by nepotism could only produce shoddy results.

It didn't matter that Viv's investigative team had never had a conviction overturned or put an innocent person behind bars, something the rest of the teams at PsyOps couldn't say.

Their work was always called into question because of the relationships between them. They were always called unprofessional.

Maybe Martin was right, Viv thought. Maybe this was her opportunity to prove once and for all that she was a professional – even if it meant pairing up with Amarynth, someone she'd found equal parts frustrating and annoying in the past. A detriment to her work rather than a boon.

"And besides," Martin continued, causing Viv to wonder how much of what he'd been saying she might have missed, "when Penny and Karen come back –"

"If," Viv said.

"When," Martin insisted. "When they come back, maybe this experience with Amarynth will make it so the two of you work together better." He lowered his voice. "Dealing with your little clashes is one of my least favorite things about my job."

"Mine too," Amarynth agreed.

Viv shot an annoyed glance at her. Amarynth was such a teacher's pet.

Amarynth smiled sweetly at Viv, unperturbed.

This was going to be a long case, Viv thought.

The images came to her as soon as they stepped onto the lot. Viv could see the building still standing, all three stories. It seemed like a perfectly normal building on a perfectly normal day. Nothing seemed amiss.

It could have been any building in Skinner's mixed-use neighborhood, Cambria Square. The downstairs level housed a convenience store. The upper two stories held apartments.

The convenience store on the ground level was open at the time of the fire, Viv saw. It was quite busy and bustling. People were shuffling in and out. Then a scream was heard, a plume of smoke seen.

People began to run from the building, stampeding into the street like cattle.

The screams continued. Flames sprouted and then quickly grew, enveloping the building.

She heard the distant wail of fire sirens as people milled about the street, unsure of where to run or if they even should.

Viv shook her head, and the vision was gone. And all that stood before her was a scorched pile of rubble.

"It must have taken a lot to burn this place to the ground," Amarynth said.

Viv nodded. "A very hot flame, one that worked exceptionally quickly."

"You'd expect there to be more left," Amarynth said, "with how quickly the fire trucks got here."

Viv pivoted to Amarynth. She nearly asked the Connections Agent how she knew this, but she caught herself just in time. Of course Amarynth knew this, just as she knew a lot of other things she wasn't supposed to know. That was her psychic power, after all, seeing connections that other people missed. It was an inconsistently useful power at best, however. Not all connections Amarynth made were helpful, for starters. Some could be quite trivial.

A team of normals brushed by Viv and Amarynth as the two detectives surveyed the scene. The passing normals were all garbed similarly, sporting matching black jackets with the word "ARSON" emblazoned on the back in tall white letters. Viv felt a pang of envy. Working for the Department of Psychic Operations didn't come with any sort of uniform.

She and her coworkers arrived at crime scenes in their plainclothes, looking scattershot and informal. In her early days working for PsyOps, Viv had made more of an effort, mimicking the wardrobe of TV detectives.

Her partner Penny had been invaluable in this capacity, guiding Viv to the best thrift stores, where Viv snatched up men's suits for pennies on the dollar. If you timed it correctly, Penny had told her, you could get to the store at just the time of day that most grieving widows summoned up the courage to offload their late husbands' clothing and get the pick of the sartorial litter.

Penny had it down to a science, one that she gladly passed on to Viv. Detective Viv Lee arrived to work in those early days in splendor. However, that splendor would not last.

It didn't take long for her smart suits to get dirty, as she crouched over bloodstained pavement memorizing the position of downed bodies and strewn weapons, snapping pictures with the oversized camera that hung around her neck so that others could see what she saw without her having to undergo a memory audit to retrieve her engrams.

After a while, Viv began to turn up to work in whatever outfit was comfortable and could get stained. Most of the time, this was Viv's paint-flecked overalls. She hadn't painted for years, not since dropping out of art school to pursue her career at PsyOps, driven by hunger and a desire to make a difference in the newly formed Psychic State, but those flecks of paint reminded her that once upon a time she had.

And in a way, they reminded her that in a future time she would paint again. But on her own terms. Only on her own terms.

The more people asked her why she quit, the less she wanted to return.

Viv stole a quick glance at Amarynth, who appeared to be deep in thought.

"You've figured it out already, haven't you?" Viv asked Amarynth.

Amarynth considered the question and nodded slowly and tentatively. "Sort of," Amarynth said.

"Care to share?" Viv prompted her.

"I would love to share it with you," Amarynth said. "I just… can't."

Viv grumbled. "See, this is why everyone thinks you're full of shit."

"Everyone?" Amarynth said.

Viv didn't answer the question.

"Even you?" Amarynth said, asking the question she really wanted to know the answer to on the second try, as a lot of people did.

Viv didn't answer this question either.

"You'll figure it out yourself," Amarynth said.

"When?" Viv asked.

Amarynth shrugged. "Eventually." She tipped her head. "I'm not exactly sure about the time. But I'm positive you'll solve this case."

"Before the arsonist strikes again?" Viv asked.

"That I don't know," Amarynth admitted.

Viv sighed, frustrated. "Okay, so if I'm solving this arson case on my own, tell me why you're here. What are you going to do? Other than obnoxiously tell me you've solved the case already and not share what you know, that is."

Amarynth took a deep breath in and out, struggling to maintain her composure. The last thing she needed to do was meet Viv's fiery temper with an outburst of her own. She knew that her limitations as a Connections Agent were frustrating because they surely frustrated her. Amarynth imagined if their roles were reversed, she might react as Viv often did to her.

True, Am wanted to punch Viv in the face, a feeling not at all unusual for her to have when Viv began to lose her temper and lash out at her verbally, but Amarynth also knew that while punching Viv in the face would feel good in the moment, it would solve nothing.

Amarynth breathed the love of punching in and breathed it back out.

"My role here is important. I can just see the edges of it, Viv, but I know for sure that my role isn't to solve the crime. It's to protect you while you solve it."

"Protect me?" Viv said. She laughed. "You're not exactly bodyguard material, Amarynth. I've got... five inches on you. And a good twenty pounds of muscle."

Amarynth nodded and considered this. "There are many ways of protecting someone else, Viv," she said finally.

Viv sighed. "When you talk like that, a sack of fortune cookies would be a better partner than you. They'd make more sense."

Amarynth bit the inside of her cheek. "Don't you have pictures to take?" she said.

Viv rolled her eyes and began to photograph the scene. Amarynth pulled out a notebook and a pen and began to take copious notes, details that leaped out to her and would certainly become important later and more meaningful as she hung them up on her causality board back at PsyOps, a visual aid that she used to better organize her insights and find meaningful links that she might otherwise miss.

"Don't worry," a familiar voice inside Amarynth's head said. "It'll all become clear."

"I sure hope so," Amarynth responded.

Viv whipped around. "Did you say something?" she asked.

"Nothing important," Amarynth replied.

"Do you ever?" Viv shot back.

Viv was great at scathing rhetorical questions, Amarynth thought.

It was dark by the time they returned to PsyOps. Viv noted with great alarm that Martin was still there in his office.

"Hope you didn't wait up for us," Viv said, pulling out a chair in front of his desk. She turned it around so it faced backward and sat down on it, straddling it so that the chair back covered her chest like a breastplate.

"Is it that late?" Martin asked. "I guess I lost track of time."

It was plausible, seeing as the entirety of PsyOps was underground, only accessible through an elevator housed in an unattractive storefront that escaped the notice of normals. Martin's office didn't have any actual windows, just a convincing painting of a skyline view of Skinner. The portrait was photorealistic enough to fool most people who came in there. The only giveaway was that the sun never moved, and the light never changed. In Martin's office window painting, it was always about 1:00 pm.

Fluorescent lights lit the room of course.

Still, there was something strained and dishonest in Martin's voice that gave Viv pause. It was at times like these that she missed Karen most. As an empath, she'd know instantly whether Martin was full of it. Karen would know if Martin was really worried and faking calm.

Martin could rarely fool Karen, but he could fool Viv all day long. *Like sunlight that never moves.*

"So what did we find?" Martin prompted.

Amarynth opened her notebook and summarized the key positions of debris they'd found at the scene of the fire and what seemed to be the fire's point of origin. They hadn't been able to identify much of anything. It didn't look like a normal building fire at all.

"I would estimate," Amarynth said, "that the temperature reached, or even exceeded, cremation levels."

"Which is?" Martin asked.

"Around 1800 Fahrenheit," Amarynth answered, before adding, "give or take."

"Give or take, give or take," Viv muttered mockingly. It always chafed her how Amarynth lazily heaped the false modesty on after the fact. Either own your intelligence or not. This half-in, half-out game Amarynth played was exhausting. Just own it already.

"Did you have something to say?" Martin asked.

Viv shook her head. "Nothing important."

Do you ever? The words flashed through Amarynth's head briefly, an echo of what Viv had said to her earlier. It was what Viv would no doubt say in her situation. She thought of saying it at this moment but took a deep breath in and one out. Breathing in the love of snark and breathing it back out. Yes, that was good.

Martin looked back at her. "I take it that 1800 is very hot?"

Amarynth chuckled. "You could say that." She consulted her notes. "A house fire *can* get up to 2000 degrees, but they're typically around 1100."

"And this one got hot instantly. There was no ramp-up," Viv said. She snapped her fingers. "It was like that. A few seconds of smoke, and then instant cremation."

"What makes you say that?" Martin asked.

"I saw it in a vision," Viv replied.

Martin looked to Amarynth as Viv groaned, annoyed to have her work checked. "What do you think?"

"I think Viv's right," Amarynth said.

"I suppose it'd be futile to ask you how you know Viv's right," Martin ventured.

"You know me so well," Amarynth replied.

"How sure are you?" Martin asked.

"Very," Amarynth said. "It's just as Viv said. Instantaneous."

Martin gritted his teeth and glanced up at the ceiling of his office, noting that one tile appeared to be disconcertingly loose. There was nothing for it, however. The maintenance budget, already slim to begin with, had been cut back severely in recent months. The Psychic State was tightening its belt in a million painful ways, and it must simply be tolerated. At least in a subterranean office, one didn't have to worry about rain dripping through the roof. You took your victories where you found them, didn't you?

He looked back down at both Viv and Amarynth, meeting their gaze. "Well, you'd better get to work on this, shouldn't you? There could be lives at stake."

Amarynth and Viv nodded in unison, a similar resigned look crawling onto both of their faces. Curious, Martin thought, how they looked so alike when they had that same expression. It was funny how two nemeses could somehow converge, despite seeming to have so little in common.

"Dismissed," Martin said, waving them away with his hand. They slunk out of his office quietly and closed the door behind them.

"Your place or mine?" Amarynth asked brightly as they emerged from the storefront onto the street.

The moon hung high above them, full, illuminating the street outside of PsyOps headquarters more intensely than either of them was accustomed to seeing it.

"What do you mean 'your place or mine'?" Viv said, scowling.

"We have work to do," Amarynth said.

"We always have work to do," Viv grumbled.

"Viv," Amarynth said firmly. Viv cringed at her name coming out of the Connections Agent's mouth. Amarynth plowed on anyway. "This case isn't going to solve itself."

"I know that," Viv said.

"So I was thinking while we're working on it, we could stick together," Amarynth said.

"I can't think of anything I'd like less," Viv admitted.

"I'm not exactly a fan either," Amarynth said.

"Then why are you suggesting it?" Viv asked.

Amarynth sighed. "Because we're in dire straits, if you haven't noticed. Both of your partners have disappeared. You're paired up with me of all people. We're on arson duty, another terrible sign. Off homicide and onto the scut work. And this is our only case." She flung her hands expansively to the sides for emphasis and dramatic effect. "It doesn't take a Connections Agent to realize that this is your last chance, Viv. That this is our last chance."

"What do you mean by last chance?" Viv asked.

"Ah, so you're in denial," Amarynth snapped.

Like most people who could dish it, Viv preferred not to take it. "In denial? You take that back."

"Once you face the truth, I will," Amarynth replied, defiant.

"Face *your* truth, you mean," Viv said.

Amarynth said nothing. Instead, she breathed in the love of punching and breathed it back out.

Viv spoke first. "Okay, so let's have it."

"Have what?" Amarynth said.

"Your truth. What am I not facing? What do you mean by last chance?"

Amarynth studied Viv's face. It seemed markedly open, for a change. Perhaps she'd gotten through to her stubborn coworker.

"If we can't solve this case, we're done. This is a test, one we better not fail." Amarynth said.

"What makes you say that?" Viv pressed.

"When have we ever had only one case?" Amarynth asked.

Viv nodded. "That's a good point."

"Anyway," Amarynth continued, "you live with your partners normally. You're used to solving cases that way. It only makes sense that we live together while we work on this one. You never know what kind of insights you're going to have at the dinner table. Over coffee. Whatever. Things that wouldn't occur to you if you just had a regular nine to five working window."

Viv considered this. "You might just have a point."

"I usually do, Viv," Amarynth said. "Even if it's not obvious at first."

"Or ever," Viv replied.

Amarynth rolled her eyes.

"Mine," Viv said.

"I Im?"

"My place," Viv said. "I have a house on Bell."

"Okay," Amarynth said. They walked in silence. It was about a 10-minute walk if the crosswalks were timed in their favor. Not too bad, considering it was about five minutes to drive there, perhaps a bit longer if those same traffic lights decided to go the other way.

Still, Viv often drove to a public parking lot near PsyOps headquarters, particularly when a case had them driving a long distance to investigate.

The recent arson had been different, however. It had been a short walk from PsyOps, so no need to drive. In fact, Amarynth had realized uncomfortably as they first received the address from Martin, the arson had happened only a few streets away from where she lived in Cambria Square.

The convenience store that exploded into flames had once upon a time been Cambria Market, where Amarynth often bought the stray grocery item she had forgotten. The prices were terrible, but you paid for convenience, didn't you? The markup was how little places like that stayed in business.

Nearly everything in that snarl of streets was named Cambria, including the small coffeehouse next door to her apartment building, where they sold expensive Italian espresso and champagne from late in the morning until late at night.

It would be nice to get away, Amarynth thought suddenly, glad that Viv had suggested she stay at her house. The smell of burnt matter from the Cambria Market fire lingered in the neighborhood air, fragrant even from her apartment patio two streets away.

Her parakeet Tesla could fend for himself. She'd left enough food and water for several days. And she could always swing by to check on him or bring him to the house on Bell if the case stretched on.

This could be fun.

Before she knew it, they were there. Viv pulled up in front of an adorable little house. It was a modest dwelling, to be sure, a far cry from the chic appointments of Cambria Square, but it had clearly been loved by its occupants. And particularly by Penny, whose uber-feminine touches were apparent everywhere Amarynth looked.

Yes, it was clear that the illustrious Penelope Dreadful lived here. The woman was walking human sunshine. Amarynth reflected that Viv was different without her. Not that Viv was ever exactly sunny – but something about Penny had a way of brightening up Viv.

Perhaps it was a mercy that Karen was gone as well, off on some sort of personal development journey. Karen could be rather gloomy in the best of times, and these certainly weren't those.

Though it was the middle of summer, Penny's absence had a way of making things quite wintry indeed, Amarynth reflected. Autumnal but without the vibrant leaf colors.

As Viv led her up the front steps, Amarynth glanced down and laughed aloud at what was inscribed on the doormat. GO AWAY.

Ah, so Viv did live here, after all.

"Penny got that for me," Viv told Amarynth, smiling.

"It's amazing," Amarynth replied.

Viv shuddered, uncomfortable at being complimented by Amarynth but pleased nonetheless.

The inside of her house was small of course but well-appointed. Wood floors everywhere. Well taken care of.

"It's not much," Viv said. "But it's home."

"It's lovely," Amarynth replied. Because it was.

"So what now?" Viv asked. "Do we braid each other's hair and pop popcorn or something?"

Amarynth blinked, staring at her.

"I've never done this before," Viv said.

"Done what?"

"Had a slumber party," Viv replied.

"You live with two women though," Amarynth said.

"Umm... Amarynth... don't take this the wrong way... but..."

Amarynth studied her face.

"I don't think you want to do a lot of what I do with Penny and Karen. At least not with me," Viv said.

"That's not what I meant!" Amarynth said, flushing a deep red.

"I mean," Viv said, picking up on Amarynth's embarrassment and leaning into it, delighted to be making her uncomfortable, "I probably have a copy of the *Kama Sutra* kicking around here somewhere if you wanted to give it a go. But I have to admit you're not exactly my type... and I'm not sure Penny or Karen would be happy about it."

"Viv!" Amarynth protested. "That's not what I meant!"

"I wouldn't blame you though. Chicks dig me. It's just the way I am." Viv grinned broadly. As she did, it reminded Amarynth of the proud smile a little boy flashes when he drops a worm down the back of a screaming person's shirt.

"Not all chicks," Amarynth said.

"We'll see about that," Viv countered.

"I think you're projecting," Amarynth said.

Viv laughed uproariously. "Oh, you think I have it bad for you?"

Amarynth shrugged.

"That'd be a cold day in Hell," Viv said.

"Anything's possible," Amarynth replied.

"I'd argue with you, but this is Psychic City," Viv admitted.

"Popcorn was a good suggestion," Amarynth said.

Viv raised an eyebrow.

"For our sleepover," Amarynth said.

"Yes, ma'am," Viv replied, snapping to faux attention and giving an exaggerated salute.

Amarynth rolled her eyes but sank onto the couch, anticipating the sweet smell of buttered popcorn.

Maybe this wouldn't be so bad, after all.

Viv's phone rang. "Yes?" she said.

Amarynth watched her face and noted that it fell sharply. "Was that tonight?" A pause. "Geez, you don't have to be like that about it. I forgot, okay?" Another pause. "Well, it's not like I don't have a million things going on. Some of us aren't sitting in our mother's house, mooching off her dwindling fortune, Love." Another pause. "Yeah, yeah, I'll be there. Calm down. Quit your bitching." Viv pressed the call end button and shook her head.

"I guess I better find something other than pajamas to wear," Amarynth said.

"It's my sister Love," Viv explained. "She's having a stupid party. I forgot about the whole thing."

"I gathered," Am said.

"Oh right," Viv said. "Of course you did. You're like that."

Amarynth grinned.

"Well, follow me. I think Penny has a few things you can wear. You're not exactly the same size, but you're probably closer to her size than mine."

"Thanks, Viv," Am said.

"Oh you're thanking me now, but just wait until you meet my sister Love," Viv replied.

Love Is a Many Splendored Thing

"Oh, Viv, darling," Viv's sister Love cooed, "it's so wonderful you could make it." Her tone was saccharine, dripping with sweetness, but her eyes gave a different impression. Love looked like a person who feels trapped.

Viv knew instantly that it had been courtesy that compelled her sister to send her an invitation and that Love had been hoping that Viv simply wouldn't respond. The follow-up call, too, had been etiquette. Love probably had thought Viv wouldn't even answer her phone. Love certainly hoped Viv wouldn't show up.

And now here she was.

Love's neck was dripping in costume jewelry. Glass diamonds. She smelled strongly of musk, as though she had bathed herself in cologne. Viv noted that her sister was also a distinctly different color than the last time she'd seen her. Love's skin wasn't quite orange and wasn't quite golden. It looked to Viv like what an amateur artist might get when trying to make either orange or brown and ending up with something in between.

A poorly applied fake tan. The cheap kind.

It appeared to Viv as though her sister was wearing a corset under her low-cut frilly blouse. Her waist appeared unnaturally thin and her breasts were conspicuously larger than the last time Viv had seen them. They poured up through the top of her shirt like a can of readymade biscuit dough after the foil wrapping is removed and it's hit with a spoon.

Why hello, Mini-Me, Viv thought. It hit her all at once. Her sister was impersonating their mother. Poorly. But impersonating her nonetheless.

"And who's this with you?" Love exclaimed, gesturing towards Amarynth.

"This is my PsyOps partner, Amarynth," Viv said.

"Partner?" Love asked. "Did you break up with Penny and... what was the other girl's name?"

"Karen," Viv replied. "And no. We're not that kind of partners."

"We're just coworkers," Amarynth said.

"Of course," Love winked at them. "I won't tell Penny and Karen if you don't."

"No, Love," Viv said. "For real. We just work together."

"So, Amethyst," Love said.

"Amarynth," Viv corrected.

"That's what I *said*," Love said.

Viv folded her arms.

"I didn't catch your last name," Love said.

"That's because she didn't say it," Viv replied. This was another way her sister seemed to be imitating their mother, as their mother typically always wanted to know people's last names. For some mothers, this might be so that they could reach out to the parents of their child's new friends, but their own mother had done it for a distinctly different reason: She was a snob, a social climber.

Their mother had always wanted to know the socioeconomic background of each potential new acquaintance of her children, and by extension, her. Anything that she could use to elevate her position was appreciated.

Viv knew this was the case with her sister Love, too.

"Amarynth Watson," she said.

Love gasped. "A Watson?"

Viv waited for what she knew was coming, the correction Amarynth always made. The Watsons were one of the Four Families, unassailable, all-powerful, who controlled a lot of what went on in the Psychic City and even the Psychic State for that matter.

The Skinners and Watsons were particularly noteworthy, moneyed, and respected. You really couldn't escape their legacy when you lived in the Skinner-Watson metro. Not only was the area named after them, but a great number of important buildings and organizations were also as well.

Amarynth wasn't one of those Watsons. Watson was a fairly common surname, after all, and Amarynth was very clear that her roots were a great deal more humble. Invariably, Amarynth would make this known after people assumed that she was connected to the dynasty.

"Yes," Amarynth said this time, however, surprising Viv. "I'm a Watson."

The color drained from Love's face. "Oh dear," she said. "I'm afraid I haven't prepared for someone of your caliber to join us." She looked frantic. "Come in, have a seat. Here, you can have mine."

Amarynth nodded demurely and did just that. The chair and a half that Love had indicated was quite comfortable indeed, although it did have the effect of trying to swallow her when she sat upon it. Amarynth perched on the edge of the chair, leaning forward to resist being sucked into it. This had the effect of making her look quite pensive. She stole an impish glance at Viv.

Viv stifled laughter. *Our first private joke*, she mused. *I didn't think Am had it in her.*

Love clinked a spoon against a wineglass. "Everyone, could I have your attention please?"

Every head in the room swiveled towards her.

"I'm happy to announce we have a *Watson* in our midst," she said. "Friends, meet my very good friend, Amarynth *Watson*."

Oohs and *ahhs* rolled throughout the room. A Watson. My goodness.

One by one, party guests formed a queue in front of the cannibalistic chair and a half. Amarynth found herself attending to a receiving line. Everyone wanted to greet her, let themselves be known.

After a small handful of names, the introductions began to wash over Amarynth and blur together, as did the greetings and naked pandering. It was paradoxical, Amarynth thought. Supplicants were so desperate to be notable and special, but they were so uniform in their efforts to achieve that aim that they had the opposite effect.

I guess that's what happens when you try too hard to stand out, she thought. *You guarantee that you'll blend in. Maybe it's better to just risk being boring or forgotten. Maybe that's how you end up being memorable.*

"Or by lying about your identity," a small voice within her said.

"Quiet," she said aloud.

"Oh—oh… oh, I'm sorry," the supplicant before her blustered.

"Oh, not you," Amarynth said. She wasn't sure how she would explain it. It wasn't exactly normal to hear voices, and typically other people would judge you for it. Hers had no link to madness of course. The inner voice she heard was a crucial part of her sanity – yet another thing that was hard to explain to others, that she heard a voice that made her saner. She'd been hearing it for all her life, but the few times she'd tried to explain that to other people in the past, she'd found herself brought in front of psychiatrists. And those psychiatrists had been quick to respond to her explanations by pressing handfuls of pills into her hand. Those pills hadn't even taken away the voice. Instead, they'd taken away everything else that made her happy, made her whole.

It wasn't madness, this voice, but a strong inner monologue, one that always helped her and never harmed her.

She'd learned early on that there was plenty that you shouldn't explain to other people. Over time, shouldn't explain became couldn't explain. The years of abstaining had a way of training her to be unable to explain anything, even when she desperately wanted to.

Thankfully, the person in front of her didn't expect for her to explain herself at all. They accepted her "not you" and didn't question her.

This was what happened when there was a perceived social power differential. People became inordinately deferential. It was kind of silly, but it was useful.

"Amelia, darling," Love said.

"Amarynth, please," Amarynth said. "Or Am, if you can't manage that."

Love's eyes narrowed. Even without empathic powers, the emotions darting across Love's face were clear not only to Amarynth but to everyone around them. At first, there was a pained look – as though Love had been backhanded across the face – understandable because socially she had been.

Then the pained look fell into a defensive one. Love briefly showed signs that she might counterattack and protect her honor. But even as this was about to happen, something else within her intervened, reminding her of Am's high status and the likely large consequences to be paid if she were to slight such an important person.

Making enemies with a Watson would be social suicide. Self-preservation kicked in, and Love curtsied low. "Of course," she said, managing a smile. "Am… or perhaps I should say Ms. Watson, there's someone I'd like you to meet, one final – but very important – introduction."

 "Oh?" Amarynth said.

"I present to you… Mr. and Mrs. Baker," Love cried, clapping her hands together frenetically.

At first, no one else clapped, but Love looked around frantically with a panicked look, and others joined her, creating a rolling wave of applause.

"Alexander," Mr. Baker said, taking Amarynth's hand in his own and kissing it. The best word for Alexander Baker would probably be *substantial*. He was tall and thick but not overly pudgy, and his voice was deep and booming. Everything about him seemed imposing and difficult to ignore.

He was… substantial. Yes, that was the word.

Mrs. Baker, however, was not. She crept out from behind him. She waved weakly at Amarynth. She was a very tiny woman, perhaps four foot nine inches tall and small-boned.

"Betty," Love urged her. "Go on, introduce yourself."

Mrs. Baker looked warily at Love. "It's Liz now," she said in a high-pitched quavering voice. If it had been lower in frequency, it would have been impossible to hear her at all.

Amarynth had heard stronger voices whistling in the wind. There was an undertone of baby talk in it. It reminded Am of the voice that daughters sometimes affect when asking their parents for favors, hoping to evoke a baby-parent dependency.

"Liz Baker," she said to Amarynth in that same evanescent, nearly imperceptible voice. She didn't extend her hand as her husband did.

"You'll have to forgive Betty," Alexander said in that booming, commanding voice. "She's a sweet girl, but she doesn't get out much. And she isn't used to interacting with people of... your caliber. I myself have much more experience in that area." He leaned in closer and added in a voice that was meant to be softer but still projected because of how substantial it was, "And I'm always looking for more opportunities. Just something to keep in mind." He smiled suggestively.

Ugh, Amarynth thought. *Your wife is standing right there.*

It was a very foreign feeling to have this man hitting on her. Am wasn't used to receiving this kind of attention at all. She had her own sense of style, a firm sense of who she was, and she did her best to look nice – although her rebellious hair rarely cooperated – but she was never the woman whose appearance commanded attention from other people. She wasn't the fashionista who made a splash by appearing impeccably coiffed. And she certainly wasn't the vixen who caused others to fantasize about her.

This man was either indiscriminate, a social climber, or both. "Both," the voice within Amarynth confirmed.

"My name is not Betty," Mrs. Baker squeaked in protest.

"It was," Alexander replied.

"Well, it's not now," Mrs. Baker said. "It's Liz."

"It's different every week," Alexander explained. As he did, he draped one giant arm over his wife's shoulders. She snuggled into the warmth of his body. Alexander looked up into the air indifferently, barely registering the adoration she beamed at him. "Let's see," he said. "Elizabeth has been... Betty of course. Which is what she was when I met her."

Elizabeth Baker sighed.

"And then she was Bette for a while. Eli, Eliza, Beth. Uhh... Liza. And now Liz, I guess," Alexander said. "Did I get that right, honey?"

Liz shook her head. "You missed Ellie."

"Of course," Alexander said. "How could I forget?'

"And Elle," Liz said. "And Ella."

Alexander frowned. "I miss calling you Betty, sweetheart," he said.

Liz looked like she was about to cry. Amarynth felt quite sorry for her. "It's been nice meeting you, Ms. Watson," Liz forced out while she still had her composure, before walking away.

Alexander pressed a business card into Amarynth's palm. "If you ever get lonely," he said, "I hear I'm excellent company." He winked before turning and walking away.

"Isn't he amazing?" Love said.

"He's something," Amarynth replied.

"That wife of his though," Love said. "She's a painful creature."

"I'd say she's more pained than painful," Amarynth said. "What's the story there?"

"She just has no confidence in herself," Love explained. "She starves herself, the poor thing, thinking that if she can lose a few more pounds that she'll be worthy. And as you can see, she doesn't have anything extra left to lose."

"No, she doesn't," Amarynth observed.

"She's gotten a little bit better than she used to be," Love offered.

"Oh?" Amarynth said.

"She used to apologize constantly, no matter what she did. Practically every other sentence. I'm sorry, I'm sorry. Even when she was doing what you wanted her to do. It was pretty damn annoying," Love said.

It must have been even harder for her to live that way, Amarynth thought, *feeling like everything she said or did had to be apologized for. It had to be unbearable.*

"She doesn't do it in words anymore, but she still does it in her body language. The way she talks. You can still see she doesn't feel worthy, that she feels like she's putting other people out by just existing," Love said.

Amarynth nodded. It had been rather obvious.

"She's had that hair color and cut for about a week. Next week she'll have a different one. It actually gets hard to recognize Betty – er, Liz. She keeps getting makeovers. It's like she thinks that if she can just find the right look that... I dunno," Love said, shrugging.

"I think it has to do with that husband of hers," Am said.

"Alex?" Love laughed. "Oh no, he's wonderful. He's a dreamboat, haven't you noticed?"

"Of course," Amarynth said. "He's attractive. But that's not the issue. If anything, it makes it worse."

"Oh?" Love said.

"He clearly has a wandering eye. I'd say he's.... pretty popular," Amarynth said.

"Well, you don't exactly expect a man like *that* to limit himself to a woman like *her*, do you?" Love said in a suspiciously wounded tone.

Ah, Amarynth thought. *You're one of his conquests. Taking after your mother, Viv's mother, are we?*

Aloud, Amarynth said, "I imagine it makes her feel really insecure. And maybe that's why she's changing hairstyles and names so often."

Love laughed. "Okay, Dr. Freud," she teased. And then remembering she was talking to Amarynth *Watson*, she quickly backpedaled. "Which is a compliment by the way. Why, he was the riot of Vienna! A genius. I don't care what anyone said about him being a quack. Or the cocaine. Oh... Oh no, I didn't mean..."

Amarynth rose from her chair, looking for Viv and an opportunity to extract herself from this den of pit vipers.

The Strong Silent Type

The most important things are the hardest to say. They are the things you get ashamed of, because words diminish them – words shrink things that seemed limitless when they were in your head to no more than living size when they're brought out. But it's more than that, isn't it? The most important things lie too close to wherever your secret heart is buried, like landmarks to a treasure your enemies would love to steal away. And you may make revelations that cost you dearly only to have people look at you in a funny way, not understanding what you've said at all, or why you thought it was so important that you almost cried while you were saying it. That's the worst, I think. When the secret stays locked within not for want of a teller but for want of an understanding ear.

-Stephen King

"So how's it going staying at Viv's?" Amarynth's mother asked her.

The dreary party at Love's was over, and Amarynth had been about to turn in for the night when her phone rang. For some people, it might have been a strange time for their mother to call, but Amarynth's mother lived a relatively asynchronous existence, sleeping when she pleased and staying up when she didn't. It had been this way so long that her mother had forgotten that not everyone in the world worked that way.

Amarynth paused before responding, wishing suddenly for the phones of her childhood, the ones with heft and weight that required you to cradle the receiver between your shoulder and ear. Those were phones you could cuddle with, that you *had* to essentially cuddle with in order to have a conversation with someone else.

A cell phone was considerably more convenient than an old-fashioned phone in practically every aspect. Lightweight, portable, came with voicemail automatically installed instead of requiring an accompanying answering machine system.

Really, a cell phone was superior in every way, except for one: It didn't cuddle you back the way a traditional phone did.

Well, and Amarynth wasn't sure if she were imagining it, but it seemed like the sound quality had gone downhill in the age of cell phones. She supposed it could be she was losing her hearing though as she aged, but her instincts told her that phone companies were skimping on sound quality on the calls she took on these tiny computers.

"It's a big adjustment, for sure," Amarynth replied.

"Is that because of Viv or because you're used to living alone?" her mother said.

"I don't live alone," Amarynth protested. "I have Tesla."

"A parakeet doesn't count as a roommate," her mother replied.

"I don't know why not," Amarynth insisted. "I have to pick up after him. He makes a lot of noise. And he's been known to wake me up in the middle of the night if he's having a nightmare and squawks."

"Oh okay," her mother said sarcastically. "I guess Viv and your parakeet are exactly the same then." Or at least Amarynth thought it was sarcasm. She'd never been good at identifying sarcasm and often mixed it up with earnest statements. It had been particularly bad when Amarynth was a little girl, but she'd gotten better with it over the years, those subtle calculations that were effortless to so many other people, the ones that would let you know when the person you were talking to was only joking with you.

It had gotten easier, yes, but she still wasn't always confident. She didn't know if she would ever be.

"Nah," Amaryllh conceded, deciding to interpret what her mother said as sarcasm. "You're right. It's a big adjustment."

"Of course I am," her mother replied.

Amarynth smiled. She had guessed right. She was finding it was safer to assume sarcasm when she suspected it at all than to err in the opposite direction.

There was dead silence on the line. This was why Amarynth didn't call her mother as often as she would like her to. She never knew quite what to say to her on the phone, how to fill the empty spaces.

All her life, it seemed to Amarynth as though she and her mother were living in entirely different realities. When Amarynth looked back at her childhood, she saw a confusing muddle, a minefield of social tests and traps, which she never seemed to quite navigate as well as her mother wanted to. When it came to social niceties, Amarynth had been born a klutz. A social disaster.

Making friends hadn't come easily to her. And it was easy for her to embarrass her mother when she spoke to others. She never meant to of course. But Amarynth didn't learn the important lessons quickly. She hadn't figured out when it was better to lie and when it was better to tell the truth.

Amarynth had been quite talkative as a little girl, but she had a habit of not understanding which topics were weird, inappropriate, or boring. She didn't come with a filter, and despite all her mother's attempts to help her develop one, she couldn't quite hack it.

And invariably her teacher's disappointing reports of Amarynth's social development, or lack thereof, would travel home to her mother.

It was at this point that her mother had instilled the one lesson Amarynth took to quickly. The one lesson that stuck.

"If you care about something, keep it hidden from other people," her mother had told her.

Since Amarynth cared about a great many things, this had the immediate effect of making her a quiet child.

Amarynth noticed that her mother wasn't like the mothers of other kids in her class. She was stunningly beautiful of course, which made her stick out all by itself. But it was more than that, wasn't it?

It would be many years before Amarynth knew the word that described her mother: Agoraphobic. An expensive-sounding word, evoking rare materials like angora, exotic locations like Angola. The deep sonorous "o" vowel gave it a roundness and beauty that made agoraphobia seem classy simply based on its sound. But despite all this superficial glamour, it was a word that belied a difficult anxious existence.

Amarynth was quite young the first time she had been tasked with running an errand for her mother. It wasn't something most kindergarteners did, trying to walk with purpose due to safety concerns while out in public alone, clutching a child-sized purse to her body.

She walked up and down the aisles of the grocery store as quickly as her small legs could carry her, focused on the list she held in her hand.

That first trip, her hands sweated so much from sheer nervousness that the ink ran, and she had to guess on a few items, made even more difficult because she had only just learned to read and was a little iffy on the list as it was.

Still, she did her best. And her mother thanked her profusely when she returned home with what she asked for.

It was a task she continued to this day. "I'm ready for the list," Amarynth said on the phone, breaking the uncomfortable silence.

"Well here's what I was thinking," her mother began, before launching into the recitation.

Amarynth had the pen ready in her hand but found she only had to write down a few items. Most of what her mother asked for, she asked for every week, and as such these items were burned into her brain.

In fact, if her mother hadn't requested them, Amarynth would probably find herself picking them up anyway, partially out of habit – because these shopping trips had become so routine over the years it felt wrong not to go through all the usual steps – but also because she would suspect her mother had simply forgotten to ask for them.

She had done this several times in the past when her mother had neglected to ask for her grocery staples. And every time Amarynth had taken this logical leap, she had been correct. It had been an inadvertent omission, and her mother was glad that she had picked those items up anyway.

Amarynth's intuition was uncanny. It always had been. Even when she was provided with the wrong explicit information by her mother, she could usually guess what her mother meant. And it wasn't just her mother. The same ability extended to practically everyone else in her life.

When teachers wrote an assignment wrong, Amarynth had no difficulty ascertaining what they'd meant, and she'd complete her work accordingly. While this earned her high grades, it often angered her peers, who would complain to the teacher about how the assignments were written, only to have the teacher remark, "Well, *Amarynth* figured it out. Why couldn't you?"

And just like that, all the other heads in the classroom would swivel towards her and glare at her at once.

Amarynth ruined the curve. Strike one.

Amarynth said very little, and what came out was inevitably awkward. Strike two.

The frizzy-haired girl couldn't take a joke. Hell, she couldn't even recognize a joke. What a weirdo. Who wanted to be friends with someone like that? Strike three.

And so she sat with her mother in silence in the evenings, with her nose buried in a book to keep her from overwhelming her mother with talk she didn't want to hear. Talk that would result in her mother reminding her once again how boring, awkward, and just plain annoying her only child was.

No, it was better not to speak. And to let her actions speak for themselves.

"Thank you, Amarynth," her mother would say, as her daughter arrived with groceries. "You are such a good girl."

Amarynth would smile, but instead she would think, *You only think that because you don't know the real me.*

And as the years wound on, not speaking her mind became less of a conscious effort and more of an ingrained habit. One day Amarynth woke up and realized that she lacked the words to express what she was feeling, what she was thinking.

She could see everything clearly. Picked up quickly on connections that other people missed. The underlying context and background.

Even previously inscrutable social interactions suddenly made sense.

But now she had no way to explain it to other people. Her words were gone. Whether they had been stolen somehow by a supernatural force or those words had simply left her when she wasn't looking, she would never know.

But she knew the words were gone. And she suspected it would be that way forever.

It had a way of making phone conversations with her mother awkward. Despite advising her to say less and to keep more to herself, her mother often seemed quite obviously frustrated with Amarynth's inability to hold up her half of the conversation.

"You're holding out on me, Am," her mother said.

On the other end of the phone, Amarynth shrugged in response to this.

"Hello?" her mother said, the pitch of her voice rising. "Are you still there?"

Right, Amarynth realized. Shrugs didn't travel over phone lines so well, did they? "I don't know what to say," she said.

"You never do, do you?" her mother replied.

Amarynth said nothing.

Her mother audibly scoffed. Nonverbal indignation, Amarynth registered.

"When would you like me to bring your groceries to you?" Amarynth asked.

"Whenever you get a chance. I've got a few days' worth of stuff left. After that, it starts getting weird."

"Weird?" Amarynth asked.

"You know. I'll have to start putting peanut butter on everything just to make a meal."

"Okay," Amarynth said. "I'll be over later this week."

Are You Ready for Your Closeup?

"Rise and shine, Princess," Viv said to Amarynth, throwing on the living room light.

The Connections Agent looked positively larval curled up on the couch like a boiled shrimp. When the light hit her face, she squirmed reflexively and covered her eyes with one inexpertly flailing arm.

"Murmlefutz," Amarynth said.

"Am not," Viv countered.

Amarynth groaned and stretched out both arms, growing like a feral cat. "Tiemizzit?" she said.

"I didn't catch that, Princess," Viv said.

"I said," Amarynth said, exaggerating her enunciation, "what time is it?"

"Oh," Viv said. "It's early."

"As always, you're a veritable fount of information," Amarynth replied, sitting up on the couch and rubbing her eyes.

"Well, I'm sort of in the dark myself," Viv admitted. "All I know is Martin wants us to come to the office."

"That's it?"

"He didn't go into *War and Peace* in his text message," Viv jabbed.

Amarynth scowled. "First or second shower?" she asked Viv.

"Your turn up to bat. I already took care of that."

"Thus the wet hair," Amarynth said, feeling a tiny bit embarrassed she hadn't noticed. She was also acutely aware that she'd slept through Viv's getting up and showering. Sometimes being a heavy sleeper had its benefits. For example, it made it rather easy to crash on a friend's couch. At other times, it had a way of making Amarynth feel more vulnerable, as though she were destined to spend a full third of her life completely defenseless.

"Always making those disparate connections," Viv teased her.

Amarynth winced.

Viv led Amarynth to the bathroom. "Fresh towels in there," she said, pointing to the appropriate area of the closet. "That lever is shower-tub toggle. The knob on the left is hot water. Right is cold. Mix it up like a DJ."

Viv turned to leave the bathroom.

"Hey Viv," Amarynth said.

"Yeah?"

"This is a waste of time," Amarynth said.

"Showering?" Viv said. "Last I checked, it was a requirement for being part of polite society."

"No, going to see Martin. It's a complete waste of time," Amarynth said.

"And how do you know that?" Viv challenged her.

Amarynth rolled her eyes.

"Oh right, that's your 'mystical psychic power.' Just knowing things," Viv replied, making exaggerated air quotes with both hands.

Amarynth sighed. "We're starting up with this again first thing in the morning?"

Viv relaxed. "Maybe it's a waste of time, Princess, but we have to do it anyway. That's how it works with your boss. If you've gotta waste your time making him happy, you do it. You never know when you'll need the goodwill."

"Alright," Amarynth said.

Viv could sense there was more on Amarynth's mind, but she couldn't think of how to begin to get at it. She stood there for a moment trying to riddle it out.

"Um," Amarynth said.

Viv snapped out of her thoughts.

"I kind of want to take my shower without an audience," Amarynth said.

"Oh right," Viv said, fleeing from the room.

It was a strange sensation to feel embarrassed in your own home, Viv thought as she shut the bathroom door firmly behind her. Perhaps that was what guests were for, to remind us of what a home normally meant by making it temporarily less safe and predictable.

They arrived at PsyOps headquarters less than an hour later. It was a quick trip underground as they didn't have to wait for the elevator at ground level, and the hallways were largely empty other than a skeleton crew of security guards.

It was funny since the facility was ostensibly open 24/7, 365 days a year, since crime took no holidays, that there would nonetheless be slow and busy times. But there were.

Viv had noted that while some dark hours were notoriously unsafe, others were much more serene. Particularly quiet were 5 am to 7:30 am, the hours for early risers, after most of the party animals and street prowlers had crashed.

Arriving at PsyOps during that quiet window always made her feel like it was her own private fortress. She could pretend as she walked through empty hallways, by closed offices with the lights turned off, that she owned the place.

They reached Martin's office quickly. Unlike every other door in this wing, Martin's office door wasn't closed. It was cracked slightly ajar.

And he wasn't alone. The sound of strange voices hit Viv's ears well before she could get close enough to get a visual.

In fact, his office was crammed with people. Martin was there, of course, looking rather grumpy and small, tucked in behind his desk where he sat stewing in his office chair. Standing next to him there was a young woman with impeccable makeup and sleek shiny blonde hair. She was tall for a woman, perhaps 5'9," but the two men who stood with her towered over her. They had to be 7 feet tall. Their heads came perilously close to scraping the low ceiling of Martin's office.

"I see you brought friends, Martin," Viv cracked, as she and Amarynth stepped into his office.

Amarynth felt her blood pressure rise. Martin's office was snug quarters no matter the occasion, but with the two hulking men in the mix, she was feeling a little claustrophobic.

"Care to introduce us?" Viv prompted.

The blonde woman stepped forward and offered her hand. "Regina Withers sent me," she said, as Viv shook her hand.

"That's a helluva strange name, Ms. Sentme," Viv teased her.

"Oh... I... didn't mean..." the woman stammered.

"Relax," Viv said. "I was only messing with you. I know who Regina Withers is."

How could she not? Viv thought. Regina Withers was a legendary TV personality– known as the Queen of True Crime for her long history of hosting documentaries on murders, abductions, and anything else that was dark and scary enough to get her ratings.

Withers had also been an integral part of their last major case, the one that had gone so terribly wrong, in which they'd been investigating a series of murders targeting the city's psychic population. For a while, Withers had been their chief suspect before she was cleared by a blood typing test that confirmed she couldn't have done the deed.

Viv had accepted that Withers wasn't guilty of the murders, but she wasn't about to pronounce her innocent. The woman was a vulture, Viv thought. There was something distinctly untrustworthy about her.

And of course, she'd send her henchmen to PsyOps instead of coming in person. "Was Regina too busy to show up herself?" Viv asked this underling.

"Well, you know how it is," the blonde henchman began, "Ms. Withers has been getting more into producing content these days. She's spending less time in front of the camera."

"Must be nice," Viv said. "Good change of pace and all."

"Ms. Withers sent this crew along," Martin explained. "Dale, Ed, and…?"

"Mitzi," the blonde replied.

"Mitzi," Martin said, nodding. "The network is working on a new project, a documentary series about what it's like to live as an intuitive. They wanted to feature the everyday work of PsyOps agents in it."

Viv shook her head. "Hard pass. This job is hard enough without a film crew tagging along after us. Right, Am?"

Amarynth looked down at her feet.

"Good to know I can count on you to back me up," Viv grumbled.

"Arguing isn't going to get us anywhere, Viv," Amarynth said.

"She's right," Martin said. "We're signed up for the project. You're doing this. This comes from the top."

"You take orders from Regina Withers now?" Viv challenged him, raising an eyebrow.

"No, not Withers. President Minot," Martin said.

That got Viv's attention. "The President?"

Martin nodded.

"Why would he care about some stupid TV program?" Viv said.

Mitzi and company looked a little hurt at that remark but said nothing.

"It's part of his new cultural initiative, Viv," Martin said. "Don't you keep up on current events?"

Viv shrugged. The answer to that question was no. It was true that she'd never cared to watch the news much... really, ever. But it had become much more difficult to find the time and energy in the past few years that she'd been a PsyOps agent. "You keep me pretty busy," Viv said.

Amarynth, however, knew exactly what Martin was talking about. If she closed her eyes, she could see the announcement President Minot had made and hear his high-pitched drawl speaking the words:

"The Psychic State is a proud new country, a strong one. We have every possible resource on our side, except history. That is the curse that follows all young countries, a lack of history. When I was a young man breaking horses, I used to have a friend who worked at a used car dealership. That was the height of control. Talk about creating or destroying history! If he wanted a car to appear shiny and new, all he had to do was turn back the odometer and give it a quick wash.

That's normally what you do when you're selling a used car. You're trying to make the old look new.

Well, we're the new car, and we want to be old. Why do we want to be old? Because people love new cars, but they hate new countries. You want to be an old country, one with legitimacy, weight.

If I had my way, we'd just turn the odometer way up in the other direction and take that sucker through the mud a few times. Maybe even hammer a couple of dents right in there. Yessir.

But you can't do that to a country, can you?

So we're going to show them that we may be young but we ain't simple. We ain't immature. We have substance. Character.

We have... culture."

In Minot's speech, he hadn't gone into the particulars, what the plan would entail. That was Minot for you – incredible at pitching an idea, not fantastic at announcing the realities of it. He had his own henchmen for that of course. People who could make the consequences happen in the shadows, where they wouldn't distract from his glorious appearances on national television.

But a film focusing on the psychic population wasn't beyond the pale. It would show the populace that there was diversity in the Psychic State. It would highlight their chief resource: Talented people who would work hard and work cheap.

Some cultures had technology. Others had good relations with other nations. The Psychic State had cheap labor.

And they were on the cusp of harnessing forces that maybe they didn't *quite* understand, but they'd work out those details when they got there, wouldn't they?

Amarynth saw this all unfold near instantaneously, as her eyes blinked exactly once. As always, the words to share this with present company eluded her.

And then another intuition hit her. There had been another incident.

"There's been another fire," Amarynth said aloud.

"Yes," Martin replied. "I was just getting to that."

"Viv, we've got to go." Amarynth strode out of the room.

"Get back here!" Martin yelled.

Amarynth poked her head into the doorway.

"You need to do that again for the cameras," he said.

Amarynth frowned.

The cameras whirred to life. The crew got into place.

Amarynth tried to recreate the moment. But every time she did, it sounded wooden and awkward.

"No, not like that," Viv said. "Do it like you're an actual person."

"What does that even mean?" Amarynth protested.

Finally, they got a usable take.

Mitzi sighed. "I think it's better if we just run continuous live tape on the team. See what we can catch organically. Edit out the rest."

"Fine," Viv said. "But you're not coming inside my house to film."

Mitzi hesitated. "You're hardly in a position to be making demands of us," she said. "But okay."

Viv and Amarynth exited the building and walked to the car, moving with what seemed to them to be glacial slowness, so that they didn't lose the film crew.

"I don't know why they say 'where's the fire?' when someone's in a hurry," Viv said. "I used to know. But not anymore."

"It's because the fire department books it," Amarynth said.

"I know that," Viv said.

"But you said –" Amarynth stopped. "It was a joke," she said.

Viv nodded.

I've guessed wrong, Amarynth thought, wondering if there would ever come a day when she could flawlessly tell if other people were joking. And wondering if she were the only one who struggled with this.

The Extreme Makeunder

The second arson site was the same old story. Another building had reached cremation temperature and burned to the ground faster than seemed possible, leaving virtually nothing behind, just charred scraps that didn't tell much of a story on their own.

The arson investigation team from the normal police department came and went in a perfunctory sweep, and then PsyOps's dynamic duo was called in.

Well, it was almost the same old story. Because this time there was a witness who had seen the whole thing and wasn't preoccupied with the frantic task of fleeing the scene.

Sugar Silva had been leaving her office across the street at just the moment the blaze started.

Immediately upon entering Sugar Silva's suite, Viv found her senses assaulted by a dizzying array of shag-trimmed throw pillows, strewn all over understated black pleather couches.

The entire room engaged in a similar visual tug of war. It looked as though a couple was arguing how to decorate it. One half of this hypothetical couple would want a stripped-down bachelor pad, reflected in sturdy pieces and basic black finishes that perhaps leaned futurist in their design, IKEA but with a hint more musk.

The other half of this hypothetical couple would argue for psychedelic shag in every imaginable color. This point of view warred and clashed primarily with itself, although these "accent" pieces did look rather incongruous placed next to the barebone macho spaceship accoutrements.

The shag throw pillows and rug reminded Viv a bit of the Tribbles episode of Star Trek.

The front room was empty when they approached, but there was a small sturdy desk with a call bell on it. The desk was black and would look perfectly at home on the bridge of a starship. Of course.

Viv hit the call bell three times.

"Coooooooming," a voice rang out.

A woman emerged, and at once it was clear that she was responsible for whatever was going on décor-wise in this room. She matched it.

Her entire body was clad in skintight black pleather, and she wore a shaggy bright pink boa over her shoulders. On either wrist was an assortment of large gaudy fluorescent bracelets that clattered as she moved.

"Sugar Silva?" Viv confirmed.

"In the ravishing flesh, darling," Sugar said. "But you can just call me the shabby chica," she added brightly, making eyes at the film crew and giant camera that followed the detectives.

"I'd rather not," Viv replied.

"Suit yourself," Sugar said shrugging. "Everyone who is anyone calls me the shabby chica these days. But it's your funeral, you know." She looked a little hurt.

"I've always hated that expression," Amarynth piped up.

"Shabby chic?" Sugar asked.

"No," Amarynth said. "It's your funeral. It's so rarely true. People throw it around like every bad decision is deadly."

"A lot of them can be," Sugar insisted. "Take your home, for example. A lot of people think your design choices are just a throwaway decision, a superficial pursuit, decorating and outfitting your home. But a home is very important. It's where you rest, relax, and rejuvenate. You have to get that exactly right, or it'll easily affect everything else that happens in your life. You never know quite where that could lead."

"Ah, so you're into that feng shui stuff," Viv said.

Sugar glared at her. "No. Nothing that done. Nothing that overdone. You wound me, you do. I'm at the cutting edge of better living for a new age. The shabby chica doesn't practice feng shui. No. No. My clients get much better than that. They get the Sugar Method."

"What's the Sugar Method?" Amarynth asked, eliciting a groan from Viv. They had an arson to investigate, Viv thought. The last thing they needed to do was get lost in the rabbit hole of exploring the passions of some kook.

"I'm so glad you asked," Sugar said, her eyes gleaming. "As you can plainly see, the Sugar Method is all about resolving conflict. Settling duality. Where most interior design methods look to blend similar complementary pieces together into one coherent style, the Sugar Method leans into dissonance and contradiction."

"You take things that don't go together and force them to?" Viv prompted.

Sugar sighed. "Yes, I guess that's one way of putting it, but it doesn't exactly do my practice the justice it deserves, you see."

Viv smirked.

"How do you work with someone so... artless?" Sugar asked Amarynth.

"Hey, I'm standing *right here*," Viv said.

Amarynth ignored Viv's protest. "I'm still figuring it out myself."

Sugar giggled conspiratorially.

"If you don't cut that out, Am, I'm leaving you here to rot with the Tribbles," Viv warned.

"Oh lighten up, Viv," Amarynth shot back.

"Indeed. She needs a drink. Or seven," Sugar replied.

Viv scowled.

"Luckily," Sugar continued, "I have a full bar out back. If you ladies will excuse me, I'd be happy to make us some refreshments." She grinned broadly. "What's your pleasure?" she asked them.

"Uhh," Amarynth said, "I'm not sure we should be drinking in front of the camera crew."

"Not to worry, I have enough for them, too," Sugar said brightly.

"No," Amarynth said, "I mean... I'm sure the department wants to project a positive image and all."

"Oh, screw the camera crew," Viv said, "and screw the department for that matter."

"Viv!" Amarynth exclaimed.

"If they can't use the footage, they can't use the footage," Viv said, shrugging. "Plus, they can edit around it if they have a problem with it." *Hopefully they won't be able to*, she thought, a smile creeping onto her lips.

"Welllll...." Amarynth said. "Would a Negroni be too much?"

"Not at all," Sugar replied. "And you, detective?"

Viv pursed her lips. She considered asking for water or tonic. She wasn't exactly supposed to be drinking alcohol while on duty, and having drinks with Sugar and Amarynth wasn't exactly her idea of a good time. But a psychic detective's salary left little for extras, certainly not booze, which was generally difficult for Penny to "acquire" even with her myriad ways of bringing home abandoned goods. Outside of a rare misdelivered package for a neighbor's wine of the month club or a PsyOps holiday party, where the bar wasn't exactly open but a few drink tickets were available, Viv didn't often get much of a chance these days to drink.

Most of her drinking had been back in college, a time when things were simpler.

Aw, Hell. Why not seize the opportunity? Viv decided. Penny would want her to if she were here. She'd ask Sugar for something pink and sweet. That was how Penny was, pink and sweet.

And Viv? Viv was classic and a little bitter. "I'll take an old fashioned," Viv said.

"Sure thing," Sugar said. "I'm glad I picked up bitters."

"And for you?" Sugar asked the film crew.

"Nothing," Mitzi replied. "And please pretend we're not here. It makes for better film."

That's a tall order, Viv thought. Sugar seemed like one of those people who played to the metaphorical camera even when a literal one wasn't around. A person who was incapable of ever acting naturally.

Sugar curtsied and disappeared into one of the back rooms, ostensibly to mix up their drinks.

"An old fashioned?" Amarynth said. "Pretty classy, Viv."

"Well, you ordered a Negroni," Viv said.

"I guess we're both kind of fancy," Amarynth said.

"Don't get the wrong idea," Viv said. "I'm only half-fancy."

Amarynth laughed. "Which half is that?"

"My fancy half?"

Amarynth nodded.

"I guess you'll have to wait and find out," Viv replied.

"And you say *I* have the wrong idea about us," Amarynth teased.

"That's *not* what I meant!" Viv protested, and she noted with horror that she sounded just as Amarynth had on the first night she stayed at her house. She had the same tone of voice, the same cadence. Everything.

It bothered her to have anything in common with this maddening woman. What a disaster.

Sugar emerged with breathtaking speed carrying a tray that had three drinks expertly perched atop its surface. She handed the detectives theirs and then set the tray down on the desk and picked up her own.

"I was devastated, you know, after the fire. At first anyway," Sugar said, as they all sipped their respective drinks.

"Devastated? How come? Did you know someone who passed?" Viv asked.

Sugar shook her head. "No. Well, not well anyway. They were neighbors, but we weren't terribly close." She set down her drink. "My other showroom was over there."

"Your other showroom?" Viv asked.

Sugar nodded. "Yes. It was more conceptual than this one. Clear plastic furniture meshed with lace. Doilies. That sort of thing. An ethereal concept. Like blocks of ice that had frosted in the thawing and refreezing cycle. I had invested quite a bit into it. Quite a bit of time, money." She sighed. "Passion."

"That had to be quite a hit," Amarynth offered gently. "Like losing a child."

"Well, yes, at first. I wept. But then..."

"Then?" Viv prompted.

"Then I realized it was an opportunity. An opportunity in disguise," Sugar said.

"How so?" Viv said.

"The fire gives me an opportunity to start anew. Just you watch. I will rise from the ashes, like the mighty phoenix." Sugar took a long sip of her cocktail. "Renovation means to make things new, does it not? And there has to be space for the new, doesn't there? Perhaps this was preordained. A sign from above. Like a forest fire can clear the way for new trees, sometimes destruction gives birth to new things," Sugar said.

"And sometimes a forest fire just destroys an ecosystem," Viv countered.

"I suppose," Sugar replied dismissively.

"I imagine it was still a big financial loss," Amarynth said. There was a shakiness in her voice that Viv recognized instantly as deception. Curious. Amarynth wasn't typically a person to bait another with something she knew to be untrue. But that was a big part of being a PsyOps detective, wasn't it? Perhaps the Connections Agent was learning from her, from being on the job.

Sugar shook her head. "Not at all. I was fully insured." She beamed. "To being prepared for anything," she toasted.

"To being prepared for anything," Amarynth and Viv chorused.

Viv shot a glance at Amarynth. Clever. They'd have to do a complete background check of Sugar Silva after the interview was conducted. With insurance money in the mix, she was now a prime suspect.

Besides, with all her eccentricities, would it be all that surprising if arson were another hidden passion? It could very well be that the shabby chica considered herself to be a mystical phoenix and that this was just another form of performance art.

Oddly, Viv felt all of this as she met Amarynth's gaze, reflected back at her. Neither of them had any form of telepathy, but at that moment, she swore that there was a deep understanding between them that rivaled telepathy.

After the toast, Amarynth deftly directed Sugar to recount her experience as a witness. Sugar gave a rather labored account, embroidered with high-flown prose that defied credulity. Viv wondered what Amarynth could possibly be writing down, as she took notes dutifully of the account.

Other than that grandiosity, there was little new in what Sugar said. Her account matched Viv's former vision of the earlier inferno almost perfectly. While this pointed at both fires being set by the same person, it gave them little in the way of leads. Sugar hadn't seen a suspect fleeing the scene, and neither had Viv in her vision.

They were essentially back at square one. Well, aside from having a new name on the suspect list.

Still, the drinks were strong, and as she finished hers, Viv found herself considerably numbed to the strangeness of her surroundings and the company. Perhaps this was why people developed drinking problems, she mused. It didn't take much alcohol to make life quite a bit more bearable. True, if you overdid it, you'd have a hangover to contend with in the morning, but the worst hangover wasn't much competition for the most obnoxious people and situations that life could throw at you.

They had such a wonderful time that for a few minutes both Viv and Amarynth were able to forget that the film crew was capturing every moment.

Sugar Silva didn't. She couldn't help herself. She was painfully aware of where the camera was and kept mugging for the audience it implied.

This turned out to be a good thing when everything was said and done. Due to this incessant break of the fourth wall, much of the film was rendered completely unusable.

"Take that, Regina Withers," Viv said to herself as she fell asleep in her bed that night.

A Dozen Eggs, a Loaf of Bread, a Carton of Milk

Grocery shopping with a hangover wasn't exactly Amarynth's idea of a good time, but you did unpleasant things for people you loved, didn't you?

Yes, Amarynth told herself, you did.

Besides, Viv sleeping off her own hangover allowed Am to sneak out and make the journey to her mother's place. It was a fairly simple thing, to call a car to pick her up, but sleeping housemates asked fewer questions, didn't they?

Yes, Amarynth told herself, they did.

She could see all the potential questions that would go unasked.

"Where did you get the money to hire a car like that?"

"Where are you going?'

"What are you doing?"

"When will you be back?"

Amarynth didn't feel like answering any of them, so it was a good thing she didn't have to. It would be hard to explain her situation to anyone who hadn't lived the life she had. She had a lifetime of incredulous looks and cocked heads to confirm that.

Like anyone else, her upbringing seemed completely normal to her, because it was the only one she'd had. But to others, it seemed bizarre.

No, it was better to not give Viv yet another reason to dislike and mistrust her.

Because Amarynth had been insisting for years that she
wasn't one of *those* Watsons.

Thank goodness for other people's hangovers, she thought,
while cursing her own.

The car pulled up in the street outside of Viv's house, a sleek
black luxury sedan. The front passenger's side window rolled
down, revealing the driver. He wasn't dressed in the style of
a classic chauffeur. He wore a medley of inoffensive business
casual – pressed khakis, a button-down shirt. No tie. No cap.

But he nonetheless reflexively reached for a hat brim that
wasn't there, in a pantomimed show of respect, tipping
his invisible cap to her. "Morning, Miss Watson. To your
mother's? "

Amarynth nodded. She reached for the door handle.

The driver made a frenzied clucking sound. He jumped out
and sprinted around to her door and opened it. "Let me get
that for you," he panted.

Amarynth shook her head as she climbed in and he shut the
door behind her.

"Could I make a request?" she said to him after the car had
begun rolling.

"Of course, Miss Watson, always," the driver replied, his voice
bright and chipper.

"The next time you pick me up at this address, could you be
a little more discreet?" she ventured.

"Discreet?" The driver scoffed. "I am always the height of
discretion. It is part of our profession."

"Well yes," Amarynth said delicately. "I'm sure you keep confidences. But what I mean is…" She searched for the words.

He wound the long black car through a maze of streets that all seemed to be in the process of being used for other things. On one avenue, children flailed about in the roadway, drawing landscapes with sidewalk chalk. On another, several large trucks were idling next to the street parking while visibly sweaty workmen hoisted furniture onto a half-dead lawn.

"If you could refrain from opening my door for me when you pick me up in this neighborhood, I think it would be for the best," Amarynth finally said.

"Are you sure, Miss Watson?" the driver said.

"I am sure."

"But it's part of my duty," he insisted.

"I understand that," Amarynth said. "But it's also part of your duty to do what I ask of you, isn't it? Within reason of course."

"Yes," he replied. "Within reason."

"It's best not to attract attention in a neighborhood like this," Amarynth said. "Drivers opening doors… well, it's a lovely gesture, and I do appreciate your kindness and your concern… but people would talk. It could cause problems."

"I understand completely, Miss Watson," her driver replied. "It will not happen again."

"Thank you," she said.

They rode the rest of the way to her mother's home in silence.

Not quite a mansion, it was still a rather impressive house and well situated in a zip code that carried a hefty price tag regardless of what size structure you lived in. Most intuitives couldn't afford a shed here.

Amarynth felt fortunate as she strode from the carport into the entrance she preferred to use, one that took her between a pair of stone lions that regarded her nobly, as they always did.

Her mother had an affinity for statues of all kinds, but these two had always been her favorites. When she was a little girl, she used to pretend they were Aslan, the patriarch of C. S. Lewis's *Chronicles of Narnia*, and Aslan's evil twin, Waslan, an antagonist that she'd completely made up.

The space between these two statues was a place where two worlds collided, she had surmised as a little kid, and as a result, this path was a location that experienced complete balance – a precarious balance but balance nonetheless.

She spent many hours there, spreading her other toys along this path, coming up with elaborate stories surrounding how this balance could be upset and then restored. In her earliest stories, Waslan was always a meddler, up to no good, looking to destroy others just to watch the world burn, the trickster god in this tale. Aslan would sweep in and save the day, restoring balance.

But as time went on and her thinking grew more sophisticated, she found herself enacting stories where hero and villain weren't so clear cut.

As she swept through this short path, she could feel all those memories coming to her at once, like a sharp gust of wind.

Was that important? She stopped mid-trail.

"No," her inner intuitive voice told her. She continued on.

The house was over 6000 square feet, spread between two living levels and a small finished basement.

"I'm home," Amarynth called out into the house. Her voice echoed back at her.

Her mother had never been one to keep many possessions. "The things you own end up owning you," she'd explained, smiling. A relatively empty house was easier to clean, and fewer possessions meant less upkeep on them.

As a result, her mother's home was cavernous, and one's voice inevitably reverberated.

It was too early for lunch, and her mother didn't eat breakfast. She was often an early riser, so there was only one place for her to be, Amarynth concluded: Her study.

Or at least that's what they both called it. The walls were lined with empty bookshelves. Books were out of the question. They were heavy, created dust.

Other people when presented with so many shelves would have felt a need to fill them, but not Bella Watson. Amarynth's mother didn't respond to pressure, of any kind. While this sometimes caused problems, Amarynth generally admired this quality about her mother.

Social pressure was no influence on her. A shelf certainly couldn't tell her what to do.

Amarynth had inherited just enough of this quality to perplex others, who noticed the Connections Agent played by her own rules. But compared to her mother, Amarynth was a conformist.

Amarynth walked into the study to find her mother sitting in her favorite chair, staring out the window. From the second floor, Bella had an excellent view of the neighbor's property. Unlike her estate, their home was tended to by a wide variety of "help," staff members who were always up to something. Some of this was what they were paid to do, but most of it was… extracurricular.

No matter how many times her mother filled her in on the complex web of relationships, Amarynth could never keep all the affairs straight. Which of the neighbor's maids were dallying with the head gardener?

Now that the gardener's son was working there, it had become even more convoluted.

"Am, come here!" her mother said.

Amarynth did as she was told.

Her mother pointed out Gardener, Jr. "Look at him. If he isn't a spitting image of his father! The laundress is going to have her way with him, just you wait and see. I'd be willing to bet she's gauche and hits all the same places she did with his dad." She smiled. "People can be like that, you know. They have their moves, and they just repeat them over and over again, even as the cast of characters changes. Disgusting, really."

Amarynth laughed. "I don't know how you see anything. They look like little ants to me from up here."

"Scheming, dreaming ants," her mother confirmed. She smiled. "I eat a lot of carrots," she said.

"I know, Mom. I buy your groceries, after all," Amarynth said.

"Vitamin A. Keeps your eyes good. You should try it, dear."

Amarynth wondered how much vitamin A it took to see into other people's souls. Her mother had probably ingested at least that amount, maybe more. She could see it now, her mother morphed into a large robot shooting orange laser beams out of her eyes. This was what happened when you overdosed on carrots.

"You're having one of your daydreams again, aren't you?" her mother said.

Amarynth nodded. Her mother was odd by most people's reckoning, but to Amarynth she was a relief. She never had to explain around her mother. Bella just got her, in a way that few others did, even if she found her daughter embarrassing.

"You could stay here, you know," her mother said. "I certainly have the room."

"I know," Amarynth said.

"I get it," Bella said. "Big city adventures. Making a difference. It's noble, you know, working for the State."

"For now," Amarynth replied. The words were out of her mouth before she knew she was even speaking. She certainly didn't understand what she meant by it after she said it. But she knew it was true.

And so did her mother. "Ah, it'll change then," her mother said, accepting her daughter's pronouncement as fact. "Well, we might as well enjoy it while it lasts."

Too bad my mother can't teach Viv to trust me, Amarynth thought. Aloud, she said, "Wait a second, is Gardener, Jr. taking his shirt off?"

Her mother nodded. "See, your eyes adjust after a while. They start looking like very detailed ants. Then you get to watch your ant farm dance."

"I thought it was carrots, not time," Amarynth said.

Her mother flashed a Mona Lisa smile in response. "Are you ready for your grocery list?" she asked her daughter.

Amarynth nodded. They had already done this over the phone, but this confirmation phase was another ritual she was used to humoring.

Her mother pressed a small note into the palm of her hand. "A dozen eggs, a loaf of bread, a carton of milk," she began to intone. Amarynth drifted away on the music of it. The list was long enough for her to do that. It was also long enough for her to drift back before the list was over.

Finally, her mother finished the list and said, "We can visit more when you get back. I'll cook you brunch."

"I'd like that," Amarynth replied. She was getting a bit tired of the meals that Viv scraped together at her home, if they could even be called meals. As best as Amarynth could tell, Viv didn't exactly eat meals, not like a normal person. Viv sort of subsisted on the margins of other people's meals, intaking just enough to not die, not exactly particular about what that nourishment tasted like.

And sometimes Amarynth wondered if Viv's math were sound. Her colleague had always been thin, but ever since her partners had left unexpectedly, Viv looked practically skeletal. Still well muscled but for how long?

"And maybe I could pack a doggy bag for my coworker Viv," Amarynth said.

"Sure," her mother replied. "We could do that."

As Amarynth returned to the car and told the driver the name of the grocery store, she thought again of how difficult her life would be to explain to others.

She thought of all the questions she was glad she wasn't being asked.

"If Bella Watson has so much money, why doesn't she just pay someone to bring her groceries?'

"Why does she bother to cook for herself?"

"She could afford a bigger staff. Why does she only employ a driver?"

Amarynth ran over these questions repeatedly in her mind, like a stone she was trying to smooth. She knew the answers of course, and it was a reality that made perfect sense to her but sounded absolutely cracked to anyone outside of her family.

Bella Watson was worried about being poisoned, so she could only trust her daughter to procure the supplies, and she had to cook her meals herself.

Her mother didn't like people snooping on her or her affairs – despite her propensity to spy on the neighbors, or perhaps because of it—so a full-time house staff was out of the question.

No, it was safer to hire a driver, send her daughter out for groceries, and have a cleaning service come in and do the works once a month, during which time Bella Watson would be on her best, blandest behavior. She would give the cleaning crew nothing to gossip about, nothing to take to those who knew her and would malign her.

Bella Watson had been through enough already in her life. More than enough. Certainly more than she'd expected she would go through when she was a little girl living in the lap of luxury, pampered by nannies, catching glimpses of her glamorous mother and hard-working father.

Amarynth wasn't clear on the exact location and the depth of her mother's emotional wounds. But she knew they were there. She had always known, even before her mother made her first attempts to tell her young daughter, to try to explain why she was different than the other mothers, something that other children she met would certainly bring to her attention.

"I understand, Mama," Amarynth had said, even before Bella had really gotten anywhere.

She was good like that. Amarynth always got things without an explanation.

Sometimes this meant people didn't ever give her one. This was fine – up until the moment that someone else demanded one from her. Amarynth had a hard enough time explaining the idiosyncrasies of her own life to others. The words were slippery and elusive.

She had *no* hope of explaining her mother's proclivities. None whatsoever. Even though she grasped intuitively that they were internally consistent, logical, and nothing worth getting worked up about.

Still, leading someone else through the process that would enable *them* to get it... well, Amarynth got exhausted just thinking about it.

It was better to avoid answering those questions, by never giving anyone else a reason to.

Amarynth moved through the grocery store as if moving through a dream. She'd devised a clever system for optimizing her time in the store, making shopping runs as quickly as possible. She sorted the items on the list by aisle, and over time, she'd come to also sort items by their positions within the aisle in ascending order of distance from the front of the store.

When she had first figured it out, her process had required her to take pen to paper and revise the grocery list by hand, rearranging it into such a form. But with practice, she'd gotten so she could mentally sort items simply by glancing at the list and then hold that mental list in her head for the duration of the shopping trip.

It always annoyed her when they moved the positions of items – due to some misguided notion that refreshing category management would drive customers to purchase new products. Good consumer psychology but obnoxious to people who were as organized and efficient as Amarynth. And forget about end caps – they were the bane of her existence. It foiled her well-laid plans any time she'd arrive in the correct position on the aisle only to find that all of the items that should be there had been relocated to a display that could be anywhere in the store.

Thankfully, none of those shenanigans happened this time. She was at the front of the store in eight minutes, waylaid solely by a slow-moving grocery line. Only one lane was open, and the self-scan checkout had an "out of order" sign hanging on it.

The shopper in front of her was earnestly digging through a giant purse, extracting coins to pay for a large grocery bill. From the look of it, they were a few pennies short of a dollar, Amarynth mused, in more ways than one. She scolded herself for being so judgmental, even though it was just frustration.

As she stood there waiting, she looked out the front windows of the store and busied herself watching the hustle and bustle of the shared parking lot and sidewalks of the strip mall.

Most of the people who passed were strangers, but one was a familiar face. As she saw them, she instantly knew who was setting the fires, but she didn't have the foggiest idea of how to explain it to anyone else.

"Next customer," the cashier said.

"C'mon lady, that's you," the guy in line behind her said to Amarynth.

Amarynth stepped forward to pay.

The Torch Singer

Another fire.

This time they were investigating on a day when the air itself felt like it was burning. Lucky them.

Summer in the Psychic State would probably be better if you were incorporeal, Amarynth thought. This was particularly the case when the heat index climbed to 111 – which it often did in June and July.

The outside world looked beautiful with sunny skies and the trees all blooming with flowers.

It was like walking through an oven, but if you could just shed your body, it wouldn't be so bad.

But that usually took some violence, Amarynth reflected. For most beings, she added as an afterthought. She was sure other beings found it to be a routine matter, corporeality versus incorporeality.

She wasn't sure how she knew, as per usual, but she was certain. Yes, summer hit the residents of the Psychic City differently, depending on their corporeal status.

For her, it was oppressive.

Perhaps if Viv's car had been equipped with a remote starter and fully functioning AC, it would have been a bit more bearable. But Viv's PsyOps-issued vehicle was a beater, and it less had air conditioning than the suggestion of it. Something was coming out of the vents. You could detect a whisper of semi-cold air if you placed your hand in front of them. But it wasn't all that cold. And it wasn't coming out all that hard.

The effect was less like functional air conditioning and more like a person was half-heartedly blowing on soup that was too hot to eat.

Does that make us dinner? Amarynth wondered, doing her best to lean forward just enough to create distance between the small of her back and the burning car seat without tweaking her back muscles in the process.

There was no time to waste, however. No time to allow the car to cool down, if it even could with the anemic AC sputtering and failing to deliver. Not with the camera crew hiding somewhere in the wings. Viv and Am had sprinted out to the car, jumped in, and driven away, hoping that the crew wouldn't be able to follow them.

Glancing behind them, Amarynth concluded that they'd managed to disappear before they could be followed. No camera crew in sight.

She wondered how Viv even wore her sunglasses in heat like this. It was probably a good thing she hadn't left them in the car, Amarynth reflected. Otherwise, the shades would burn the flesh around Viv's eyes, leaving strange mask-like scars.

Amarynth giggled a little at the thought.

"Something funny?" Viv asked.

"No," Amarynth said. "Well, yes," she admitted. "But not really. I mean, I don't think you'd find it funny."

"Probably not," Viv agreed.

If they'd been just a bit further west, on the other side of the dryline where they'd been suffering a terrible drought and the fire risk had been extreme for weeks, the string of fires would have probably been dismissed as accidents, climatic disasters.

Here in Skinner, where it had managed to rain in the past month, the fire risk was significantly less.

It's like they wanted to get caught, Amarynth thought. No, that wasn't quite it. It was like they didn't care if they got caught.

Because if they'd driven just a bit further west – no more than an hour – they could set fires with total impunity.

For some reason, they hadn't done that. Instead, they set the fires where everyone would notice. That meant something, Amarynth was sure of it.

The targets themselves weren't presenting much of a pattern. First a convenience store and then a designer furniture storeroom. This time around, the arsonist had targeted a nightclub owned by Lake Meadows, a local entertainer.

Viv pulled the car to the curb. Turned off the engine.

Amarynth stepped out of the car and looked up.

So this was where Lake Meadows lived. She'd expected something more bohemian and distressed from a torch singer. But Ms. Meadows had done well for herself, and apparently this was where she wanted to live –whether it matched her professional image or not.

And apparently where the divine Lake Meadows wanted to live was in a townhouse with a neutral-colored stone exterior. It reminded Amarynth of the mini-estates that developers were so fond of putting in high-end housing developments – McMansions they were sometimes called. They were cookie-cutter homes all themed the same way, each with the same modern finishes and large garages, planned and distributed perfectly on plotted private lanes, usually gated with a guard.

Skinner-Watson had more of them every year. For some reason, a lot of people wanted to live in them. Amarynth had never reasoned out why. To her, it seemed like the worst of both worlds – like you were playing at luxury but never quite getting there. Overpaying for what you got.

Besides, you always had to answer to the Homeowner's Association, didn't you? It was a strange thought, buying a home, taking on that level of responsibility, and still having to follow someone else's rules.

But then again, even people who lived in standalone houses had to answer to the State at the end of the day, didn't they?

Still, Amarynth wasn't a fan of McMansions. And this little townhouse was a curiosity in its own right – since McMansions were shrunken down imitations of something grander, and this townhouse was basically a shrunken down imitation of a McMansion. A copy of a copy, losing a little something on each duplication.

The townhouse was wedged between two identical tiny McMansions, sharing walls with both. Glancing up and down the street and taking in the chain of shrunken McMansions, Amarynth was reminded of paper dolls whose arms linked one to another.

Viv knocked on the door of the paper doll in question, Number 2031. The door snapped open immediately, as though someone had been on the other side, expecting their visit.

Lake Meadows stood before them, dressed like a showgirl, a flurry of red and black feathers and sequins. "Do come in,"

Lake half-sang, spinning around in place and leaving the door open behind her.

Viv followed Lake inside with Amarynth trailing behind. As Amarynth closed the door, she toyed with leaving it open. It was a strange impulse that sometimes hit her – particularly when someone trusted her to do the right thing. She wasn't sure exactly why, but these urges had plagued her for her entire life.

What would happen if she left the door open? She wondered. Would she let in insects? A house lizard? An ambitious grackle? She'd let out all the home's precious air conditioning, that much was certain and could be accomplished quickly. But what else would happen?

She wasn't about to find out because she closed the door. Like she always did.

Nearly always, she reminded herself. There had been times when she had succumbed to these urges. Those experiences were, after all, how she knew it was usually better to resist, as tempted as she might be.

The torch singer led them to a large sitting room. She sat down carefully, doing her best not to muss up her Mardi Gras costume, and as she did so, she gestured to the surrounding furniture. Viv and Amarynth settled in, joining her.

Lake pulled out a pack of cigarettes and lit one. "Mind if I smoke?" she asked.

"Do you always ask for permission *after* you do things?" Viv challenged her.

Lake shrugged.

"Oh wow, you have a baby grand," Amarynth said.

"I do indeed," Lake replied.

"Do you play?" Amarynth asked.

Lake shook her head. "No, honey, I sing." She took a long drag off her cigarette. She held in the smoke for a few moments before exhaling luxuriously. "A piano's more of a platter I serve myself on, you see."

"A platter?" Viv asked.

Lake nodded. "Or a canvas, if you prefer. I look delicious draped across a piano." She set down her burning cigarette in an ashtray and walked over to the piano.

"See?" she said, draping herself across it, revealing a pair of exquisitely shaped legs.

"I do," Viv replied.

Lake beamed, sliding off the piano and returning to her chair. She picked up her cigarette, took another drag, before adding, "That's how you succeed in business, you know. It's not about how much talent you have. It's about self-knowledge. To succeed, you need to know what you do well and what you don't – and from that, you figure out how to apply what you've got."

"I'll keep that in mind if I ever decide to go into show business," Viv shot back.

"Oh, that's just not show business," Lake countered. "That's every business." She smiled, took another long drag, and exhaled. "Anyway, speaking of business, you're here on yours. What can I do for you, honey?"

"Well, as you know, your club burned down last night," Viv said.

Lake nodded, frowning. "It's an awful thing. I'll be fine. Don't you mind about that. But I feel horrible for everyone else who performs there. We're like a family, you see. They depend on me. They depend on the club." She took another drag, shaking her head. "I'm a big name these days. I'll have no problem finding another gig... but some of the acts we host... well..." She shook her head again and sighed. "I don't like to think about it."

"Well, we need you to," Viv said.

Amarynth sighed. Viv Lee could always be counted on to be a blunt instrument. Her coworker wasn't a scalpel but a sledgehammer.

But then Viv surprised Amarynth by adding, "I'm very sorry by the way to be bothering you at a time like this."

"No, it's fine," Lake replied. "For all you know, I set the fire myself."

This, too, surprised Amarynth. It was unusual for witnesses to go there on their own. Typically, it was something that they came to as a matter of defensiveness, once the detectives had asked enough leading questions that they began to wonder if they were a suspect.

But nope, Lake cut to the chase. Amarynth supposed it fit her, this bluntness. There was nothing subtle about this woman, after all, on stage or off. Had she been a burlesque dancer instead of a torch singer perhaps there would have been more of a dance back and forth, the tease part of striptease.

"We have to consider every angle," Viv replied. "Everyone's included as a suspect before they're excluded."

Lake nodded. "Of course." She took another long drag off her cigarette. "You're just doing your job. This is the way you drape yourselves across your piano. This is your platter. Or your canvas, if you prefer."

Amarynth laughed. "Never thought about it that way before."

Lake shrugged. "We artists speak our own language. Practically live on our own planet," she said. "Why would you think like us?"

Viv bristled at the word *artist* because it had described her once. She'd gone to painting school, after all, had majored in art once upon a time, before she dropped out and gave it all up to join the Department of Psychic Operations.

Dropping out of school most people understood. Why pay extra for classes and certifications if you were going to do something else career-wise? But she'd also stopped painting when she dropped out, and that was harder to explain. Sometimes people would ask her why, and she could come up with some answer on the spot if pressed – although she usually just found another way to end the conversation.

But as far as the true answer as to what drove her to quit painting, she wasn't quite sure herself. Every time she thought too hard about painting, she felt sad, and yet she felt no desire to return to it... but why? The question persisted in nagging at her, as much as she wished it would just go away. She suspected that the answer to that question would scare her, that it was hidden behind things she didn't like to think about, because it hurt her to even think about painting.

Aloud, Viv said, "You'd be surprised."

"Oh?"

"There are a lot of artists who do other things for a living. You never know. We could both be creative types," Viv said. She didn't dare be more direct. She hated the series of questions that followed: What kind of artist? What do you like to paint? And of course, once those questions had been answered, the inevitable – why don't you paint anymore?

Even now, Viv dreaded Lake asking something probing like, "Are you? Are you a creative type? Are you an artist?"

But Lake didn't do that. "Fair," she said. "It's good to not make assumptions." She inhaled on her cigarette, paused, exhaled. "Although you can't really help it, can you?"

"Help what?" Viv said.

"Everyone makes assumptions," Lake said.

"I don't know about that," Viv replied.

"Well, I do. Oh sure, not everyone *makes assumptions*," she said, waving her hands in the air around her head for emphasis. "Not the way that people usually mean when they say that. They're talking about an edge case, the narrow-minded person who jumps to conclusions all the time and goes off the deep end with it. But that's a lazy way to define 'making assumptions.'" She shook her head. "That's the funny thing... we're always making assumptions and we're not even aware that we're doing it. Like today. I opened the door and let you in. I assumed you were here from PsyOps, but did I check your identification? Did I verify it?"

"And you assumed I would close the door after I came in," Amarynth piped up.

"Sorry?" Lake said.

"You walked away without looking back at us. I was the last person in, and you just assumed that I would close the door. That I wouldn't leave it hanging open. Let out the AC and let in critters," Amarynth explained.

Lake smiled. "Yes. That's a good example. A person who didn't ever make assumptions wouldn't fit into society at all. They'd come off as odd and grating."

Amarynth nodded. She sometimes felt as though she were close to that reality. It had been worse when she was a little girl, but over the years, she had worked hard on creating scenarios where she felt comfortable making a few assumptions. Enough that most of the time she could kinda maybe sorta fit in... so long as people didn't spend too much time with her. And so long as she was in a context where she knew how people were supposed to behave before going in. It was significantly harder for her to judge novel contexts, however, particularly without either experience or formal study.

"You can't help but make assumptions," Lake said. "I can't help but make assumptions. So it's less about never making assumptions, you see, and more a matter of making the correct assumptions. The correct assumptions, the correct amount."

"When you put it that way, everyday life sounds exhausting," Viv said.

"Isn't it?" Lake replied.

Viv laughed.

She gets it, Amarynth thought.

"Anyway," Lake said. "Here's what you probably wanna know. Yes, I have insurance on the club. I have the papers on my desk if you want to take them with you, enter them into evidence or whatever. I submitted a claim this morning using scanned electronic copies so you're welcome to borrow them."

"If I just study them, we'll probably be fine," Viv replied.

Lake cocked her head quizzically.

"I can store them in my visual memory," Viv explained.

"Oh! You're an eideticist!" Lake exclaimed.

Viv nodded. "Yes, I have an indelible photographic memory." She beamed proudly. It was strange to feel proud of her psychic powers. Usually, people became suspicious or nervous when they realized she was a walking, talking camera, but Lake seemed thrilled.

"That means my beauty will be forever in your thoughts, doesn't it?" Lake asked.

Viv laughed. "Of course."

"That's a nice thought," Lake said. "Although I suppose I mustn't be a bad sport about it. Puff myself up. Be too cocksure. Because that will also be preserved forever in your memory, too, won't it?"

Viv grinned, nodding.

Amarynth rolled her eyes. Boy, with Karen and Penny gone, Viv was starved for positive attention. She was really soaking it up, wasn't she?

"That has to be tough," Lake said suddenly. "Like... when someone does something wrong. When someone does something to hurt you." She stubbed out her cigarette. "How do you ever forgive them?"

Viv considered this. "Sometimes I don't."

"But can you?" Lake said.

"Can I?" Viv asked.

"Can you forgive? Is it possible, I mean?"

Viv thought for a moment. "There are plenty of people who aren't eideticists who never forgive," she replied.

"That doesn't answer my question," Lake said.

"I'm still figuring myself out," Viv admitted.

Lake smiled. "Aren't we all?" She rose, brought the insurance paperwork to Viv, and set it in front of her so she could visually absorb it.

"As far as my alibi at the time of the fire," Lake said. "I was at Ballhaus dining with... a moneyed friend. One of my admirers, you see."

"And his name?"

"Apollo Watson," Lake replied.

Amarynth snorted. "Moneyed is right." Apollo Watson was a rich man among rich men. She didn't know him well herself, but she was positive her mother did. He was a distant cousin of hers, but this was of course something she couldn't tell Viv without blowing her cover.

"Well, people are all the same, really," Lake replied. "But some of them buy you nicer dinners."

Viv felt her blood go cold. She was reminded of her mother, who had targeted men as a source of income and validation her whole life, only to end up losing her mind. These days her mother was locked up behind bars, kept on a permanent

Black Square status, deemed too dangerous for society, but when Viv was a little girl, her mother had been a regular in the society pages. And yes, her mother had certainly depended on wealthy men for meals.

Viv closed her eyes and brought the memory up. She could still hear and see the conversation she'd had with her mother when she was just a little girl. "Men have two purposes," Viv's mother had said. "To disappoint us and to feed us."

"All men?" Viv had asked, wide-eyed.

Her mother had nodded. "The disappointments never get any better," she'd said. "But if you find a good man, the meals do."

Viv's eyelids flew open as her memory stopped and her speculative imagination took over.

And men like Apollo Watson could get you meals at Ballhaus, her mother would say.

Viv had eaten food *from* Ballhaus herself but had never dined *at* Ballhaus. Instead, her partner Penny had "rescued" extra food that the cooks had conveniently delivered to the dumpster and brought it home for their family. Even that had been a special occasion, getting the discarded leftovers.

That was the best they could do on a psychic detective's salary – or three. There wasn't a lot left after you were taxed for basically existing, told that it was to support public safety and services necessary to protect the non-psychic population from what intuitives were theoretically capable of. Never mind that they hadn't done any such thing in reality. At least not yet, was the State's reply, as though they could see a future that was still largely unclear even to the State's most skilled precognitionists.

"You can check with Apollo directly of course," Lake said, snapping Viv out of her thoughts. "But it might be easier to check with the staff at Ballhaus. We had a reservation, and I'm sure the waiter would remember us. Apollo is... well, he's Apollo of course, and I'm sure the waiter would remember him – and the tip. And me? Well..." She paused, flashing a coquettish smile. "As you can plainly see, I'm a snappy dresser."

"You are at that," Viv replied, fighting the sickness rising in her stomach. It did no good thinking about her mother. That door needed to be kept shut. She suspected there would come a time when she'd have to face that, but not now.

Absolutely not now. She wasn't ready. She didn't know if she'd ever be fully ready.

"Well, I would have dressed up a bit more for the interview of course, but I came directly from rehearsal." Lake shrugged with affected helplessness.

"If you were any more dressed up, you'd be a parade float," Viv observed.

Lake laughed. "You're a brave soul." She smiled. "I like you... Detective..."

"Lee," Viv offered. "Detective Viv Lee."

"Ah," Lake said. "Of course." She nodded. "I know your mother."

Don't say you're sorry, don't say you're sorry, don't say you're sorry, Viv thought, wishing fervently at that moment that she were an expressive telepath and could send the thought into the torch singer's head – or better yet that she had psychic powers that would allow her to compel others to do, or not do, things. That would certainly come in handy in a way that being a perfect documentarian often didn't.

Thankfully, Lake didn't apologize. "Anyway, I was at Ballhaus, witnessing another fire," the torch singer said.

Viv raised an eyebrow.

"They flambeed our dessert tableside," Lake explained playfully. "Not exactly the kind of inferno I suppose you investigate."

Viv groaned.

"Anyway, Detective Lee, if there's anything you think of that you need to ask me, don't hesitate to reach out." She rose and walked them to her front door. "It was a real pleasure," she said, closing the door.

Amarynth and Viv turned to find the camera crew waiting for them on the street. Mitzi was glaring at them with her arms crossed over her chest.

"Whatever you did in there," Mitzi said, "you'll have to do it again."

Viv groaned. "Yeah, that's not happening," Viv said.

"I can't believe you took the interview off camera!" Mitzi protested.

"Lots of things happen off camera," Viv said. "Most of life happens off camera, Mitzi. Deal with it."

"But what am I supposed to tell Ms. Withers?" Mitzi said.

"She's your boss, not mine," Viv replied.

Amarynth studied Mitzi's face. She wasn't sure exactly how, but she knew at once what she must do. She reached out and grabbed the car keys from Viv.

"What the Hell, Amarynth? I'm not letting you drive my car," Viv protested.

"That's not what I had in mind," Amarynth said. She pointed her thumb towards the front door of Lake's townhouse.

Viv rolled her eyes. "Really?" she said. "You're going to side with Mitzi?"

Amarynth nodded. "And Dale and Ed," she said, gesturing to the cameraman and sound guy.

Viv shot a glance at her car. Walking home from this nightmare wasn't an option. She couldn't leave her car behind. Sure, it probably would seem like a heap of junk to some others, but it was a prized possession to her. Owning her very own car, even a work vehicle, was a big deal to her. She felt like her car was almost her child.

Besides, it was over 100 degrees out. She didn't have any water. It wasn't safe. Heck, even standing outside on the sidewalk arguing about what to do for too long probably wasn't great for her health.

"Fine," Viv said, sighing. "Let's just get this over with."

The camera crew got into position as Amarynth knocked on the door. Confusion flicked across Lake's face for a split second before she registered the camera crew. At that moment, her expression broadened, and she began to perform for her audience.

Amazingly, she needed no explanation to know what to do. They repeated the earlier interview, not word for word, but as a kind of paraphrase – only this time Lake projected her voice more and gestured more expansively.

It was like Lake but with the drama turned up fifteen percent. She never broke the fourth wall, however, showing professionalism that Sugar Silva had lacked when in the same position.

Once the cameras were off, the two detectives and the camera crew all walked to the front of the townhouse to leave when Mitzi froze in place.

"That's beautiful," Mitzi said, pointing to a painting on the wall that Viv and Amarynth had looked past.

"Thank you," Lake said. "Are you one of us?" she asked cryptically.

"No," Mitzi replied. "But I have close friends who are."

"Ah, you should really consider joining," Lake replied. "It's the best decision I ever made."

"Are you a level 15?" Mitzi asked.

Lake shook her head. "Very few people are, you know." She frowned. "How do you know about the levels?"

"My friend told me," Mitzi replied.

"Well, you should warn your friend about talking about things like that with outsiders," Lake said. She caught herself. "I mean…. With people who aren't practitioners."

Mitzi nodded. "I didn't mean any harm."

"It's fine," Lake said. "It's just… not appropriate."

Their second sendoff was a little more stilted and uncomfortable, Viv noted. And maybe she was imagining it, but it seemed like Lake closed the door a lot harder than the first time around.

"What was that all about?" Amarynth asked Mitzi, as she and Viv walked the crew back to their van.

"She's a member of the Grounded Temple," Mitzi replied.

"Really?" Viv and Amarynth said in unison.

"She doesn't look the part," Viv said.

Once an obscure faith, the Grounded Temple had sharply gained in numbers recently. Viv had known about them for a while, however, since her partner Karen had a family link. The Grounded Temple had been originally founded because of Karen actually, when Karen's father, Augustus Cross, realized his daughter was an empath. It had started as a way to avoid having Karen tested for psychic powers. He founded an entire religion to have a valid religious exemption since the existence of psychic powers was considered by the temple to be a test sent from God.

With careful discipline and hard personal development work, any person experiencing psychic deviation could overcome their nature and become a normal citizen. The Temple offered extensive courses in conversion therapy for psychics who wished to pursue this path. Not only that but normal individuals could work with the Temple to learn to better regulate their own emotions. To feel less, react less. To gain control over their lives.

It was the Temple's view that when it came to emotions – of any kind –the less a person felt, the better.

Lake Meadows was a dramatic, expressive entertainer. She was a torch singer, after all, and everyone knew that torch singers were vocalists known for their sentimentality, their deep dark longing and personal suffering, usually for some form of unrequited love.

None of this seemed to make her an ideal candidate for Temple membership.

"They've been recruiting more celebrities lately," Mitzi explained.

"Like Regina Withers? Is *she* your friend?" Amarynth ventured.

Mitzi sighed. "You know I can't answer that. Anyway, I don't think Ms. Withers would appreciate it if I told someone else she was my friend. I don't think she'd like it if I were even under the mistaken impression for a minute that she was my friend. She considers me beneath her. Well beneath her."

"That doesn't answer my question," Amarynth pointed out.

Mitzi didn't say anything else.

Amarynth turned to Viv. "We were supposed to do that twice," she said.

"The interview?" Viv asked.

Amarynth nodded. "It was important for us to go back in with the camera crew." She handed the car keys back to Viv. "That's why I took your keys."

They began to walk back to their car together. "You know what's infuriating about you, Amarynth?" Viv said.

"What's that?"

"Hanging out with you, working with you… it's like trying to watch a movie I'm really into, and you've already seen the thing. And you're not giving me spoilers *per se*, but you kind of are. Well, not the kind of spoilers where I can solve the crime myself, but…" Viv's voice trailed off.

"Enough so you don't enjoy it," Amarynth finished.

Viv nodded.

"Well, for what it's worth, I don't enjoy it," Amarynth said. "I don't know if that helps at all."

Viv thought about it for a second, before replying, "You know, it does."

Amarynth smiled.

"Okay," Viv said. "So clearly it's important that Lake is in the Grounded Temple."

Amarynth nodded.

"I guess it's time to figure out if the pattern holds," Viv said.

"You mean, to see if the other targets were Temple members too?"

"Exactly," Viv said.

Amarynth considered this. "That is exactly the right approach."

"I don't know where it'll lead us," Viv said.

"Me neither," Amarynth admitted. "Not exactly. But it's the right direction. I'm sure about that."

"You know," Viv said. "Sometimes I wish you gave me a detailed map, but Amarynth…"

"Yeah?" Amarynth said.

"You're a good compass," Viv said. She started the car. "And sometimes that's all you need."

KAREN'S INFERNO

The Lobby

It looked like Oz's castle in the Emerald City. Yes, exactly like that.

The edifice was 15 stories tall, plunging high up into the clouds that were hanging over the handful of small towns sprinkled west of Watson. Well, calling them "towns" was perhaps a bit generous, Karen thought. The word "town" implied a sense of identity, and these zip codes weren't entities with identities of their own but bland settlements that sprang up because people wanted to be close enough to the city to shop or even commute to work without too much trouble but didn't want to sacrifice country-based comforts like having your own plot of land and a small buffer between you and the neighbors.

To an earlier version of herself, to the wide-eyed girl who had just left the Maine woods, Karen would have thought these faceless towns *were* the big city. She would have been easily overwhelmed by the number of people that sifted through these generic streets, moving mostly in one direction, towards the massive metroplex of Skinner-Watson.

A suburb would have looked like a thriving metropolis to her back then.

But now the people who drove past looked like folks who wanted to have it both ways, who wanted to keep one foot in each world and fully relate to neither. Well, good for them, she thought.

What was a skyscraper doing this far out in the suburbs, all 15 stories of shimmering green glass stabbing the sky from below like a shiv plunging into someone's chest?

It didn't look right, flanked on all sides by housing developments, strip malls, and state highways.

The tower looked like it had been picked up by a mischievous giant and placed here, like a flower being transplanted into a new garden.

It hadn't been easy to get here, out to the sticks. A series of city bus drivers had taken pity on her, waving at Karen to get on even though she lacked the fare to ride. She was a tiny woman, slender and short, and she could feel the pity rising from others in response to the sight of her. Many of them mistook her for a child or teenager, particularly when the hood of her sweatshirt was raised, obscuring her facial features, the only thing that could give her real age away.

There had been other times of course when the bus drivers showed up and had shaken their heads at her lack of money and drove unceremoniously away, causing her to slink back to the bus stop and wait for another opportunity.

It was a drive that normally took about 45 minutes in a car. This time it took Karen 12 hours. But she never doubted for one second that it was the right thing to do.

There had been something about the flyer she'd found on her front lawn that spoke to her. Something that seemed familiar.

> *Overwhelmed by your own emotions? Become the master of your own mind.*

And most importantly, the subsequent words: *Free course.*

She'd extracted the flyer from where it had been snarled between blades of overgrown grass, torn out the address segment, and thrown the rest away.

And now here she was.

The sliding doors of the 15-story green glass shiv opened, and a man and a woman strolled out. They were both smiling and well dressed, attractive in that inoffensive way that's so prevalent in the photographs that come with picture frames.

"Why hello there!" the woman exclaimed.

"I'm sorry," Karen said. "Do I know you?"

"Not yet," the man said. "But here at The Mentus Center, there are no strangers. There are only friends who haven't been properly introduced."

Karen wished suddenly that she had not come. These were not her kind of people. These were people who woke up easily in the morning, completely refreshed, ready to attack the day.

These were people who looked back fondly on their high school years.

These were people who whitened their teeth.

"Oh, it's okay, dear, don't be shy," the woman said, mistaking the look of regret on Karen's face for shyness.

They were trying at least, this photo frame couple. Karen had to give them that. Besides, it had been a long journey out here, and it would be easily just as long of a journey home. Maybe longer, if she happened to time her buses wrong and end up stranded somewhere during the dead hours when buses were only running along a few busier routes – and likely none of them at the periphery of the metro, the swath of roads that cut through the jungle of faceless towns she would be navigating.

Maybe she should give them – and this program –a shot.

"So what brought you to us today?" the man asked

"I found one of your flyers," Karen replied.

"Oh? Where?" the woman prompted.

"In Skinner," Karen said. "Near Bell and Blitz." She lived three houses away from the intersection, which was handy since Blitz was a major thoroughfare, but Bell was a quiet route, good for walking since most people zipped along other major arteries. This meant that it was easy to hop on Blitz to get somewhere, but there was enough of a buffer that Karen and her partners weren't suffering from constant traffic noise whenever they sat in their house.

Best of both worlds again.

"In Psychic City?" the man asked. "Well, you've come a long way then, haven't you?"

You don't know the half of it, Karen thought. Aloud, she said, "Takes a while to get here by bus."

"By bus?" The woman raised an eyebrow.

"I think she'll excel in our program," the man said, turning square to face the woman.

"With that kind of persistence? That kind of grit?" the woman replied. "Certainly."

Karen began to feel awkward. It felt momentarily like they'd forgotten she was standing there.

They swiveled back to face her, in eerie coordination. Everything about them, their movements, and their manner seemed rather synchronized as though they had been practicing an elaborate choreography.

It was very... controlled.

Yes, it was eerie, Karen thought, but wasn't control the reason she was here? Wasn't she looking to gain self-control?

Perhaps these strange greeters that reminded her so much of summer camp counselors had something to teach her.

"Anyway," the woman said sweetly, "if you'll just follow us inside, we'll get you registered, and then we can start the process of improving your life."

"Improving my life?"

They nodded in unison. "That's why you're here, aren't you?" the man said.

"I suppose so," Karen replied.

"Then you've come to the right place," the woman exclaimed, clasping her hands together and smiling so broadly it looked a little unnatural and even loose to Karen, a bit like what happens to a dog's face when it hangs out of the open window of a moving car.

"I suppose so," Karen said again.

And as she followed them into the building, she noted with great surprise that she had sensed no emotions coming from either of them.

This was highly unusual. *Is it me?* She wondered. *Has being around them calmed me to the point where my empathic hypervigilance dissipates? Or is it something peculiar about them, some kind of absence? Have they achieved such inner calm that I feel nothing when I'm around them?*

There were other options of course, but those were far more unsettling: The last time she had experienced so few emotions, it had been in the presence of the emotional avatars who would visit her on occasion. Anger, Fear, Grief, Sadness. When they visited, she didn't sense that they felt anything. Emotions didn't feel emotions; they embodied them.

Her current hosts were clearly not emotional avatars, but perhaps they were something else otherworldly and unnatural that was separate from the realm of human emotion. Like robots. Or the undead.

This was a deeply unsettling thought.

No, better not to dwell on it, Karen resolved. She intentionally shifted her focus to putting one foot in front of the other as she followed her hosts into the sliding doors of the shimmering green skyscraper.

The building was quiet. So quiet.

When it came to noise, certainly... but also... emotionally silent.

Karen was used to feeling complex webs of emotional layers any time she stepped into a public place in general but especially so in large buildings like this one, one with multiple floors, packed with people.

She would feel the emotions of the people in the building before she even saw or heard them.

However, she felt nothing as she stepped into this building. It was as emotionally empty as a long-abandoned warehouse.

And yet... there were certainly people here. The lobby was quite open and spacious. No one else sat in the lushly padded chairs that were centered around a working fountain.

A receptionist sat behind a large white marble reception desk shaped like a fresh staple still in the box. She looked impeccable in a white suit with her auburn hair swept primly into an updo.

Karen felt nothing emanating emotionally off this receptionist. Unlikely, even for someone who was at work. Typically, she'd sense *something* coming from the receptionist – even if that feeling were boredom or agitation. Perhaps impatience, a natural thing to feel coming from a worker who stared at the timeclock, counting the minutes until quitting time.

Plus, there was a sassy smirk plastered on the receptionist's face that seemed to suggest that she was feeling *something*.

Then why wasn't it detectable? As far as Karen's empathy was concerned, it was like no one was sitting there. It was the same lack of emotion she had felt from the hosts who had greeted her outside. As though summoned by her very thoughts, the photo frame couple walked up to the desk at that moment, craning over it and speaking softly to the receptionist about something. Karen presumed the conversation had to be about her.

She walked over to the plush chairs and lowered herself into one. It wasn't until she was seated that she realized how tired she was. Her eyelids closed.

When Karen opened her eyes again, the glass walls were a different color. Or at least that's what she thought.

A few moments later, she realized that it wasn't the walls at all that were changing color but the quality of light shining through them. Oh. It had been that long.

Night had fallen.

She sensed some motion in her peripheral vision and started when she saw that one of her hosts was sitting in another of the chairs, just outside the range of her direct vision – because the woman was staring at her.

Has she been watching me sleep this whole time? Karen wondered.

Now there was another unsettling thought.

"Good," the woman said. "You're awake."

"I'm sorry," Karen replied. "I didn't mean to fall asleep."

"It's common actually," she replied. "It happens a lot of times when people first tour our facility."

"Really?" Karen said. "That's strange."

The woman shook her head. "Not at all. It takes some time, you see, to adapt to the ambients."

"The ambients?" Karen asked.

"You really don't know much about us, do you?" the woman asked.

"I guess not," Karen said. "Although it's kind of hard to know what I don't know." She paused. "You know?" she added.

Karen briefly imagined the woman countering, "Would I know if I didn't?"

But of course, she didn't. That kind of witty banter wasn't in the cards, not coming from the mouth of someone who to Karen looked like the walking embodiment of a summer camp icebreaker. Karen sighed, while she waited for the woman to say something, anything at all.

Predictably, the woman launched into what struck Karen as her predictable spiel, one she'd likely given countless times to other potential students. "Our center is a place of tranquility. Of calm. Ideally, during your time here, you'll learn how to cultivate a place of calm within yourself. Until then, we have the technology to help you along. Like the ambients," the woman explained. "They're hard to explain. I don't quite understand them myself." She smiled sheepishly. "I don't have a technical background."

"Me neither," Karen admitted.

"In practice, they work like emotional dampening fields. They vibrate at a frequency that helps you relax. You, me, everyone," the woman finished.

"So this sense of calm," Karen said. "It'll only stay with me while I stay here?"

"In the short term, yes," her host admitted. "But the work you do here will help you take it with you."

"Is this something you know from personal experience?" Karen asked.

The woman nodded enthusiastically. "I'll warn you – it's not easy. But it's achievable." She rose and walked to the reception desk.

Karen realized with surprise that the same receptionist from when she arrived was still sitting there, with the same implacable smirk on her face.

Had she been there all this time while she slept? Karen dismissed that idea. No, that was too preposterous. That would be a ludicrously long work shift.

But as she surveyed the large lobby area, she realized that she was the only student she could see, at least in this part of the building, which was admittedly massive.

Normally, Karen would have felt a sense of deep unease at this realization, but at the moment she was having trouble feeling much of anything. It dawned on her that the emotional dampening effect was also muting her own emotions and not just those of the people around her.

Comfortably numb, she got it now, that lyric from a Pink Floyd song she only knew about half of the words to. She knew what comfortably numb felt like. Finally.

She knew what Viv would say if she told her that, too. "Karen," Viv would say. "That's not what that song is about."

"I know, Viv," Karen would answer.

"It's about drugs," Viv would unhelpfully explain.

"I know," Karen would repeat, getting agitated but not showing it, instead feeling the agitation well up inside where it couldn't harm anyone.

"D-R-U-G-S," this hypothetical Viv might say.

Karen shook her head, not wanting to get lost in her thoughts. She'd never had a problem with daydreaming before. Perhaps there was more room for that in her emotional inner life when she wasn't constantly bombarded by emotions – whether other people's or her own.

Even when spending time with Viv and Penny, she had still felt her own emotions. Those hadn't left her alone. No substance – legal or illegal – had completely freed her of her own emotions.

Whatever technology they were using in this building was impressive. If nothing else, Karen resolved, she'd have to figure out what it was. She didn't have much for resources, and she imagined ambients were expensive, but maybe if she had Penny barter for her or Martin called in a few favors…

Karen stopped herself mid-thought. She was getting ahead of herself. She should see what the course had to offer.

Karen rose and followed her host to the front desk. As they began the registration process for the course, the elevator bell dinged, and the doors flew open.

A white-haired man who had to be about seven feet tall stepped out. He was thin and slightly bent as well, making him look like he'd been stretched long like a piece of taffy. He wore a white coat. His complexion was disconcertingly pale, and his eyes had a pink tint to them.

Her host and the receptionist immediately dropped what they were doing to greet him.

"Dr. Mentus!" they chorused in unison.

He nodded as he approached the desk. "Your hand," he said to the receptionist.

She held her right hand open before him, and he placed a note in her palm. The paper appeared to be intricately folded. It reminded Karen of that children's origami game—a chatterbox or a cootie catcher, where a paper is transformed into a small puppet with options for a player to choose from to tell fortunes.

But she only got a glimpse of it because the receptionist closed her hand quickly and slid it underneath her desk into... a drawer? One of her pockets?

Karen couldn't quite tell. It happened too fast.

Damn, Karen thought. *I wish Viv were here.* Her partner's photographic memory would allow her to replay the scene as many times as she wanted, even slow it down so she could get a better look. Ah, to be an eideticist. There were times when Karen would gladly trade being an empath for pretty much any other psychic power.

Dr. Mentus nodded at her. "Good evening," he said.

"Good evening," Karen said back. She couldn't remember the last time someone had actually said those words to her in earnest. Good evening. It seemed so old fashioned that it was charming.

"We're so glad you've chosen to study with us," Dr. Mentus said. A warm smile spread across his face. It looked natural, like it belonged there.

He probably smiles a lot, Karen thought. This was a good sign. She imagined being a doctor could be stressful, the expectations people had of you, the pressure of others always assuming you knew what to do... but you couldn't always know, could you? Everything seemed simple when you were training, when you in a classroom, but nothing could prepare you for every real-life situation that would come up. Even doctors made mistakes.

When she was little, Karen had viewed doctors as nearly separate from humanity, as though they were a different species. This was before the Psychic Phenomenon, of course, and certainly before she realized that she was part of the intuitive population. She had always thought there were gifted people among us of course – people who stretched the boundaries of what people could be. But before that time, those people didn't possess psychic powers or perform feats that some would consider miracles. No, these people possessed degrees and performed specific professions.

Being hospitalized so many times in psychiatric institutions probably didn't help. There had been a series of doctors then, each successive one as useless as the last. They couldn't fix what was wrong with her. They couldn't make her empathy even marginally more bearable – and in fact, many of them had done her active harm in their coldness and their callousness.

The psychiatrists who worked on locked wards were often judgmental. Instead of being sympathetic to the plights of their patients, they had a way of treating mental patients as though they were less than, subhuman. Certainly irredeemable.

Indeed, Karen had come to note over the years, there seemed to be an awful lot of psychiatrists in active practice who weren't driven to the profession at all because of a genuine desire to help people but because of a seeming need to be an expert and to feel better – saner, smarter, more competent – than their charges.

Or, in other words, many psychiatrists craved the company of those they considered subhuman because spending time with their patients made them feel superhuman in comparison.

It was ugly but obvious to Karen, particularly as she could feel the smugness and superiority radiating off the psychiatrists. Even the ones who were fairly good at concealing how they felt – and not all of them were – couldn't fool Karen and her empathy.

Over time it had destroyed her faith in doctors. She had stopped looking up to them, and her inclination these days was to default to looking down on them until given a reason to feel otherwise.

The fact that Dr. Mentus smiled so warmly and so naturally was a good start.

"Thank you," Karen replied. "I'm excited to get started."

He nodded politely. "Great to meet you," he said, before walking away.

The receptionist turned and watched him as he did. There was a faraway look on her face. Karen felt something then coming from her, something that bled through whatever dampening fields the facility had in place. Adoration. No. Not adoration. Not quite. Exaltation. Worship. The receptionist had Dr. Mentus up on a pedestal.

Karen sighed. She remembered feeling like that once upon a time. Life had a way of disabusing her of that notion, however.

Once Dr. Mentus had disappeared into the elevator, the receptionist swiveled back around. "We don't see much of him down here on the first floor," she explained.

"Oh?"

The receptionist shook her head. "No, Dr. Mentus lives here, up on Floor 15, but he keeps mostly to himself. His work is completely limited to those who have attained that level."

"So I won't be working with him?" Karen asked.

"Not right away. And some never do, no. But if you work really hard…" The receptionist let her voice trail off.

Karen nodded. "I always work hard."

"Of course," the receptionist said, nodding, but using a weak tone of voice that suggested that she was just being polite and didn't necessarily agree with Karen's self-assessment.

"It's hard work just being me," Karen explained.

This got a laugh out of the receptionist. "Let me give you some advice," she said.

Karen craned closer.

"The work is the work," the receptionist said.

"What does that mean?" Karen asked.

"A lot of people come in here looking for some kind of catch. Some of them do this because they're impatient and are looking for shortcuts. Which never goes well of course." The phone next to her rang. "One second," she said to Karen, before scooping up the receiver.

"The Mentus Center, Emily speaking," the receptionist said in a practiced rhythm that suggested that she'd said it so many times that it had become logistically one word to her rather than two phrases.

A long silence ensued as whoever was on the other end of the call effectively told their life story. Karen could hear the voice, as the caller was speaking loudly, but not exactly what the voice was saying. Emily rapped her fingers on the desktop as she waited for a break in the conversation. When one happened, she asked a few questions about scheduling.

"Perfect," Emily said finally. "We'll see you then." And then, to Karen, "Sorry about that."

"No worries," Karen said, "It's your job."

"Anyway, where was I?"

"You were talking about people who try to take shortcuts on the course," Karen reminded her.

"Oh right," the receptionist said. "Yeah, don't do that. And the other big thing is people who want to take... longcuts, I guess you'd call them."

"A longcut?" Karen said.

"Yeah. They enter the lessons and instead of just doing what's asked of them, they assume there must be some kind of trick or trip. And that the real lesson is hidden. So they start doing other things, thinking that the real test requires snooping around and getting creative." She shook her head in disapproval. "Don't do that either. The work is the work. All you gotta do to complete the program is to do what's asked of you. Nothing more, nothing less. It isn't always easy, the work. But it's straightforward."

"The work is the work," Karen said. "Got it."

"Here's your bunk assignment," the receptionist said, sliding a printout across the desk. "The student hostel is down that hall, to the right."

"Oh," Karen said. "I didn't know that this was a residential program."

"It isn't always," Emily said. "Some students commute in and arrange their own accommodations. But considering how far you came and your…" She searched for the words before proceeding. "Lack of resources, it was either this or put you up with a host family. Which I could do if this is unsuitable."

"No," Karen said. "This is absolutely fine." She didn't like the thought of imposing upon a family, especially since she suspected that they, too, would look like they had stepped out of a photo frame filler. "It's quite generous," she added. "And I appreciate it."

The receptionist nodded.

"Are you sure there's no charge?" Karen asked.

The receptionist laughed. Strangely, Karen felt no joy emanating off her. "Of course there's no charge," Emily said. "The work we do here is rewarding enough."

Karen nodded and shuffled down the hall, holding the printout in her hand. As she put Emily behind her, she felt a strange sense of unease pushing up against the deadening effect of the ambients. The unease fought the ambients hard but sunk back down. Karen couldn't quite manage to worry properly, even though something within her insisted that she should.

The Hostel

Like most hostels, the one provided for the center's residents was nothing all that elaborate or impressive.

The students for the Mentus Center were all housed in one large room that seemed to have been filled with as many bunk beds as mathematically possible, given the room's dimensions.

The Mentus Center generally employed a rather futuristic, fantastic design scheme that reminded Karen for all the world of a spaceship or a lab. The décor in the hostel was different than that, featuring a wash of light brown neutral wall paint and linens, a light hardwood floor, and wooden bunks.

As Karen moved through the room, she noted that half of the beds seemed to be occupied, although many of the inhabitants weren't currently in them, possibly away at a class or something. This struck her as odd given the time of night, but the printout she'd been handed at reception had mentioned that different learning schedules would be accommodated. If her partner Penny were here, Karen thought, she would most certainly have opted for night classes.

Karen worked out the bunk numbering scheme and noted that her bed was set away in a back corner. There was a paper tag slipped into an identification slot on the end of the bed on the lower level: *Cross, Karen.*

She doubled checked that the letter-number combination H7 – which had reminded her very much of playing Battleship – matched the one on the bed. It did.

"You can put your things in that cabinet," a voice called down from atop the bunk bed.

Karen looked up.

A small wiry red-haired woman with a freckled face looked back at her. "Marilou," she said. "Although you'd know that from looking at the bed tags, I suppose."

"Karen," Karen replied. "And same."

"Right, right, well, get on with it," Marilou said.

"Get on with…?"

"The ginger jokes. Jokes about freckles. The Marilou jokes, about people who have two names or how redneck you think that is. Whatever jokes you have to get out of your system, now's the time," Marilou said.

Karen smirked. "I'm fine."

"No, you're not," Marilou said. "You have jokes to make, so out with it. I have heard them all before by the way. People always think they're being so clever when they make the jokes they make. But they make the same ones over and over again." She shook her head. "There's nothing new under the sun, you know. But people are so fixated on their own damn little lives that they think they've invented everything. It'd be sadder if it weren't so annoying. So come at me. I'm ready for you to call me Wendy or make Pippi Longstocking references."

Karen sat down on the bottom bunk.

"Hey, aren't you going to put your stuff away?" Marilou said.

"I didn't bring any," Karen said. "I didn't know I'd be staying."

"Wait, what?" Marilou said. "You have a story. I just know it!" She scrambled down the side of the bunk bed and sat down beside Karen. "What happened? What are you doing here?"

Karen studied Marilou's face. It was odd spending time with another person and not being constantly accosted by their emotional inner life. Normally, any time Karen opened her mouth, she could feel the other person reacting in real time to what she said, before even *they* were consciously aware of what they felt.

It was distracting, made it hard to tell a proper story sometimes, because their emotions were constantly butting in and essentially interrupting what she was trying to say by diverting her attention from her words.

Karen realized as she began to explain that the ambients were preventing that. And surprising herself, she opened up completely. She told Marilou all of it. Her background, her struggles with mental illness, the brief respite she'd found in the form of Penny and Viv. She recounted Penny running off, finding the flyer, and taking the bus out here. She even told Marilou about the strange hallucination she'd had in which the emotional avatars had attacked her.

All the while, Marilou let her speak, and Karen had no idea what was going through her bunkmate's mind.

Finally, when Karen had finished telling the tale, Marilou opened her mouth and spoke. "So what's your last name?" Marilou said, not addressing one word that Karen had spoken in the last several minutes. She craned her neck around and peered at Karen's bunk tag.

"Karen Cross?" Marilou exclaimed, laughing.

"I'm sorry?" Karen said.

"I already know the kinds of jokes you're used to hearing," Marilou said, struggling to maintain her composure. "Get down from the cross, Karen, someone else needs the wood."

"What?" Karen said, for she had never heard such a joke before and wasn't sure she even got it.

"Because you have a martyr's name. It sounds like 'carrying the cross.' And considering your gloomy disposition…" Marilou started laughing again.

Karen shook her head. "No one has ever pointed that out before," she said sotto voce.

"You must not get out much," Marilou said flippantly.

It stung. "Well, I don't care what your last name is," Karen shot back. "If it's anything other than Pain-In-the-Ass, it's false advertising."

"Yeesh," Marilou said. "Someone's sensitive. Alright, alright. Don't cry. I take it back. I mistook you for someone with a sense of humor."

Karen scowled at her.

"Let's start over," Marilou said. She stuck her hand out. "I'm Marilou. Feel free to get whatever jokes you're going to make out of your system now."

Free accommodations, Karen thought, shaking Marilou's hand to get it over with. *Yeah, right. Nothing's ever* really *free, is it?*

"You put the hostile in hostel," Karen spat at Marilou.

Her bunkmate grinned at this. "I knew you had it in you," Marilou replied, climbing back up the side of the bunks and into her bed.

"Oh shut up," Karen said.

On the top bunk, Marilou stared at the ceiling and grinned.

Floor 1

After a long night tossing and turning and a cursory shower in the common women's locker room area provided for those staying in the hostel, Karen was eager to get out of her quarters and on to the first day of classes.

The Floor 1 program would serve as orientation, her welcome packet instructed her. And the next session would be starting shortly, taking place in the large auditorium that branched off the lobby in the other direction away from the hostel.

It was a sizeable auditorium, with about the same capacity as a large freshman college course. Glancing around, Karen felt it could easily fit 200 students, perhaps 300 if there were a need to seat that many.

Karen noted with great surprise that she was the first one to arrive.

Is it going to be just me? She wondered as she settled off into a distant corner, well into the back of the auditorium, looking for a place where she would be as inconspicuous as possible to the lecturer. It was a carryover to earlier days when she tried to hide in class. She'd been a good student when she was young, the kind of girl who raised her hand constantly and knew all the answers. But that same quality that generally pleased her teachers had driven her classmates to first mock her and later bully her, shoving her face into deep snowbanks during recess.

"Whitewash! Whitewash!" her tormenters would cry.

And after a while, her teachers also seemed less than enthusiastic that Karen always had her hand up. "Yes, Karen, I see you," they'd say. "Anyone else? Anyone besides Karen?" Now that she was an adult, she could see the situation from the teacher's perspective. They had an entire class to teach and not just one pupil. It wasn't that being so eager to provide answers was bad in and of itself, but they needed to have other students participate because otherwise they'd loaf, let Karen take the stage, and learn nothing.

At the time, however, Karen had no insight into this. She had instead just felt invisible and confused, as behavior that had once been rewarded was now discouraged.

Her response was to slowly shrink into herself at school. At first, this was a matter of never raising her hand, fearing her teacher's dismissal. Then she found her posture beginning to sag. The hoods on her oversized sweatshirts – a uniform she wore even then – crept up so she could hide under them.

And then as the months and years wore on, she sat farther and farther into the back of any given classroom.

She had learned that it was best to not be noticed in a crowd, if you could help it.

"I can't believe there's no one here yet," she muttered to herself. Her voice was rather soft, but the sound still carried more than she expected due to the lecture hall being so empty.

She *was* nearly a half an hour early, but there was little else to do at the hostel, especially without risking more social interaction with Marilou, and Karen had decided Marilou was best avoided as much as possible. Perhaps if she'd brought entertainment, something to read, she would have been less inclined to be here so early.

But that was how it worked.

Karen was relieved when a few minutes later other students started to pour in. Her packet had indicated that this course was open to the public and could be registered for just before entry. A lot of people seemed to be taking advantage of that option.

The people who filtered in were a motley mix. There seemed to be no pattern to them, nothing unifying. They were of all professional backgrounds. Some appeared to have come directly from blue-collar work, wearing a variety of well-used uniforms, perhaps on an extended lunch break. Others looked like they'd never worked a day in their lives, having that easily recognizable sheen of money and prestige bestowed upon birth.

The crowd also varied in age. The course had specified that this location only taught adults – and that children needed to study at other satellite campuses (*with details available upon request!* the promo materials breezily added). That much was plainly evident watching the other students enter.

However, when it came to the ages of attendees, there were young adults, seeming octogenarians, and everything in between.

True, it was difficult to figure out people's ages just by looking at them. But to Karen, it seemed like a much more diverse class in terms of biological age than a college setting, where older adults were normally considered "nontraditional students."

No gender seemed to dominate the audience. And while again tough to pinpoint precisely by simply looking around, it seemed to Karen like the assembled crowd was rather racially diverse as well – something she wasn't at all expecting based on the milquetoast appearance and demeanor of the staff.

In other words, Karen was pleasantly surprised by the diversity, in just about every dimension.

I wonder, she found herself thinking, *how many of them are intuitives.*

That was perhaps the trickiest dimension of all to suss out by simply looking around. It was arguably the most important one to her – but the visible evidence of likely diversity in other areas made her feel more optimistic than she had been coming into the class.

Just as the room seemed at risk of reaching capacity and Karen started to eye the empty seat next to her nervously, worried that someone might sit there, her hosts – the would-be photo frame models – entered the room, noisily shutting the heavy doors to the hall behind them.

"Good morning everyone!" the woman called. "I'm Daisy Jones!"

Of course, Karen thought. *Of course, that's her name.*

"Hope everyone's a happy camper this morning!" the male host called up.

Karen stifled a giggle. Seriously, this *was* an awful lot like being at summer camp.

"Doug, you need to introduce yourself," Daisy said to him sharply.

"Oh yeah," he said. "I'm Doug Jones! As you can see, Daisy does all my thinking for me."

Daisy beamed. "Behind every good man is a woman," she intoned.

"Oh boy," Karen grumbled to herself.

The guy sitting in front of her turned around and glared at her. Karen shrugged at him and raised the palms of both hands.

Shaking his head, he turned around.

"We're here to help YOU get YOUR life in order," Doug said, punching the air every time he emphasized a word. "Oh yeah, oh yeah, oh yeah," he said, boxing the air, seemingly psyching himself up.

The other people in the lecture hall started clapping.

Oh dear, Karen thought, careful not to speak it aloud, lest she evoke the ire of the gatekeeper sitting in front of her. *I should not have come here.*

She wondered idly about what she'd signed at registration. She'd been tired when she arrived and hadn't read it carefully. What was in that paperwork? What had she done? Was there a way out of this situation?

With her empathic powers dulled by the ambients, it was difficult for her to get any sort of read on the room. She noted that there wasn't another egress. The way out was blocked by heavy doors.

And she'd have to walk right past Mr. and Mrs. Jones to get there. Not to mention the hundreds of other people who seemed to be enjoying this monstrosity of a presentation.

No, Karen decided. She was stuck.

"Here at the Mentus Center, we'll teach you all of the skills you need to finally get disciplined and get ahead in life. You'll learn willpower, emotional self-regulation," Daisy said.

"And TIME MANAGEMENT!" Doug finished, punching the air in a flurry.

"TIME MANAGEMENT!" someone in the crowd yelled back.

Doug flashed them peace signs with both hands.

Daisy forced a very unconvincing smile and pressed a button on the console in front of her. A lecture screen unfolded, the lights dimmed, and a video presentation began to play.

As the film started, she and Doug shuffled off to the side of the auditorium. Because of the strange angle, Karen could still see them but only just. They were faintly illuminated by stray light. Even just silhouetted it was clear to Karen that their expressions had completely changed. Gone were the camp counselor façades. Doug was scowling in a way that struck Karen as predatory. Daisy looked incredibly bored.

Perhaps if her emotions were working properly, if they hadn't been deadened by ambients, Karen would have felt fear at this, unease. But at the moment, it seemed oddly comforting. They were showing a bit of humanity, after all. It was clear to her that they'd done this presentation countless times. Of course, they were over it. Anyone would be.

And as the video played, Karen realized that this "class" was mostly a sales presentation, for a product she had already signed up for.

Well, no matter, she thought. It was better than dealing with Marilou. And the video did explain the program a bit better than the booklet and the quick pitch they'd given her before.

She would be trained using a series of modules. The easiest classes would be taught on the lower floors of the building, and as she mastered the program, she would ascend to the upper floors.

There were two payment options available to students. There was cash pay of course. Karen hadn't chosen this route because she didn't have the money. But many students did finance their education by directly paying the center.

And for those who couldn't pay, there was the referral program. Upon graduation, Karen would be required to go to an off-site training center where she would learn how to recruit new students.

There were no recruitment quotas, the video assured. All the Mentus Center asked was that former students try. And as part of that expectation, they even provided recruitment training.

Being asked to simply try something didn't sound so bad to Karen. And she probably wouldn't finish the program anyway. It sounded like most students didn't. The recruitment commitment could probably be sidestepped simply by walking away from her classes before that happened, catching a series of buses back home.

No big deal. No big deal at all.

Karen thought to herself as the video switched to testimonials of satisfied students that it was a wonder that anyone paid cash for the program, given those easy terms.

Suckers.

Floor 2

Karen wasn't sure what she had expected from the classes at the Mentus Center, but this wasn't it.

She found herself once again gazing longingly at the door. True, it was a different door, a different room.

She had entered the session rather hopeful – and feeling oddly like a VIP. There had been an unmistakable moment of satisfaction when the proximity key fob she'd been provided after orientation beeped agreeably and allowed her entry into this course.

She had access to something others didn't, the little beep told her. She was on her way to great things.

It was a feeling Karen wasn't at all accustomed to having. She was used to being at the bottom rung of every ladder she found herself on.

And now here she was sitting in a circle with a bunch of other dorks, cradling a dictionary in her hands.

"You may think you know this book," her instructor said, "but you don't. I assure you that you don't. If you did, you wouldn't be having the problems you were having. We tend to think of misunderstanding as something that exists on the global level. It's a Big Problem with a Big Solution. No, no, no." The instructor shook his head as if to punctuate this point. "It is a Big Problem, but it starts in a Small Place. It starts on the level of discrete meaning itself."

He smiled and opened his dictionary onto his lap. "It's time to rediscover meaning, dear students. Please begin."

"Begin what?" a classmate said.

"Begin reading the dictionary," the instructor said.

"What? Just read it? Like it's a book?"

"It is a book," the instructor replied.

"Not one with a plot," another student said.

"Real life doesn't have a plot either," the instructor said. "Movies have corrupted your brain. It's time to correct that."

Karen expected her classmates to walk out. She felt an urge to herself, even over the calming field of the ambients. She didn't want to do it alone, however, but perhaps she could join those who were about to leave.

But shocking her, no one made a move to leave. Instead, her classmates all opened their dictionaries and began to read quietly.

Karen opened hers as well:

a

[ə, eɪ]

DETERMINER

1.   used when referring to someone or something for the first time in a text or conversation. Compare with the.

2.   used to indicate membership of a class of people or things.

3.   in, to, or for each; per (used when expressing rates or ratios)

Floor 3

Karen watched with amusement while her classmates debated one another on the meaning of dictionary definitions.

"Now that you *think* you understand what all those words mean, now is the time to challenge yourselves and each other," her instructor had said.

When he'd first described the exercise, it sounded to Karen like they were going to be having some kind of semantic bee – like a spelling bee but focused on meaning instead of orthography.

But instead, he meant for them to debate one another on supposedly incontrovertible facts. They were to find the loopholes inherent in the definitions, the secret connotation hiding behind denotation.

Now they were arguing about water – whether the term strictly pertained to the molecular combination of one oxygen and two hydrogen atoms – or whether it was acceptable to refer to any liquid that was mostly water, even when containing other trace elements within it, as most water did, as *water*.

The conflict was getting strangely emotional.

Karen felt almost like an observer outside of her own body as she leaped into the fray.

"If you take such a purist view of language, if you restrict a term to only the most prototypical representation of what it points to, you are rendering language practically useless. Such prescription isn't just annoying and aggravating – it threatens to unravel civilization." The words flew out of her mouth and startled her.

"Very good, Karen," her instructor urged her. "Counterpoint?"

Several volunteers came forward. "Words have to mean *something*. Without an exact meaning, what is the point of communication? We might as well be waving our arms and grunting."

"Isn't that what communication is?" Karen said. "On its most basic level, isn't that what we're *still* doing?"

"Perhaps," her opponent said. "But we're doing it precisely. Take out the precision and what do you have? You have a bunch of animals who think we understand one another but don't."

Karen laughed. "You're good at describing humanity."

"Pardon?"

"Clear definitions are no safeguard against miscomprehension. There's so much behind words. There's nonverbal communication. There's the emotional subtext. And there's how people project their own life experiences onto any given situation. All that blends together and colors the meaning and the words. It's never just about the words," Karen said.

Her classmate frowned and turned to the teacher. "I thought we were supposed to be getting past our emotions here."

"No," the instructor said. "We're supposed to be gaining control of them. It's hard to gain control of something if you won't acknowledge it even exists. Who would want to wrangle invisible cattle?'

Karen smiled. *That's exactly what it feels like sometimes*, she thought. *Like wrangling invisible cattle.*

The instructor rose to the board, which he had filled out in an elaborate scoring system. He adjusted the points based on their recent flurry.

"Okay," he said, pointing to one of the students. "Next concept. Family."

The student rose nervously. Karen went to sit back down.

"No," the instructor said, pointing to Karen. "You go again."

Karen nodded. Her heart was beating fast, and her legs felt weak. She squeezed her hands tightly into fists as her opponent began his argument, doing her best to focus on each word he spoke to her even as blood rushed into her ears, pounding, making it difficult for her to hear what he was saying.

Floor 4

As Karen looked around the next classroom, she noted that while there were a few familiar faces in the mix that most of them were unfamiliar. As always, she received the news that she had passed the course offered on the previous floor via the interoffice mail system, which simply notified her in a flyer stuck in the mail slot at the end of her bunk informing her that the proximal key fob could now access the classroom on the fourth floor.

On the first few floors, her class had almost entirely graduated with her. Not this time.

Only a few of her peers had ascended to the next level with her.

I guess I'm one of the quick learners, Karen thought.

"If you're just joining us," her instructor said. "Good work."

Karen beamed, feeling an odd warmth enter her body. It reminded her for all the world of those early times at school before she stopped putting herself out there and obviously excelling over her peers. It felt like the times before she was sure that silent others probably seethed and deemed her a teacher's pet.

The times before she cared and dimmed her aptitude to make those around her more comfortable.

It was a strange and unexpected transformation – not at all what she'd expected to find at the Mentus Center when she picked up the first flyer off her lawn and made the trek out here – but a welcome one.

"And if you've been here for a while," the instructor continued, casting his gaze on others whose faces Karen didn't recognize, "get your shit together."

A few individuals visibly trembled at this. Karen felt the warmth drain from her. Perhaps she had been a little premature in her celebration.

The instructor gave a quick rundown of what they'd be studying in this class. "I'd go into greater detail, but your peers would probably die of boredom," he snapped, throwing a sour gaze over the class. "Anyway, if you have any aptitude whatsoever, you probably won't need much instruction. Fair warning though. The fourth floor is where most of our students get stuck. A lot of you will never advance. Many of you will withdraw, disgraced. And some of you... will waste my time considerably before you put me and the rest of us out of the misery of your company."

Someone's bitter, Karen thought. *Bitter or just big on power trips.*

"You," the instructor said, pointing at Karen.

"Me?" Karen croaked out. It was early morning, and her voice hadn't had much chance to warm up, since she'd successfully escaped from Marilou's conversational clutches once again.

"What was that about?" the instructor said.

"What are you talking about?" Karen said.

"You made a face," the instructor said.

"Did I?"

The instructor nodded.

Karen shrugged. "Sorry," she said. "I didn't mean to."

"It's that kind of sloppiness that strands you on Floor 4," the instructor said. "What you say with your body language

– even in the small movements of your face – it speaks volumes. If you can't control your facial movements, then you can't control your emotions. And you certainly don't deserve to be a Mentus Center graduate with that lack of discipline."

"Yes, sir," Karen replied, hanging her head.

"Take that look off your face, too," the instructor said. "Give me a blank slate. That's what the goal is. Not misery. Not remorse. You are not here to become someone that other people trod on."

Karen did her best to clear her mind, to relax the muscles in her face. At first, it seemed impossible, but as the seconds rushed by, she let herself sink into the constant emotional white noise of the ambients.

"Very good," her instructor said.

He told them to split into pairs. Karen felt a jolt of anxiety at this request. She hated the process of pairing off, always expecting she'd end up left out – because she had been so many times. She stood waiting for someone to approach her, but they all chose one another until a single student remained.

One she had somehow completely missed up until this point, dragging herself through early morning stupor. Marilou.

Oh no.

"Heya Cross, guess it's just you and me, huh? It's like it's meant to be," Marilou chirped.

"Guess so," Karen said.

They sat across from one another. The objective of Floor 4 was simple but deceptively difficult. They were to perfect sitting across from someone else in silence, gazing at their partner, not breaking eye contact – although they were allowed to blink. If either party changed from a blank facial expression or neutral physical posture, then they failed the class for the day.

To pass Floor 4, they had to maintain this silent mutual regard for four hours.

The class started well enough. A full five minutes crawled by at an interminable pace before one person lost their composure and broke into laughter.

Others failed their test not long thereafter. Laughter was contagious, after all.

Karen bit the inside of her cheek, hoping to stave off laughter herself while simultaneously wondering if that slight movement changed her facial expression enough for her to flunk the test.

At any moment, she expected Marilou to crack up. Or flash a weird face. Or, well, do something very Marilou.

But her partner sat there placidly, and before long, they were the only students left who hadn't failed the day's class.

The other students gathered around, watching them in closer proximity than Karen would have liked. All those hovering people made her nervous enough that she felt her face beginning to betray her.

Each time, however, she sunk back into the ambients, which washed over her like a great white wave. She felt herself plunging down into them. The ambients were never quite as deep as she wanted them to be – she felt like she was trying to completely submerge herself in a bathtub that simply wasn't large enough to hold the requisite water.

But the trying helped. It at least distracted her from the feelings that pulled at her.

She had no idea how long it had been, but eventually, her instructor said, "Okay, you've passed."

Marilou and Karen both rose.

As they did, the instructor laughed. "I was lying of course," he said. "That was only two hours."

"But you said..." Karen started.

The instructor shook his head. "It doesn't matter what I said. You didn't do what was asked of you. Tomorrow we begin again."

The work is the work. No tricks or traps, my ass, Karen thought bitterly but had the good sense not to say aloud.

Marilou shrugged as they left the classroom.

The next time they sat down for the test, Karen came prepared. They had developed a counting system. It was rudimentary and crude, but she and Marilou determined that the ambients swelled to their tangible apex approximately 10 times a minute. It was a little more than that, but just to be on the safe side they decided that they would sit for 2400 apical beats, no matter what anyone said or did.

They would not break the exercise until 2400 beats passed. Once that happened, one of them would rise. Hopefully, the count would be correct.

"We'll take turns," Marilou had said. "One day you'll count, the next day I will."

"Okay," Karen had replied. "I'll go first."

On the second day, Karen rose after 2400 beats.

"I'm sorry," the instructor said. "You're 17 seconds short. See you tomorrow."

On the third day, Karen felt more than a little defeated but worked hard to not let it show on her face. It seemed like the water levels in the proverbial bathtub were lower than normal, but at least she had experience on her side.

It was beginning to feel oddly natural to be this unreactive.

Perhaps that's the point of the exercise, she thought, noting her face stayed perfectly still.

Karen and Marilou sat in the stillness, even as others erupted around them. Again, they were the last pair of students left sitting.

It feels like forever, Karen thought. *Is this what it's like to be immortal?* She thought of the crushing ennui, the pointlessness, the emotional vertigo that must result from being so removed from everything and everyone else. She'd often wished she could live forever, but after three days on Floor 4, she wasn't sure she'd wish such a thing on her worst enemy.

Finally, Marilou rose. The instructor nodded in acknowledgment.

"Good luck on Floor 5," he said to both of them. "I'll send a note to the registrar about access."

Floor 5

On Floor 5, they were informed that they'd be doing the same exercise as on the floor before – except this time several people would actively antagonize them while they attempted to stay still and silent.

Karen sat, bristling internally while people invaded her personal space, screaming insults into her face.

She did her best to count. It was only 2400 beats. Was that so hard? Surely, she could do it.

But she discovered, just as she had last time, that she rose 17 seconds too soon.

"Add an extra couple of beats onto the end," Marilou unhelpfully advised after they failed their first Floor 5 attempt.

"I *am*," Karen insisted. That was what was so strange. No matter how much she tried to pad the counts, she was always short. And always by the same oddly specific margin, by 17 seconds.

Marilou easily counted the time correctly on their next day in class, causing them to pass Floor 5 with flying colors.

"Maybe you should do the counts from now on," Karen offered. "I keep screwing it up."

Marilou shook her head. "No, you can do it. I know you can," she said. "And anyway, it's probably good practice for us, having to do the material twice."

Maybe good practice, Karen thought. *But demoralizing and tedious.*

She found herself wondering about the ambients. Could it be that they pulsed differently for her? She had timed it with Marilou and a stopwatch in their bunk – multiple times at this point – but perhaps there was something about Karen's physiology in particular, and the fact that she was an empath, that was complicating things.

Whatever the case, she didn't relish repeating floors. Hopefully, they'd be done with all this silent-game-staring-contest nonsense soon.

Floor 6

Disappointingly, the exercise on Floor 6 was quite similar to both of the two previous floors.

Where Floor 5 had people yelling insults into their faces, Floor 6 took a wilier tactic. The examiners on Floor 6 told jokes. Hilarious jokes. Nonstop, constant jokes.

A lot of what they said Karen didn't find funny, which was a huge relief. But fiendishly, the would-be comedians seemed to be practiced in launching jokes in a calibrated manner, appealing eventually to all different senses of humor, including hers.

Someone put an awful lot of thought and effort into developing this part of the curriculum, Karen noted. Because the jokes were different every day they showed up, having failed the class from the day before.

There was something different about humor. It worked on a deeper emotional level than self-preservation or ego or anything else. There was something very primal about responding to absurdity. Karen felt herself scrambling to contain this response.

She had never quite understood how comedians kept from laughing on set while others around them told jokes. She supposed part of it was repetition – hearing the same lines over and over again until they were no longer funny.

In this curriculum, however, semantic satiation wasn't an option. Nor was just garden variety desensitization. The jokes changed too much to ever get used to them.

Instead, the students were left to herd subconscious cats.

And once she finally did, Karen was despondent to learn she had screwed up her timing once again. She'd miscounted the four hours by... 17 seconds.

Shit, she found herself thinking. *You'd think I'd gain some kind of implicit instincts by now. Some kind of sense. But nope.*

If Marilou were disappointed, she didn't show it. However, Karen thought, that would be a pretty easy thing for her to mask, given how much practice they'd had keeping anything they were feeling hidden away beneath the surface.

The next day Marilou counted them successfully through the test. It was on to Floor 7.

Floor 7

To the bunkmates' relief, Floor 7 did not feature the obnoxious exercise they'd been enduring since Floor 4.

In fact, Floor 7 did not resemble any of the previous levels at all. Instead of having a layout designed around a large central classroom, Floor 7 had a few dozen tiny chambers. It reminded Karen of how the music department of large colleges will have a floor full of practice rooms set aside for musicians to use to practice individually. Some practice rooms will have a piano inside but not all. And none of them will be large enough to accommodate more than two musicians.

The Floor 7 chambers each had similar dimensions and were also soundproofed, again calling back to practice rooms.

Additionally, each student had their own instructor for this part of the course.

They were cautioned going into Floor 7 that nothing they discussed on this level could be shared with their fellow classmates. This was a general rule of the Mentus Center, but a violation on Floor 7 would be taken particularly seriously. Students would be expelled immediately and banned from the program for life.

This seemed a bit overkill to Karen, and she wondered what the big deal was.

"The purpose of Floor 7," her instructor finally revealed to her, "is to set down anything you brought into the center with you that might be encumbering your studies."

"Encumbering my studies?" Karen said.

"Yes, it's particularly important that you share your wrongdoings with me. That you clear your mind and your conscience," her instructor explained.

"Ah, so this is like going to confession?" Karen said.

The instructor bristled at this remark. "We prefer not to call it that."

"I'm telling you my sins, and you're absolving me. What else would you call it?"

The instructor smiled. "It's not absolution. That's not what Floor 7 is about. It's about clarity. Lightness of being. Moving forward unencumbered."

Karen frowned. "If you wanted me to have a mind that's unencumbered, then why wasn't this done earlier in the program?"

"Excellent question," her instructor replied, grinning. "Exactly the kind of question you should be asking me, if you're adhering to the program and learning everything you should."

"And the answer?"

"Well," her instructor explained, "it's hard to know what's encumbering your learning if you haven't had a chance to experience the learning process, isn't it?"

"I don't follow," Karen said.

"Any revelations you would have made before you started our program would be ones made by a confused mind. One lacking discipline. Could you have had some benefit from revealing yourself to a certified instructor then? Possibly. But you'll benefit so much more now."

"What happens if I don't have anything I need to get off my mind?" Karen said.

"That's impossible," her instructor said. "Everyone does."

"But if I don't?" Karen replied.

"Well, then you're not human," her instructor said. "And you won't pass Floor 7."

Karen combed her brain for anything she could offer. However, between the reassuring wash of the ambients and all the non-reactive training she'd been working on for the last handful of floors, she was finding it difficult to feel guilty about anything.

Nothing encumbered her thoughts.

"Maybe I'm not human," Karen suggested.

Her instructor leaned forward in his seat. "Why do you say that?"

And before Karen knew it, she felt herself telling the instructor about her upbringing, about a father who was constantly disappointed in her, a mother who took off one day without even saying goodbye, and the strange woman who shuffled in so quickly to take her mother's place.

She told the instructor about how she was just expected to accept all of it. "A good daughter would have."

"Ah," the instructor said. "See, now we are getting somewhere."

She told him about being sent away to One Eighty Acres, a ranch for troubled teens, after she started to exhibit psychic powers. How her father didn't believe she was an empath.

She told him about the strange visits she began to receive there, from what seemed to be emotional avatars or some other form of interplanar beings.

"Which sounds crazy, I know," Karen said, before telling him about all the time she'd spent dipping in and out of psych wards.

She hadn't talked to her father and stepmother in years, she confessed. She hadn't updated them on her whereabouts or her new address. And they accordingly hadn't sought her out either.

"They're probably just glad to be rid of me," Karen said.

She thought about mentioning her father by name, talking about the Grounded Temple. But it was all embarrassing enough, wasn't it? It was awful even without bringing any of that cultish shit into it.

She was really talking now, and she felt a sort of helplessness as her body followed the momentum she'd given it.

"I stiffed so many of those hospitals," Karen admitted. "I couldn't pay my bill. It wasn't the right thing to do, but I was suffering. I was struggling. It was always a game. I was always on the run, trying to figure out how to survive just a little longer. And then I met Viv and Penny..."

"Viv and Penny?" the instructor asked.

"My partners. Romantic partners, yes. All three of us live together. I know it's not a traditional arrangement, but it works for me. Well, it worked for me before Viv got sick and Penny took off."

"It sounds like you're in transition," the instructor observed. "You're actually doing really well for someone in such acute existential crisis."

"You think so?" Karen said.

"Sure," the instructor said. "And it sounds like you're making progress since you haven't had any hallucinations since you've arrived here at our facility, correct?"

"Hallucinations?" Karen said.

"The emotional avatars, I think you called them. You haven't seen them since you got here, right?" her instructor said.

"Well yeah," Karen said. "I haven't seen the avatars here at the Mentus Center... but that doesn't mean they're hallucinations."

"But you said you had a hallucination just before you found our flyer and decided to come here. They were chasing you, these emotional avatars. They were going to harm you," the instructor said.

That's different, Karen thought. *That's not even close to the same thing.* The emotional avatars, her strange visitors, had been a staple of the last decade of her life. They were there during sane times and crazy times. Their presence – or absence – was completely independent of her mental health. They frankly just seemed to be linked to what other *people around her* were feeling.

But as she studied the instructor's face, she knew that explaining this nuance would likely be futile. Such distinctions didn't generally have a place in this program. And what would be the point of making it clear to him?

She was trying to pass Floor 7. It wasn't lying. Not really. It was holding back, not making sure that the other person knew the whole truth. *Which is lying*, something within her insisted, but she did her best to ignore that doubt.

Although another nagging question remained… why *hadn't* she seen the emotional avatars since arriving here?

She imagined it had something to do with the ambients. Perhaps they impeded their entry somehow, like an invisible barrier.

Or perhaps there was something to what her instructor was saying. Maybe the emotional avatars *did* emanate from within her. Maybe as soon as her emotional lability was dialed back, she would no longer see them.

Could they actually be hallucinations?

No. Something within her was sure that wasn't it.

But she was equally sure that trying to convince her instructor wasn't a good use of her time.

She let him sweep her away into a different conversational loop and left that point uncontested.

"It's been wonderful doing this module with you," he said, shaking her hand after their session. "You really are a gifted student, and I am excited for you."

"Thank you," Karen replied.

Floor 8

Marilou again. This time they quickly chose each other as partners.

In the hostel, they'd fallen into a comfortable pattern with one another. Karen found herself making more of an effort to be semi-social, to do the normal "fake nice" behaviors she had a hard time achieving around people in general but which seemed to set Marilou at ease.

For her part, Marilou dialed her intensity back a bit. She was still gregarious and outspoken but no longer seemed like she was auditioning for a role. In hindsight, Karen could see it so clearly, that Marilou was so extra not because she thought she was amazing or insightful but because of the exact opposite: Marilou felt like she had to perform for other people for them to want to spend any time with her.

Marilou thought she had to be "on." That she had to have a big personality for people to like her.

The reality was that Marilou was a lot more fun to be around when she wasn't trying so hard to be interesting or zany.

Perhaps that was what Marilou was learning from the school, Karen reflected. They had spent many hours sitting in silence, after all. Maybe Marilou was learning it was okay just to be silent sometimes. To just *be* with other people.

Whatever the case, it was a great relief for Karen to find her old partner in the Floor 8 classroom. They couldn't talk about what happened on Floor 7, but they'd managed to talk *around* it and knew they were both proceeding to the same floor once again, having both passed Floor 7 on the first try.

I would give anything to know what Marilou told them, Karen
thought, although she knew better than to voice this aloud.

They had been hoping it would be partner work again on
Floor 8 and weren't disappointed to see the classroom set up
for just that configuration.

On the small table set aside for them was a dizzying array
of cards, spread in chaotic disorder. To Karen, the default
position looked like a paper fan that had caught against a
branch in the wind and shredded and malformed. Each card
had the same image on both sides. Front and reverse were
identical and those designations, arbitrary.

The assignment was to place the cards in a logical order
which told a story. There was just one catch: No one was
allowed to speak while doing so. And after the story was
constructed, both halves of the pair would be separated and
interviewed individually about the story. If they came to the
same conclusion about what the sequence meant, then it
would be on to Floor 9.

Karen noted that as she and Marilou studied the cards before
them that their natural inclination was silence. Good old
Floor 4 to 6 training coming in handy again.

Indeed, the entire room was silent as the pairs worked. No
one was going to fail this exercise by talking.

When the test had been explained, Karen found herself
battling a surge of anxiety. The goal sounded practically
impossible. How would she even begin to do that? She wasn't
telepathic, and neither was Marilou. Heck, with the ambients
going in full force, she wasn't all that empathic either.

However, it was oddly comfortable once they started working
– and not nearly as difficult as she anticipated it would be.
Karen found that she could practically communicate with

Marilou wordlessly and that she was perfectly understood in turn.

They worked out a sequence of cards via eye contact and slow movements of their hands.

It was painstaking work, requiring intense concentration, but gradually, the cards were placed in an order that made sense to both of them.

They were the last ones to finish their sequence, and judging by the looks of the departed pairs, no one had passed the exercise so far. Those students would have to repeat.

But Karen felt oddly optimistic as they flagged the instructor down to indicate that they had finished.

Karen didn't know how she knew that, but she did. She would have staked anything that they had a shared understanding of what the sequence meant.

Still, they were led to separate soundproof chambers in the back of the classroom – very much the same shape and structure as the ones that dominated Floor 7. Karen could not hear anything going on in the other chamber as she sat locked in there, waiting for Marilou to brief their instructor on her explanation. But she felt no anxiety as she waited for her instructor to arrive and interview her.

After both interviews were done, they were led back to the common area.

"Congratulations," their instructor said. "I don't know how you did it on the first try, but I'm impressed."

Karen and Marilou made eye contact. *I don't know how either*, both thought simultaneously. *But I'm very grateful.*

They nodded in unison.

"Keep this up, and you'll be *running* the center," their instructor said, clapping them both on their backs.

Floor 9

Another collaborative exercise awaited them on Floor 9. This time, they were seated together at small tables, each topped with a huge mound of brown clay.

A series of nonsensical sounds played over a loudspeaker, a recording that struck Karen as randomly generated. It reminded her of how language sounds coming out of the mouths of birds who are only semi-skilled mimics and can't produce recognizable phrases. They instead will recreate prosody and the flow and sound of human speech while not saying any identifiable words.

Babies, too. Babbling babies were similar.

After the sounds had finished, they were to work together to mold clay into a collaborative sculpture. It needed to be abstract, the instructor cautioned them, nothing representational or obvious but instead a shape that appealed to them both, inspired by the abstract sounds they had heard.

Again, as on the previous floor, once they had finished their creation, both partners would be led into small chambers separately and interviewed on what the sculpture meant and why they had chosen that form.

Both partners' accounts would be compared, and if they differed in any way, they would have to repeat the course.

"And don't even think of coming in tomorrow having a plan in place for your repeat exam," the instructor said. "It won't work. We've had people try to cheat that way in the past – and believe me, we know."

The room was silent after he said this. Karen suspected they were all wondering how – the thought had indeed entered her mind as well – but none of them were foolhardy enough to ask. Asking that sort of question was something much more common on the lower levels.

Past Floor 7, Karen observed, *you know better than to ask questions that aren't going to get answered and won't get you anywhere.*

Working with Marilou on the sculpture was actually kind of fun. They both instinctively moved towards a spiral shape. It looked very much like the carvings that might come off a pencil when you sharpen it.

Karen was struck by the shape and found she had a very sharp impression of what it meant. It resonated with her deeply. She studied Marilou's face and found it rather inscrutable as they worked.

Did the sculpture mean the same thing to her partner? This time around, Karen wasn't sure. Perhaps she should play it safe, she thought. Describe something that most people would take away from the sculpture.

No, she thought. *That's not what I did last time, and what I did last time worked out very well. I'm going to stick with it.*

This time she was asked to explain first. And when she did, she was completely honest about what the sculpture meant to her.

"It reminds me visually very much of the shavings that come off a pencil. Sometimes I feel like that pencil, something that has been very intentionally shaped and honed into a form where I'm going to be more effective and fit better into society. But I never quite escape the sadness that comes from discarding pieces of myself that are unacceptable, even if society tends to reward me for it. So I sculpted this piece to honor that sacrifice and acknowledge that even the things that society deems unacceptable have worth – even if circumstances call for me to set them aside at times," Karen explained.

It was hard waiting for Marilou to weigh in.

They were again the last students to be evaluated, but once Karen saw the faces of Marilou and her instructor, she realized that they'd passed on the first attempt yet again.

Floor 10

The program had somewhat resembled normal classroom instruction up until this point – although not precisely. It had never been quite what Karen remembered school being like. Not until Floor 10.

Floor 10 was rather on the nose. It looked very much like a standard public K-12 classroom. There were rows and rows of desks and a large teacher's desk at the front of the classroom which had exactly three things sitting on it: a stack of standardized testing booklets, a stack of fill-in-the-bubble answer sheets, and a pile of sharpened No. 2 pencils.

The chalkboard behind the teacher's desk was marked with information that was to be entered into the blanks in the demographic section of the answer sheet at the very top.

Karen filed into the room in silence with the other students. After everyone was at their desks, the instructor handed out answer sheets, No. 2 pencils, and finally the testing booklets.

"Okay," he said. "You may begin." And he started a small electronic timer that he set on his desk, giving them four hours total to complete the exam.

At certain intervals, he would rise and update a running tally on the chalkboard that said "___ minutes left" by erasing the former number and dutifully chalking in the next one.

The test itself was very strange. Many of the questions seemed rather subjective to Karen. There didn't, for example, seem to be a correct answer to what a person's favorite time of day or night was. But the test asked her this and framed it like this was a normal part of an objective multiple-choice exam.

Still, she noted other items that tested more objective bits of knowledge – information about the history of the Mentus Center, its vision, and its purpose.

The strange thing, she thought as she filled out the corresponding bubbles, was how much of this information wasn't what she was being taught explicitly. Instead, the exam primarily tested knowledge that had been incidentally transmitted by the organizational culture and had little to do with the explicit training, which thus far had focused on oddly specific tasks like keeping your face expressionless or learning to argue arbitrary, pointless matters.

At about two hours into the exam, other students began to rise and turn in their tests. Karen found herself naturally taking more time, reading over the answers, and sitting with them. She was again the last student to complete the task.

Welcome to Floor 11, a notice crammed into her bunk the next morning by the resident mail courier read.

It was a nice way to wake up.

Floor 11

Karen let out a massive sigh when she arrived on Floor 11. It was laid out similarly to Floor 7, a hodgepodge of small soundproof chambers.

Floor 7 had been taxing in a way that the other tasks weren't. And she'd hoped that she wouldn't have to repeat the exercise.

But the Mentus Center excelled in tedium, didn't it? Karen found herself thinking about this as she sought out the chamber that had her name on the door.

"Alright," she said to her instructor, "let's get this confession over with."

"It's not a confess—"

"I know," Karen said. "I mean, I'm ready to get unencumbered."

Her instructor grinned. "Glad to hear you say so. It's always a relief to skip past the preliminaries. A lot of students are quite resistant to go through this process again."

"Well, I'm not exactly thrilled," Karen admitted. "But I figure you must have some reason for doing so – even if it's not exactly obvious."

Her instructor nodded. "Precisely. The Mentus Center is very much like that. There's always a method. Sometimes students come in here, and they think that if they can't see the purpose or the strategy that there isn't one."

"People like to people, don't they?" Karen said.

"You say that as though you're not a person yourself," her instructor replied.

"I wish," Karen replied.

"Let's look more into that," the instructor said. Karen noted that those words had the easy rhythm of a catchphrase. They were probably a staple of her instructor's training, something he'd said thousands of times. That good ole Mentus Center repetition again.

Practice made perfect, she supposed, but it didn't make the process fun.

Floor 12

Having been "unencumbered" once again, Karen wasn't quite sure what to expect from Floor 12. She noted upon arrival, however, that the crowd had thinned considerably.

She didn't see Marilou, for one. And in fact, no one that surrounded her seemed familiar at all.

Ah, she thought. *Another bottleneck. Well, here goes nothing.*

The increase in difficulty became immediately evident when their instructor arrived and briefed them on what the next task was to be. It also revealed a lot about how the Mentus Center operated that had been completely invisible to Karen, although in hindsight, she felt foolish for missing it.

Floor 12 was nicknamed Observation and Report, their instructor told them.

All the lower classrooms were equipped with cameras and wired for sound. And their next task was to review what was being taught, how the students were being tested, and to prepare a report on their impressions of the curriculum at the Mentus Center.

What was effective? What seemed ineffective? What would they change and how?

Of the students being currently tested, who seemed to be thriving? Who was struggling?

It was a mind-numbing business to observe. As tedious as the activities had been as a student, they were even more boring to watch as an observer. Still, Karen did her best. She found herself developing a numerical system to rate various activities, a quick rubric with different levels for response and performance.

Dutifully, she watched each level for several days, scoring the activities, making notes, working out a rough kind of statistical explanation.

She set all these calculations into a table and added a section where she explained her rubric as well as how she came up with her operational definitions. Then she worked out an introduction and a conclusion to explain the issues at stake and her overall impressions and recommendations for the program.

She submitted the report late at the end of one class day, figuring it would take several volleys back and forth for her to pass – as it invariably did for her classmates.

But the mail courier delivered good news in the morning. And Karen found that her fob now did indeed unlock access to Floor 13.

"Getting close now," she told herself, stepping over the threshold.

Floor 13

As it turned out, Floor 13 wasn't a standard classroom setup, after all. It was instead simply a large meeting area, a kind of office that their next task launched from, not where the task itself would be done.

Upon arrival, Karen was informed she'd be proctoring. That she'd be given a designation and sent to other floors to help distribute materials and shadow the instructors.

When she thought about it, she realized that there had been plenty of proctors flitting around the Mentus Center. She'd seen them many times as she ascended the levels. However, she hadn't given much thought to how they got on proctor duty. She'd barely noticed them when she was absorbed in her coursework. She'd gotten so focused on getting to each successive floor that she had gotten tunnel vision.

On one hand, she felt kind of silly realizing this. It was such an obvious thing to have missed.

On the other hand, it was also kind of a relief. It meant that the students would probably notice her very little themselves. This took the pressure off.

And indeed, as Karen began her proctor duties, she noted that students barely registered her presence at all. They certainly had no reaction to her, didn't directly interact with her.

I wonder if this is how Penny's ghost friends feel when the rest of us just pass them by without saying hello? Karen thought and was glad that she'd trained herself to be non-reactive. Semi-invisible or not, she would have attracted some attention if she'd burst into laughter while proctoring a Floor 4 session, something she was tempted to do so many times watching how uncomfortable the students were staring at one another in silence.

Floor 14

When Karen was starting to feel bored with proctoring, a notice showed up again informing her that she had reached the penultimate level.

Instruction, she thought instinctively, not sure why she was so confident that this would be the task.

But it was. The next task was to become an instructor, just as she'd expected.

What a dangerous thing it was, Karen thought, to become confident, to fully believe in your ability to anticipate the unknown. It was like being full of hope. It felt good in the moment, could even get you through difficult times, but believing in yourself left you vulnerable to the kind of crushing disappointment that self-skeptics never felt.

It was a thought that never left her, even as she received her assignments and slipped into roles that only days before she had viewed from the other side.

This kind of confidence was addictive, even narcotic.

Comfortable, confident, and comfortably numb.

Part of her resisted this shift and fought it hard, but she pressed on. Because wasn't this why she had enrolled in the course in the first place? Wasn't this the state of mind she wanted to achieve?

Of *course*, growth was going to be uncomfortable. Of course, it was scary to change. That was the whole point.

She moved through teaching each floor with the kind of ease that not only shocked her but surprised everyone around her.

Still, she wasn't expecting the final notice when it arrived.

It looked different than all the rest, which had simply informed her that she had access to the next floor.

This notice also included instructions for moving out.

> *Please take everything you own with you when you reach Floor 15. You will not be returning to the hostel upon completion of the task. Thank you very much for choosing the Mentus Center. It has chosen you in return.*

Packing didn't take long since Karen hadn't brought anything with her.

Somewhere along the way, Karen noted, Marilou had disappeared. Her bunk was empty. Her things were gone. Karen knew it had happened while she was working as an instructor, but she wasn't quite sure exactly which day Marilou had disappeared. The work of teaching was exhausting, and there were many nights when Karen fell asleep as soon as her head hit the pillow.

Marilou had also become much quieter and more reserved in the time they'd bunked together, making it easier to miss her presence – something that had been impossible to ignore in the beginning.

As Karen looked up at the empty bed, she fought a wave of sadness that managed to sneak around all of her non-reactive training and the roiling ambients as she struggled with a painful reality: Her bunkmate – her closest friend at the Mentus Center – had moved out without saying goodbye.

The front desk wouldn't provide info as to where Marilou went – or the circumstances of her departure. Had she failed out? Withdrawn of her own accord? Did she graduate?

Other students shot her a disapproving look for even asking. There would be no answers there.

Karen felt simultaneously as though she'd only just arrived at Mentus Center and also that she'd been there far too long.

The only thing to do was to move onward to Floor 15.

Floor 15

It's often said that the polygraph, also known as the lie detector test, was invented by William Moulton Marston. Somewhat suitably given the subject matter, this is not strictly true.

Or you could say… that's a lie. The polygraph was actually invented in 1921 by a man called John Larson. He was 21 at the time and attending college in California. The invention's application was at first limited to strictly forensic use.

Like all lies, there's a core element of truth, however, behind the commonly held belief that Marston invented the polygraph. Marston did invent what would become a key element of the polygraph – the systolic blood pressure test. According to reports, it was Marston's wife Elizabeth who first suggested that blood pressure could be reflective of a person's emotional state, having noticed her own blood pressure elevated whenever she was angry or excited.

Marston also marketed and *popularized* the polygraph. Many believe that his efforts are why we still know about the tool and talk about it today.

Even without the attendant theatrics that a lie detector test conjures, Marston was quite a colorful character in his own right – and a forward thinker. In addition to his wife Elizabeth, he also lived with a second romantic partner, Olive. He had four children total, two with each woman.

From his work using polygraphs, Marston became convinced that women were more honest and were far more capable than they were given credit for being. Because of this, he became a champion for feminist causes at a time when this was quite rare for a man to do. He also researched and wrote on sexual taboos and explored dominance and submission as key facets of individual personality.

All of this is probably why it's easy to remember Marston as the inventor of the polygraph – even if that isn't exactly true.

But perhaps that's quite fitting because the polygraph itself has a loose relationship with the truth as well. It turns out that the way that it measures emotional response – heart rate, blood pressure, respiration rate, and galvanic skin response – may present a good analog to a person's inner life but is far from a clear window into it.

Indeed, a person can fail a lie detector test while telling the truth; conversely, a person can lie and pass with flying colors. This is why, generally speaking, lie detector tests are not admissible in court.

In the Psychic State, truth evaluators are generally employed as government consultants, and this counsel is a greatly preferred method for the State to accurately ascertain whether any given person is telling the truth or not.

But lie detectors continue to be found in dramatic movies and on certain talk shows, where they're presented as instruments that incontrovertibly sort out the truth but instead primarily provide entertainment value.

To lie easily on a lie detector test, one has a few straightforward options: The first is to lie in response to any of the calibration questions that the tester expects you to lie about and at the same time bite down hard on your tongue while you are doing so. This will produce a very pronounced physiological response that will tell the tester that you are a poor liar and that you experience dramatic easily measured signs when you are doing so. This will skew the test by throwing off the expectations of the tester, who will miss more subtle variations or write them off as insignificant. In doing so, they will miss the subtle variances that mark your actual lies.

The second option is to be a sociopath. It is an uncomfortable truth: There do exist individuals who have absolutely no physical internal reaction to telling a lie. They do not care; it does not cause them distress. If you happen to be such an individual naturally, then you will pass lie detector tests with flying colors.

"Why hello Karen," a familiar voice called to her as the Floor 15 doors beeped and slid open in response to her key fob drawing near the sensor.

"Dr. Mentus," Karen called back in greeting. It was strange to be so surprised by his voice, but she was. One of the first things she'd learned about the Mentus Center, right when she'd arrived, was that Dr. Mentus lived on the top floor of the building. That Floor 15 was his domain.

And yet... the information had gotten lost in the flurry of training that had unfolded between now and then. She had been so busy, first with learning and then with observing, and finally in learning how to teach and then teaching students, that she had completely forgotten.

Maybe that's the flip side of learning to be less emotional, Karen noted. *Maybe the numbing process has a cost. Maybe it's easier to tune out things you should be paying more attention to.*

Still, Dr. Mentus smiled at her and beckoned for her to approach.

His office was rather modern and sleek. It looked expensive because there was lots of extra space. Karen had noticed that about high-end living environments. It wasn't necessarily the expensive decorative touches that made them look luxe. It was the overabundance of space, a lack of furnishings relative to the room that was available to hold them, that had a way of making any given setting look expensive.

Well, expensive decorative touches didn't hurt, did they? She mentally corrected herself as she walked to Dr. Mentus's very well-designed desk. However, if you piled enough expensive objects into one cramped area, it didn't matter how elegant any of them were. They'd resemble a trash heap. Perhaps there was a lesson in that. Maybe even one beyond the low-hanging fruit of "less is more."

Dr. Mentus produced a small appliance, which he placed on the surface of the desk. The shape of the machine looked a bit like a plastic painter's palette, except the face was studded with a variety of dials and indicators. Karen wasn't sure exactly what she was looking at. It reminded her of both an at-home beauty system and the control panel on a spaceship.

A wire connected this palette-shaped interface to a pair of thick black rubber gloves.

"Gloves on, please," Dr. Mentus instructed her.

Karen hesitated.

"Put your hands in the gloves," Dr. Mentus said.

Karen swore she could see something strained leaking through the façade of Dr. Mentus's normally warm and sunny smile. But it was only a glimpse. She wondered if she actually saw it, or if she were simply overtired. She had heard from countless other folks at the center that he was a man of great discipline, after all – surely, he wouldn't react in such a manner, even if he were frustrated with her.

She donned the gloves.

"Wonderful," Dr. Mentus said. "Wonderful."

He walked back to his desk and spun the plastic palette around so that the indicators faced him.

"Okay, my dear girl, I am going to ask you a series of questions to test the effect that your coursework has had on your inner life, and this device will tell me if you are truly unencumbered – or if you have been faking this whole time."

"Faking it?" Karen said. "Why would I do that?"

Dr. Mentus smirked. "You would be surprised, my dear girl. Not everyone is honest with us." He turned a few knobs and stared at the dials. "I know that you *think* you've effected big changes here. You've been very committed to the program, and everyone who has interacted with you during your time here has nothing but good things to say about you. Both as a student and as an instructor."

He studied a setting carefully before nodding and making finer adjustments with the knobs on the plastic palette.

"However," Dr. Mentus continued, "that just means that you believe you've gotten something out of the program. *You* think you have become an emotionally unencumbered individual because of this course. The best liars fool themselves. And that's where this machine comes in. It will give me a clear picture of your automatic reactions, the ones that you can't manipulate." He nodded as if convincing himself. "It will tell me if you're lying to yourself."

"Why don't you just use a truth evaluator?" Karen asked and then instantly wished she had not.

Dr. Mentus scowled. "My dear girl, that's a nasty thing to say."

Karen had been well into the program before she had
discovered how deep the psychophobia ran at the Mentus
Center. They acknowledged the existence of the Psychic
Phenomenon of course – it was hard these days to claim
otherwise as more and more inexplicable paranormal
events had entered public knowledge. Not that some fringe
conspiracy theorists didn't try to take the psychic denial
route.

However, the Mentus Center claimed that psychic power
wasn't destiny. They insisted their program could purge
intuitives of the nasty social curse. That psychic powers were
a defect, a sign of a weak soul. Not front and center on their
flyers of course – but in oft-whispered conversations.

"My apologies, Dr. Mentus," Karen said. "I just... I am not
familiar with a device like this."

"Very well," he replied. "Then I will familiarize you." He
spun the plastic palette back around to face her. "I'm going
to ask you a series of calibration questions so I can get your
baseline biorhythm for factual statements and adjust these
dials to a setting that represents you. And then once I've
established your baseline, I will ask you the target questions.
These indicators right here will show me whether or not your
physiologic state matches your baseline truth-telling state."
He nodded with resolution. "That will tell me if you're lying."

"Yes, sir," Karen said, feeling her chest tighten.

Dr. Mentus turned the palette back around.

"Is your name really Karen?" Dr. Mentus said.

"Yes," she answered.

He studied the interface and glanced up at her face. "Are you
sure about that?" he said.

"Uh, yes," Karen replied.

Dr. Mentus shook his head. "Okay, okay, let's try another one. Are you really 25 years old?"

"Yes," Karen said. "I just turned 25 in April."

Dr. Mentus peered at the meters. He shook his head. "I don't understand," he said. "This has never happened."

"I'm telling the truth," Karen insisted.

"Well, okay. Let's try something else," Dr. Mentus said. "Here's an obvious one. Are you sitting on Floor 15 of the Mentus Center right now?"

"Yes," Karen said.

As Dr. Mentus watched the meters react, his features bloomed into a deep scowl. "It thinks you're lying."

"I'm not," Karen said.

"But..." Dr. Mentus shook his head. He sighed. "Well, there's nothing else to be done then, is there?" he said, as he pressed a button on the console.

"What do you m—" Karen said, as the palms of her hands filled with static and she blacked out.

Off-Site Training Center

When Karen came to, she knew she wasn't at the Mentus Center anymore. The ambients were gone. She was bobbing in a sea of emotions – most of which she knew instantly didn't belong to her.

The next thing she knew was that the carpet she sat on was hideous. And the wall art was generic, derivative. Entirely without personality. There were two twin beds in the room and an outdated television that had a laminated list of channels Velcroed onto its side.

A cheap hotel room. Probably one in a motor court. But where?

She could hear whistling coming from the adjoining room, a bathroom no doubt.

"Ah, you're awake!" a familiar voice called.

No, Karen thought, not her. What was happening?

Her wrists itched. She looked down, expecting to see bonds, something holding her wrists together. But the irritation was coming from ivory lace cuffs.

I'm wearing a white gown, Karen noted. It was surreal and disorienting.

The bathroom door swung open. Marilou was similarly garbed in a white dress that was nearly identical to hers, fussy, dated, and overwrought.

"C'mon," Marilou said, "the ceremony's about to start, we're going to be late."

Still in a daze, Karen took Marilou's hand, and they moved toward the communicating door that led to another hotel room.

"Oh wait," Marilou said. "Almost forgot." She placed a veil made of the same scratchy ivory lace and secured it into Karen's hair. When she pulled it down, Karen noted that the veil was far more opaque than she had anticipated. Under the veil, Karen could make out vague colors and large shapes, enough to help her not bump into things, but that was about it. All visual detail was lost.

"I can't see with this on," Karen said.

"That's okay," Marilou said. "I've got you."

"What are we doing?" Karen asked.

"Doing?" Marilou said. "Karen, this is *graduation*."

"Graduation? Whatever happened to the robe and mortarboard? We look like a couple of vestal virgins," Karen protested. It was a classical reference that would have made Penny laugh but fell flat with Marilou.

"Karen, you're embarrassing me," Marilou said sharply.

Strange, Karen thought. That's not at all what she picked up from Marilou. Not embarrassment. Anxiety perhaps. The veil couldn't cover that, after all.

But the others nearby seemed happy. Which was reassuring.

Marilou guided Karen into position.

Strange music began to play. Karen felt as though she recognized it but couldn't place where she had heard it. Perhaps it had been playing at the center in the background.

Then there was a ceremony conducted entirely in Latin. *Where's Penny when you need her?* Karen thought, tuning out and feeling bored. *She would be so thrilled to have her Latin come in handy for once.*

Thankfully, the Latin portion only lasted a few minutes. And then the officiant switched to English.

"I now pronounce you husband and wife, with the glory of Heaven's blessing, you may now kiss the bride."

What?

Terror stuck Karen in place. She felt detached from her own body even as she wanted to run away.

The veil lifted, and as Karen was finally able to see her would-be groom, she screamed.

It was a face she hadn't seen for a very long time.

Standing before her was Augustus Cross. Her father.

PENNY'S INFERNO

Seven Going on Seven Hundred

"So I'm… Hellspawn?" Penny said.

Kip nodded.

"My father is the King of Hell? My mother is spring incarnate? And my sister is going to be the Queen of Hell?"

"Yes, little one," Kip said. "One day."

"Wait," Penny said. "There's something that doesn't make sense."

"And what is that?"

"If I ran away, why hasn't anyone been back for me? Why haven't they dragged me back?" Penny asked.

"Ah," Kip said. "We are there again. We are back where we started. Back to the things you made me swear never to tell you."

Penny sighed. "Past me was a real pain in the ass."

Kip laughed. "You have no idea, little one."

"I'm starting to get the picture," Penny confessed.

"Well…" Kip said.

Penny sat up straighter.

"Perhaps there's a way," Kip said.

"A way?" Penny said.

"A way around that promise I made you," he said.

"Kip," Penny said, as she beamed. "I had no idea you could be so devious."

"You don't last long in Hell if you can't bend the rules every once in a while," he told her. "Otherwise, the rules will bend you."

"Or break you," Penny added.

"Very good, little one," Kip replied. "Perhaps there is a bit of Hellspawn still in there somewhere – as Earthly as you've become over these past 20 years."

"Twenty years?" Penny said. "So I was seven when I first came here."

"Seven going on seven hundred," Kip replied.

"I can't believe no one has come after me for 20 years," Penny said. "Who does that? Who just abandons their child? Even if I ran away, you would think they'd look for me."

"Well, it hasn't been 20 years in Hell," Kip said.

"What?" Penny said.

"I mean, it *has*," Kip said. "It's just… life moves a lot slower there. Things haven't changed very much at all."

"So my family?"

"Still there ruling over Hell. To Hellions, it's more like a few weeks since we left – or how it would feel on Earth anyway," Kip said.

Penny shook her head slowly. Kip had warned her, but she hadn't been prepared for… this. But there was no going back now. She had to know. "You said there was a way around your promise."

Kip nodded. "I take promises very seriously, especially ones that I make to you, so I can't tell you what happened. Not all of it. But you didn't make me promise not to tell you who could fill in the rest."

Penny smiled. "Oh Kip, you're a genius!" she said, flinging her arms around his neck, feeling an icy chill course through her as she did.

Kip pulled away uncomfortably. His bloodless cheeks stayed grayish-white, but a pained expression on his face suggested that he would blush if he could. "Well, uh, yes," he stammered.

Penny giggled.

"There's a woman on Whisper Street who knows everything. I'm not sure what she's going by these days, but I believe you know her as Gretchen Mills," Kip said.

"The woman who runs the Warrens of Persephone," Penny said, surprised that Kip said a name she not only recognized but a person she had seen not too long ago.

Kip nodded.

"I interviewed Gretchen with Karen and Viv on our last case," Penny said. "It was a weird interview. She kept singling me out. Acting as though she knew me."

"That's because she does," Kip said.

"And not just because I'm Hellish royalty?" Penny said.

"No, not just," Kip said.

"She's met me on this plane before, hasn't she?" Penny said.

Kip pursed his lips together.

"Okay, whatever, the stupid promise again," Penny said. "You would think because it's *me* asking you to break it, that would be enough for you."

"Not to be a broken record," Kip said. "But you said you'd say that."

Penny rolled her eyes.

"Anyway, if you want answers, little one, that's where you go," Kip replied. "You go to Whisper Street."

"At this hour of the night?" Penny said. "Or morning?" she added, because it occurred to her it was probably technically morning at this point, if only just, Earthly time speeding onward as quickly as it did.

"This is the best time of all to visit," Kip replied. "I don't believe Gretchen sleeps anymore. I think she's grown out of that."

As Penny approached 659 Whisper Street, the front door swung open.

"Top of the evening to you, Rhea Stygius," a familiar voice called out into the street. A tall statuesque woman stepped into view. Her hair was scraped into a perfect updo, not a strand out of place. She was adorned in a flowing amber gown that impeccably skimmed and clung to her proportions in a way that suggested it had been made especially for her.

"Ms. Mills," Penny acknowledged her.

"I had a feeling you'd be back," Gretchen said.

"A feeling or a vision?" Penny challenged her.

Gretchen laughed. "Do come in, Ms. Stygius."

Penny followed her inside, feeling more than a bit irritated that Gretchen hadn't answered the question. On her last visit to the Warrens of Persephone, Gretchen had wound the team all over the premises, which were large and labyrinthine. Viv would probably remember the layout, Penny found herself thinking, on account of her incredible memory and spatial recall.

But me, I'm hopeless.

However, this time they weren't going very far. Gretchen led her down a different hallway branching off the anteroom. From there it was a straight shot through a mere four connected rooms before they reached their destination.

There were tapestries on the walls of this room, as there were all over the Warrens. Most of these were mythological legends, however, with an unsurprising emphasis on the legend of Persephone.

But the tapestries in this room stood out in stark contrast to the décor found in the other chambers. These tapestries weren't antiquated or dusty like many of the others found around the Warrens.

The decorations in this room looked new. Modern. Less like strangely cut fringed rugs hanging on the walls and more like art canvases simply made of plain fabric.

Instead of mythological depictions, all the tapestries in this room sported a similar simplified emblem: A silhouette of a human head and neck with a flame where the brain would normally be.

There was also an inscription on the wall: *In girum imus nocte et consumimur igni.*

Latin, Penny noted. It was a palindrome and a riddle: "We enter the circle at night and are consumed by fire."

Penny racked her brain for the answer to the riddle but came up short.

"I knew you'd be back," Gretchen said again. "I guess what's surprising to me is that it took you so long to do it."

"I'm sorry?" Penny said.

"You struck me as the kind of customer who would be storming back sooner rather than later, demanding a refund," Gretchen said.

"A refund?" Penny said.

"You're probably wondering why I took you on in the first place then. And that would be a reasonable question to ask," Gretchen continued, as though she hadn't heard Penny. "Have a seat, dear," she said, gesturing to a chair beneath the largest of the fiery brain tapestries.

A bit of a sinister placement, Penny noted as she sat down. But Kip had led her here, and he'd never put her in danger.

Or would he? A little voice piped up within her.

She mentally swatted away the doubt.

"You see," Gretchen continued, "in every business, there are customers that one must take on. That you simply can't refuse. Not because they'll be all that profitable for you in the long run all on their own. No." She clucked her tongue and shook her head. "But because they'll raise your profile. Such a customer is worth serving even if you serve them at a loss."

Gretchen grinned, and even though she was an otherwise stunning woman, the smile looked ugly on her face. It revealed something narcissistic that was usually absent – or at least hidden from the outside world. "The Princess of Hell certainly qualifies."

"Certainly qualifies for what?" Penny said. The question seemed to shake Gretchen out of her soliloquy.

"Rhea Stygius, please stop messing around. You may think you can get away with disrespecting me because you're the daughter of Persephone, but this is getting ridiculous. I know you're here for your memories," Gretchen Mills said.

The Memory Eater of Whisper Street

Mnemonophagia

The practice of mnemonophagia, or memory eating, was long rumored but until recently difficult to confirm. Like many psychic phenomena, the practice of mnemonophagia destroys the evidence of the act when done well.

In recent years, however, the gaslighting division of the Department of Psychic Operations has apprehended multiple individuals for the crime of mnemonophagia. Because of this, laws have been enacted to reflect the State's dim view of the practice, laws which impose strict penalties on any that engage in mnemonophagia.

There is controversy within psychic taxonomic circles as to whether mnemonophagia is a power *per se* – or simply a taboo practice. Documented incidents of memory consumption are still rare enough that it has been difficult to determine if the ability to eat memories is a distinct power in the way that other intuitive abilities present or if mnemonophagia is a more widespread, readily available ability to intuitives who would better be described in other ways. Perhaps there are certain telepaths or empaths who can consume the content of the messages and while doing so consume other stored memories. Whether this would render them distinct from other telepaths and empaths who lack that ability is a point of contention.

Or, to put it more plainly: It is well known that mnemonophagia exists, but do mnemonophages?

Hopefully, with time and further study, this matter will be resolved definitively in objective terms. Until then, it will remain a hotly contested dinner party debate among taxonomic colleagues, rivals, and bedfellows.

from Insecta Psychica: Towards an Intuitive Taxonomy by Cloche Macomber

Gretchen studied Penny's face for a few moments. It was suspiciously blank, free of defensiveness. All Gretchen could detect was confusion.

"Of course," Gretchen said. "Of course... you wouldn't remember."

"Remember what?" Penny said.

Gretchen laughed. "You'll have to forgive me," she said. "I've been... doing this for a very long time, and yet it still manages to surprise me." She rubbed her neck, letting down her long flowing hair as she did. As it cascaded down her back, she rolled her shoulders and let out a deep moan.

"We took in a woman here who used to be a recovery nurse," she told Penny. "She would talk about her job sometimes, how it was when patients were waking up from anesthesia. It was different depending on the person. Some of them were rude and abusive. Others had a hard time waking up at all. Sometimes this inability to wake up was life-threatening. And some would be ready to leave way too quickly. They would bolt out the door, their bodies ready to go while their brains were still half-zonked, and orderlies would have to chase them down and tackle them."

"She said after a while you got used to everything – the entire array of erratic patient behavior. After a while, it got impossible to be surprised. You acclimated to the patterns. Just needed more experience."

Gretchen stretched her arms and moaned again. This time it was darker, more carnal. It stirred something confusing within Penny.

"Maybe that's my whole problem. It could be a matter of low volume. Maybe that's why I haven't quite gotten the hang of this," Gretchen said.

"This?" Penny replied.

"Oh darling, Kip really didn't prepare you for me, did he?" Gretchen said.

"Guess not," Penny said. "He just told me to find you. That you would lead me to all the things he couldn't tell me. All the things that he promised he wouldn't tell me."

"Ah," Gretchen replied. "There's no real way of putting this delicately."

"You don't have to," Penny assured her.

Gretchen smiled painfully. "That's awfully kind of you to say. But I'm afraid that any permission you give just has to do with you. I have to give myself permission as well." She stared at one of the tapestries.

"I am a monster," Gretchen said to the tapestry, not meeting Penny's eyes.

Penny didn't say anything for a moment. She let the confession sit there, let it echo.

The two women stared at one another for a moment.

"No, you're not," Penny said.

"Yes, I am," Gretchen said. "I'm a memory eater. "

Penny shuddered involuntarily.

"I suppose you'll have to report me to PsyOps. That little job of yours and all," Gretchen said.

"Why would I do that?" Penny said.

Gretchen tilted her head to the side. Her long hair shifted, dangling unevenly like a cardigan sweater that's halfway through falling off a clothes hanger. "You're a Green Star, a detective. You work for the Psychic State. I'm sure you have a duty to report, to turn me in."

Penny shrugged noncommittally. "I'm on leave," she said.

Gretchen laughed. "That's a silly reason to not report me," she said. "That's no excuse, and you know it."

"Look, Ms. Mills," Penny said. "If I turn you in, I don't find out what happened, do I?"

Gretchen grinned. "No, I suppose you don't."

"I figure we can do one another a favor," Penny said. "You help me out, I help you out by not reporting you." She nodded resolutely as if to validate the suggestion. "How's that sound?"

"That sounds like someone's bending the rules," Gretchen teased.

"Well, you don't last long in Hell if you can't bend the rules every once in a while," Penny said. Kip's words were coming out of her mouth. They felt good though. True. And familiar, as familiar as singing the lyrics of Christmas carols she'd learned in public school. Or reciting the words that introduced her favorite TV shows, the ones she'd grown up with, that had followed her from foster home to foster home when little else did.

"Are you sure you don't have a few memories kicking around in there?" Gretchen said.

"Yeah, why?" Penny replied.

"That's a Hellish saying," Gretchen said. "Usually people say it in Infernal or Impish. It sounds a little plain in English. It's better with hisses and growls. Spicier."

"I learned it from Kip," Penny admitted.

"That Kipper Dante," Gretchen said, getting a stricken look in her eyes. Penny swore it was lovesickness but couldn't be sure. *Where are Karen's empathic powers when you need them?* Penny thought, before reminding herself that she was the one who had left Karen, not the other way around. If Penny were going to be frustrated with anyone, it had to be with herself.

"So is it a deal?" Penny said. "You tell me what happened, and I won't turn you in."

"Deal," Gretchen said. "And I'll do you one better, even. I won't just tell you what happened. I'll give you your memories back."

Memory Storage and Retrieval

While the study of mnemonophagia is still in its infancy, determined taxonomists have nonetheless made great strides in understanding its basic mechanisms.

Like many concepts that are named before they are fully understood, the term mnemonophagia fits in some cases and in other cases is more of a misnomer. In many instances, memory intake and consumption function identically to the intake of food, whereby memories are ingested, broken down and digested, and absorbed into the intuitive, leaving little to no trace of the initial memory.

In other cases, a memory may be ingested and stored but not digested or broken down in any way. In that case, the memory is merely stored within the memory eater and can be later regurgitated wholesale – or, in less graphic terms, retrieved for later use.

All mnemonophagia is prohibited by law. Intuitive advocacy groups have recently emerged arguing that it is not the ingestion of the memory but the digestion of the memory that makes mnemonophagia so problematic and taboo. They argue that laws governing mnemonophagia should reflect this, that memory digestion and subsequent destruction (theoretically named mnemonolysis) should be illegal, not merely the intake of memory, which could serve a productive societal purpose, particularly if employed in service to the Psychic State.

However, these efforts so far have failed to gain traction, as those in power argue against them with a slippery slope rationale. Critics state that legal exemption for consumption and storage only give cover to those with ill intent. Would-be criminals could claim legal storage and then easily digest stored memories later privately.

Currently, the Department of Psychic Operations has no plans to utilize memory storage in any official capacity.

However, when it comes to PsyOps, there's historical precedent that the official capacity and unofficial practice often diverge from one another.

from Insecta Psychica: Towards an Intuitive Taxonomy by Cloche Macomber

"Give my memories back to me?" Penny said. "Can you really do that?"

Gretchen nodded. "I kept them whole this entire time. Like I said, I had a feeling you'd be back."

And how wonderful it is that we've made our deal, Gretchen thought to herself. She had been expecting to offer up the memories *and* get turned in. After all, how could she refuse the daughter of Persephone? She'd have half of Hell after her. No, thank you. It had never been a real choice. But the Stygius girl had sweetened the pot. She had offered more than Gretchen would ever ask for.

And better yet… they'd get to make the connection again.

"Come," Gretchen said. She led Penny to a low divan that was pushed against the back wall. The linens all had that same logo – fire in the brain. Gretchen climbed onto the surface and scooted over. She patted the space next to her.

Penny froze in place, hesitated.

"Lie down next to me, Rhea Stygius," Gretchen said, with a firm voice.

The voice blew through Penny's body like a strong wind. She felt pulled to the bed almost magnetically. Her legs started to move of their own accord. Penny squeezed her eyes shut and forced her feet to take a few steps backward.

"What are you doing?" Penny said.

"What needs to be done," Gretchen replied.

"You're not just a memory eater, are you?" Penny asked.

Gretchen shook her head no. "I'm lots of things, Rhea Stygius. And so are you. We all are, frankly. I know I've said this to you before, every time you've visited me, but that's the whole point of my organization, the Warrens of Persephone. What your partner Karen called a cult. One of our most fundamental beliefs is that all people and things have a duality to their nature. Nothing is just one thing and only one thing. Simplicity is an illusion."

"You are a spirit medium, a former foster kid, and the Princess of Hell. Your mother is spring and the Queen of Hell. Kip is... well, Kip's a little bit of everything." That strange look crept over her face again.

Penny felt uncomfortable, left out because there was clearly a private history there that she wasn't part of, but also disturbed enough by the idea that Gretchen and Kip had *anything* in common that she wasn't sure she wanted to know more.

Gretchen beckoned Penny to come closer with a crooked finger. That strange psychic wind blew through her body again, causing Penny's hands to shake. "No," Penny said, shaking her head. Something within her was telling her to resist, to wait, and to be cautious.

"Good girl," Gretchen said, and a treacherous ripple of pleasure coursed through Penny's body as she did in response to the memory eater's approval. "Very smart. You're not in any danger of course, but I could see how you would feel you were."

Gretchen relaxed. She reclined more fully on the divan, and as she did, the force tugging on Penny's body and compelling it to move forward ceased.

"It's better if you choose it yourself anyway," Gretchen said.

"Choose what?"

"The connection," Gretchen said simply. "It's how I transfer the memories back to you."

Penny hesitated again. "If that's what you wanted, why didn't you just say so?" she said finally, climbing next to Gretchen.

"Because I wasn't sure how much you remembered," Gretchen replied, before seizing Penny's forehead in her hands and pressing it against her own.

The Latin palindrome flashed into her mind as their heads met: *In girum imus nocte et consumimur igni.* "We enter the circle at night and are consumed by fire."

"Moths!" Penny gasped as they were both engulfed in flame.

What Everyone Gets Wrong About Hell

There are many things people get wrong about Hell. Like any great city with a reputation, much of what is said about Hell is at least based in truth, but the great majority of it is an exaggeration.

Hell is in fact both the name of the most major city settlement on its plane and of the plane itself. It is said that once upon a time, the settlement had been called Hell City, but that over the millennia the "city" half of the name had been eventually dropped.

Most outsiders confused the plane and the city anyway, and the Hellish rarely needed to make distinctions between the city and the plane since they so rarely left either.

Perhaps the most glaring inaccuracies about Hell – both the city and the plane – stem from literary depictions of them. Two very troubling mischaracterizations have become quite popular on the Earthly plane. The first is the references to Hell that appear in a popular religious text called the Holy Bible, or often more familiarly, the Bible.

In the Bible, for example in the books of Luke, Matthew, and Revelation, Hell is described as a place of torment, fire, and eternal suffering. In the religion that corresponds to this text, named Christianity after an especially important martyr figure, avoiding going to Hell is proffered up as a chief motivation for behaving well and being kind to others. As the teaching goes, if you misbehave you will go to Hell – and it's quite a nasty place to be.

To be clear, Hell certainly has its challenges. But the dead typically do not arrive in Hell because of misbehavior. More accurately, the denizens of Hell have been chosen by the plane because they are suitable candidates for living there.

This is not stretched upon a moral framework whatsoever. Hell seeks out and selects those who it recognizes as having a lot in common with those who already live there.

It is not a place of requisite suffering for those who belong there. True, those not meant for Hell would find it an environment that's quite difficult to bear, but souls who are not meant for Hell rarely end up there – and when it happens, it's typically because something truly extraordinary has happened.

The other greatly misleading depiction of Hell takes place in the first part of Dante Alighieri's 14th century epic poem *Divine Comedy*. This first of three parts is called *Inferno* and reads as part memoir and part travelogue, all recounted in verse. In *Inferno*, Dante travels to Hell, guided by the Roman poet Virgil. Hell is not Dante's intended destination, but instead he is passing through Hell and Purgatory on the way to meet his lover Beatrice in Heaven.

While quite celebrated, this Dante's *Inferno* gets many things wrong. For starters, routing through Hell and Purgatory to travel to Heaven simply makes no logistical sense as far as travel plans. The cost of this multi-extraplanar travel would be incredible and needless. Virgil is not the name of any known interplanar travel agent, and if indeed such an agent did exist, he would be quickly censured by the governing boards for suggesting such a needlessly roundabout travel route to his client. In addition, Dante's detailed descriptions of the structure and social order of Hell are also inaccurate.

There are a few things Dante does get correct. There are in fact nine circles in Hell, just as the poet indicates in his work. The River Styx, too, is noted as a major geographical feature.

It's fascinating that Dante manages to get these details absolutely correct – while getting pretty much everything else about Hell wrong.

In his work, Dante describes each circle as being inhabited by souls who are guilty of different Earthly sins. In his work, he correctly identifies the First Circle's other name – Limbo. However, while doing so, he incorrectly describes the inhabitants there as all having been unbaptized or pagan. Limbo is not populated in such a manner. It is more of an unorganized sub-settlement where souls live with modest means. Some might compare it to an Earthly slum.

The subsequent eight circles are all similarly misattributed – with Dante assigning a sin to the inhabitants of each one, in the following order: lust, gluttony, greed, wrath, heresy, violence, fraud, and treachery.

Dante further describes the River Styx as being home to inexorable pirate battles between ships. This is utter nonsense. Only one boat can get across the River Styx – and that's only because the river allows it.

The sin classification of Hell's circles, however, is probably Dante's greatest mischaracterization. Each circle of Hell is less like a jail for specific crimes – as the poet implies – but more like a neighborhood. While it's true that each neighborhood has its attendant idiosyncrasies (the spectacular fire fountains of the Fifth Circle spring immediately to mind), each ring is distinctly marked more by differences in the inhabitants' socioeconomic statuses than anything else.

Income inequality, while found on practically every plane, is unfortunately quite dramatic in Hell. As with the arrival on any plane – for example, the arrival proxy of "birth" on the Earthly plane – much of your fate hangs on your resources prior to getting there. But inheritance is not destiny. Upward mobility is theoretically possible in Hell – it's just awfully hard work. Some of this work is toil of course. But most of it is tolerating the incredible frustration of pushing through the nigh unbearable unfairness over and over again for millennia, only to advance a millimeter or two for your efforts.

Penny for Your Thoughts, Dollar for Your Memories

"Penny for your thoughts, dollar for your memories," Charles Huron said. It was more than natural to him. Supernatural? He shook his head. That wasn't quite right. The words had become automatic millennia ago.

The ferryman prided himself on his work. He was a small man in the scheme of things, yes, not one of the underworld's movers and shakers. Just Charon to his friends. But not a nobody. There weren't any nobodies in Hell, Charon reflected, not when you really thought about it. Everyone knew that big cities like Hell needed little people to make them work.

Big cities like Hell needed transit workers.

Really, big cities like Hell needed *more* transit workers.

It had been a rough morning, and Charles Huron felt the phantom itch that indicated that he might sweat, but of course, he didn't. It had been a long time since Charles Huron had perspired. He had long ago acclimated to the stiflingly hot climate of Hell and its environs. Like many things in Hell, it was only a matter of time. Your body could only put up a fight and continue such an effort for so long before it would, reasonably, conclude that it didn't matter. And at that point, it would give up foolish pursuits like perspiration.

The weather in Hell was always a challenge of course, but it was not a challenge you could or even should fight. Because it was not a challenge you would ever win.

Any fight was wasted energy. Energy that a Hellion could not afford.

At least it was a dry heat. That itself was a mercy. Even on the waters where he spent most of his interminable years, Charon found that the air remained disturbingly dry. It was as though any water that entered the air immediately sublimated and absconded somewhere else, somewhere mundane water stood a fighting chance.

Standing atop his boat and paddling it across the eerie waters of the River Styx, Charon often felt his mind drifting, wandering back to the first moments he saw the river.

Back then there had been no ferryman, and each new arrival had been expected to find a way to cross the river themselves. Many of them jumped in and attempted to swim across, always a risky proposition.

Occasionally, some were able to survive the swim and arrived on the other side of the river with profound strength, prepared to rule Hell as demigods.

Harry Stygius had been one of those lucky ones. But he was not the only one. A whole demi-pantheon had survived the Styx. There seemed to be no rhyme or reason why some conquered the river and other swimmers were swallowed by it, never to return.

Or at least not yet, Charon added on hastily, because after all, you had to take the long view when considering how things would unfold in Hell, and there was a chance that one day the "victims of the Styx" would reemerge, confounding everyone. One never knew.

Part of the trouble certainly stemmed from the fact that drowning in real life doesn't look like drowning in the movies does. We're conditioned to think that drowning is dramatic and involves someone yelling for help and waving and splashing all about them.

However, when drowning happens in real life, it is deceptively quiet.

When a person is actively drowning, they nearly always are incapable of crying out for help. This is because the ability to speak relies on the respiratory system. This means that if you can't breathe, because you have water in your airway, you can't speak. When a person drowns, they will sink below the water and bob up periodically – but typically not long enough for them to exhale and inhale a breath of air that will allow them to call for help and then also have enough time to do that.

Additionally, drowning people can't flail their arms to signal a need for help due to an instinctive response that causes them to thrust their arms to their sides and attempt to press down on the surface of the water, so that they can get enough leverage to try to get their mouths up and breathe. None of this happens voluntarily or consciously. During drowning, pure deep brain instinct takes over, and the body moves of its own accord, doing whatever it thinks it will help the drowning person survive. These instinctive plans include no idea that someone nearby will come to the rescue, and so a drowning person doesn't try to attract attention, even in situations where this would be the best strategy.

Does this mean that if someone is thrashing and yelling in the water, they're not in trouble? No, not at all. If someone is doing that, they're in water-related distress. But they're not drowning. At least not yet.

A drowning person can be incredibly hard to spot – only distinguished by minor tells like a mouth at or below water level or glassy eyes.

And because of this relative subtlety, people weren't entirely sure if the river had swallowed the swimmers, or if the so-called drowning victims of the Styx dove down to the depths on purpose. Because of this, there were some citizens of Hell who expected that the lost would reemerge any day now.

The Styx was arbitrary, fickle.

There seemed to be no pattern, no indicator that the river respected strength, youth, intelligence, vitality, beauty, or any of the other traditional things that living beings usually respected.

That didn't stop the victors of the Styx from becoming braggadocious about crossing the waters, however. Nearly all survivors emerged pompously trumpeting their victory.

But not Harry Stygius. He did not claim to have defeated the Styx – as many of his peers did – but took the view that the Styx had shown him mercy, that the river had let him go. Not that he had conquered the river.

And as a sign of respect and gratitude for this mercy, he took on the river's name.

The other denizens of Hell had considered this a kooky choice and wondered why the Styx had spared a nut like Harry, someone who would bow before a river like it was his master. But over the millennia, Harry Stygius steadily rose to prominence.

Charon smiled at the memory. He had seen it all unfold during his long life in Hell.

Harry had been an early ally of his when Charon espied the waters and decided there was no need to swim any longer. Where the other victors had shunned Charon and his ideas, Harry had made Charon's dream of a ferry service a reality, marshaling the resources to make the boat that could shuttle passengers safely across the waters.

For an idea that was shunned by so many of Hell's prominent business minds, Charon's ferry service was a surprisingly huge hit. Not because of what he earned from passage. The boat service barely broke even.

No, the bigger economic boom had been what happened to Hell as a result. Once upon a time, it had been a struggling frontier town with much more land and resources than the population could effectively gather, let alone put to good use.

But once the boat started making it across the Styx, the population had exploded. And nowayears Hell was a thriving metropolis.

And I was part of that, Charon thought, as the passengers *oohed* and *ahhed* at the impressive skyline that became visible so precipitously as the mists that crawled along the Styx began to thin nearer to the shore.

It was rather sudden, like the castles that sprang up in a children's pop-up book. And just as magical.

Once Charon's boat service had become so successful, there were of course imitators. Victors began to appoint ferrymen of their own and to provide them with boats that were quite similar to Charon's.

But the Styx swallowed those boats and their ferryman along with them. The Styx would allow no competitors.

It would appear that Harry had been right all along. It was up to the Styx who it let cross its waters.

For now that includes me, Charon observed, as his boat glided smoothly to the dock on the shore of Hell. He balanced gracefully with one foot on the dock and one still on the boat and tied his boat to its moorings.

"There you go," he said to his passengers, who pushed and shoved each other as they scrambled to disembark.

One lingered behind, as usually happened. "What about payment?" this last customer asked the ferryman.

Charon shook his head. "The way to Hell is free," he explained. "The way back is very expensive."

The passenger's eyes widened.

"Off you go," the ferryman half-hissed, pushing the last passenger onto the shore. Charon waved his hand at the mooring, and the knot securing the boat untied. He wiggled his fingers in goodbye at his delivered cargo. Most of them were long gone, scrambling off to see the city and its delights. Only the one straggler was still watching the boatman, frozen in place with his mouth hanging open as he watched the ferryman sail away, back to the other shore.

Goats Go to Hell

The first thing Penny realized when she regained consciousness was that the ground was moving beneath her, the color of sunset on Earth – and as that ground shifted forever under her, she felt her skin scrape as she passed over its coarse texture.

If she didn't get up, she realized, she'd get a terrible rugburn.

Almost simultaneously, the sound of a horrible cacophony hit her ears. A chorus of terrible cries and wails... or...

It hit her all at once, bolstered by the strange wealth of memories that had flooded back into her brain. Those weren't cries or wails at all. They were bleats.

And this was not ground she found herself on but a mass of squirming goats jockeying for position in an overcrowded, small pen.

She was essentially crowd surfing on a herd of panicked goats.

Glancing at the sky, she could see that it was a pale dirty yellow with a haze that struck her instantly as familiar. It was early into the multisolar cycle yet. One sun, just faithful Monosol, the only sun that never set, sometimes called the "lonely sun." She had plenty of time before the sky bled into deeper shades, creeping into amber and then oranges, and finally the flurry of reds that would usher in the danger of Pentasol, the fifth sun, and the madness of Hexasol, the sixth. At those times, the sky would burn, and the most cold-blooded of Hell's denizens would raid the plane.

That straw yellow was a comfort. It meant she had plenty of time to go home and see her family and... and then what?

Go back to Earth? How was she going to do that exactly?

Well, she'd just have to deal with that later.

The walls of the enclosure rattled. "Hey, what the fuck are you doing in there?" a gruff voice called in. Penny froze, even as the goats continued to churn under her. Taking her silence as a language barrier, the voice translated what he'd said into several Hellish dialects, making the statement more obscene and rude with each re-translation.

Penny noted with great confusion that she understood everything the voice said. In her life on Earth, she had only learned Latin and Greek for her classics program through sheer stubborn will. Spanish still largely alluded her despite the Psychic State's proximity to Mexico, its Southern neighbor, much to the chagrin of her put-upon high school Spanish teacher. And yet after establishing the connection with Gretchen Mills, she was spontaneously fluent in a variety of Hellish dialects.

"These are meat goats, you know," the voice said. "I have no problem throwing you into the grinder with the rest."

It's now or never, she thought. She crawled along the goats' backs, feeling all the while like she was hurting them, until she cleared the caprine mass and reached what seemed to be the corner of the pen.

That's when she saw him. He was part goat himself – the bottom part. His fur bore the same color scheme as his flock's. His coat was an ombre of bright sunset colors that spanned the full gamut that the Hellish sky was capable of, from the dim light of Monosol to the blaze of Hexasol. His top half was human, well mostly anyway, for he had a human face and beard but also sported horns.

The goat tender gasped. "Is that you, Stephanie Stygius?" he asked. "What is the Queen of Hell doing in my goat pen?"

Penny shook her head. "I'm not Stephanie," she said simply. "I'm Rhea."

"Rhea Stygius!" the goat tender cried.

"And if I'm not mistaken, you're a faun," Penny said.

"A faun?" the goat tender said. "Well, I suppose you're right, but it's been ages since anyone's called me that."

"What do they usually call you?" Penny asked.

"Well, my name of course," the faun said, shaking his head. "It's quite disrespectful otherwise. It'd be like me saying 'hey lady' to you forever. There's no sense to it. Why would you do that?"

"Of course," Penny said.

"I will of course pardon the Princess of Hell for being so thoughtless," the faun said, bowing.

Penny bristled at his faux-polite tone.

"My name is Napoleon," he introduced himself.

"Pleased to meet you," Penny said.

"You don't have to do that," Napoleon shot back.

"Do what?" Penny asked.

"Show false courtesy to a nobody like me," Napoleon replied.

"False courtesy?" Penny said.

"I imagine you've been on Earth for a while, judging by how much older you look," Napoleon said. "Long enough to get used to the way they do things over there. Probably lost most of the Hellion in you by this point. But it's a little ridiculous for you to be pretending to care about a working stiff like me. I am just a food supplier. No one the Princess of Hell would be pleased to meet."

"That's not true," Penny protested. "On Earth, I was poor. I worked every day myself in a job that wasn't glamorous."

Napoleon laughed dismissively.

"But it's true! There isn't a good thing that I've gotten in my life that I haven't had to fight like Hell for," Penny said.

"Except Hell itself."

She cringed. The new memories of her earlier life in Hell sat at the edge of her psyche, and as she pored over them, she could see that the goat herder was right. Before coming to Earth and living for 20 years first as a foster kid and later as a Green Star intuitive, her life on Hell had been rather... privileged. She frowned. It was an identity completely at odds with how she'd seen herself until extremely recently.

But it was true and undeniable. Very disconcerting.

She'd come into being with a team of servants. Living on a grand estate. Wearing the finest clothes. Eating the best food that Hell had to offer.

And yet... none of it had been good enough for her, had it?

She had run away as a spoiled child. And now here she was, returning to her ancestral home, a woman who had convinced herself that she'd earned everything she ever had.

And due to hiding the evidence, she'd been able to enjoy that illusion for 20 precious years.

She now understood why she'd sworn Kip to secrecy. Why she had taken such great pains to continue fooling herself. It hadn't taken very long to figure it out, after all.

"Did you come here straight from Earth?" the goat herder asked her.

"As far as I know," Penny replied.

Napoleon frowned.

Penny sighed. "Last thing I knew, I was performing a ritual with a memory eater."

"Ah," Napoleon said, "so you didn't come in the normal way, by the ferry?"

Penny shook her head. "Guess not."

"A little unorthodox, but I suppose that makes sense," said Napoleon.

"It does?" said Penny.

"You always did love goats," Napoleon said. "You came here with your family when you were teeny-tiny. Big day that was for me, royal family gracing me with their presence and all. So much work to be done to prepare." He grinned at the memory. "I imagine that visit is one of your first memories, and that you rode that memory all the way here, across planes."

Penny returned his smile. "Wait," she said. "I rode a memory across planes?"

"Boy," Napoleon said, "you didn't receive proper travel counseling, that's for sure."

He opened the gate to the goat pen, and its denizens began to plod out. "Dinner time, boys," he called to them.

They bleated in response in a peculiar chorus.

Penny watched as the flock trod over to an area adjoining their pen. It struck Penny as a junkyard, this whorl of discarded miscellaneous kipple. A dented washer and dryer combo stuck out of the jumble along with several dilapidated hoopties with doors missing or smashed windows. But there were many other items in this snarl. Stained plush toys, knick-knacks, and books. Pieces of paper and orphan socks were suspended, snagged upon the sharper bits of detritus, waving like flags in the slight wind of the unevenly heated Monosolar sky.

The goats eagerly and indiscriminately chowed down on anything they could chomp their little maws onto.

It came to Penny then – an old memory but one that felt familiar. She remembered that lost things had a way of ending up in Hell. It was unusual to go very far without running into some sort of forgotten debris, items that owners likely thought they'd misplaced but had instead absconded, wandering into the underworld.

While Hellish passage was expensive for living beings, it was essentially free for objects, who took great advantage of the reasonable rates, particularly if their owners mistreated or didn't pay enough attention to them. Although sometimes objects simply fled because they were bored.

A visitor might say that because of this Hell had a litter problem. The residents of Hell saw it differently. The litter wasn't a problem at all. It was part of what made Hell, Hell. Suddenly, it clicked in her brain. Was this why she'd been driven to dumpster dive on Earth? Part of it had surely been poverty and resourcefulness. But she found herself wondering... was she attracted to discarded items because they reminded her of home?

"You feed your flock any way you can," Napoleon told her, as Penny watched the goats graze, splitting apart fenders and chomping on massive steel fasteners. "If I only fed them on grass, they'd die, or I'd go broke."

"You can die in Hell?" Penny asked.

"Of course you can," Napoleon said, laughing. "Oh, that's right. You were a little kid when you left. Guess your parents never had that talk with you. About imps and beasts. About the poor souls who sunk to the bottom of the Styx." He leaned forward and whispered, "Or everyone else who disappears and is then promptly forgotten." He leaned back and added at full volume, "Life is long in Hell, but everyone has a short memory here, you know."

"No, I don't know." Penny frowned. "On Earth, Hell is thought of as a place you go when you die. Not the only place. And not everyone even believes in an afterlife."

"The afterlife! Ha!" Napoleon said. He stamped a cloven hoof on the ground. "I forget that they call it that."

Penny cocked her head at him.

"The afterlife is a bit of a misnomer," the Hellish faun explained. "It's like calling chickens after-eggs. It leaves out the part where chickens make more eggs. It's a lot like the answer to the famous riddle – 'What came first, the chicken or the egg?'"

"Oh, I know that one," Penny chimed in. It was one of her favorite thought experiments, even now that she knew the answer.

"Do you?" Napoleon challenged her.

Penny nodded. "A very long time ago, there was a rather chicken-like bird... but not quite a chicken. A proto-chicken, if you will. A proto-hen probably more precisely. Anyway, this proto-hen met a proto-rooster, they did their mating thing, and then the proto-hen laid an egg. That egg did something unexpected and hatched into offspring not quite like either of them. And *then* they had the chicken."

"Very good," Napoleon said.

"Technically, the egg came first, but it was only possible because of proto-chickens," Penny concluded.

"Everything that comes later owes to what came before it," Napoleon elaborated. "Somehow, in some way. However slight."

Penny nodded.

"And so," Napoleon said, "in one aspect, life itself must be contingent on something else. It's only afterlife relative to the life you came from. In an absolute sense, it's not afterlife, so much as parallel life or para-life. If you'd stayed here in Hell, you probably would have been taught this. Taught about the planes. Taught about how it all hangs together, how it's all connected." He laughed. "But here you are, the Princess of Hell... literally being intellectually one-upped by a goat herder." He grinned broader. "Life – afterlife, para-life, whatever – it's funny sometimes."

"So you're telling me that Hell isn't just a place you can go when you die," Penny summarized, ignoring the slight.

Napoleon shook his head. "I mean, that's one way to end up here, sure. Dying has a way of forcing you to switch planes." He paused. "Most of the time anyway."

"Forcing you to switch planes?"

Napoleon nodded.

"As in, get born somewhere else?" Penny pressed.

"Sometimes," Napoleon said. "Although it's usually not that simple. Dying and being born are reliable ways to shift planes. That much is true. But death and birth are not... the most optimal means of travel. It's especially expensive to be born."

"Expensive?" Penny said.

Napoleon frowned. "I worry about the state of the educational system on Earth. Okay, Princess, it's like this... birth and death will get you somewhere. But it might not be where you intended to go. And you might have to sacrifice something important for the trip... meaning, you might not arrive in the next plane in the same shape that you left the last."

"Sacrifice something?" Penny said. "Like what?"

"Well," Napoleon said. "It really depends. Depends on what a person has and what the person transporting them is looking for." He paused a moment, watching his flock graze. "In Hell, the ferryman usually wants you to pay with your memories."

On the Unreliable Nature of Memory

Childhood amnesia refers to a widely seen phenomenon in which adults largely cannot remember episodic memories – that is, memories of lived experiences and personal events – from their early lives. The exact cutoff for childhood amnesia varies by individual, but generally speaking, adults cannot retrieve memories that happened before they were two years old – and childhood amnesia can span to as late as four years old for some.

There is also a relative detriment of stored memories before the age of 10, if not complete amnesia as seen with the earliest years of life. Although most adults have some memories from that period, there are comparably few memories from those years when compared to other life periods.

Some research has suggested that quite young children – perhaps as young as a year old – can form memories. However, those memories often disappear as the child ages.

Regardless, it's well established that memory formation seems to function quite differently in childhood, and that when it comes to our memories, there is a marked difference between those in adulthood and childhood.

There are several proposed scientific explanations for this – including the lack of a coherent cognitive self-story in childhood, the fact that emotion plays a powerful role in memory and children are still making sense of their own emotions and how they interplay with the world and others, and many other potential neurobiological chemical factors.

However, while making great strides in this area of research, we are yet to definitively understand the phenomenon and why it happens.

It does not help that memory as a general process is deceptive.

For most beings, memory is not an exact and precise record of what has happened. Instead, it is an approximate recall but one which can easily be manipulated or changed based on suggestion.

This has been well demonstrated in research. Notoriously Elizabeth Loftus pioneered a series of studies into memory beginning in 1974 that completely revolutionized our collective understanding of memory and how accurate – or inaccurate – it is.

In sharp contradiction to the lay beliefs at the time, Loftus established that eyewitness testimony is often to prey to mistakes and that it's fairly easy to unduly influence recall based on the way we ask a person about their experiences.

In her most famous experiment, subjects were asked to view films of car crashes and then to answer a series of questions after viewing them about what happened in those films. Subjects who were asked "About how fast were the cars going when they smashed into each other?" reported a higher estimated speed than those who were asked if the cars "collided," bumped," "contacted," or "hit" one another. Simply using the verb "smashed" caused the participants to remember a higher speed, altering their recollection.

The subjects were once again approached a week later, and researchers found that those who had been asked about how fast the cars "smashed" together were more likely to say that broken glass was present in the car crash film they viewed – when in fact, there was no broken glass on the film.

The study demonstrated that the way that a person is asked about an event has the power to reshape their recollection of the event.

This predictably had huge legal implications – ones that are frankly still being sorted out. The Psychic State has had a huge leg up in this endeavor, as eideticist memory is not nearly as vulnerable to these same effects. It is theorized that the memory of an eideticist is entirely faithful and immune to being warped by suggestion or personal bias. However, a suitable experimental design study has yet to be developed that would objectively test this.

from Insecta Psychica: Towards an Intuitive Taxonomy by Cloche Macomber

"Pay with my memories?" Penny said. "Is that what happened to me?"

Napoleon shrugged. "Your guess is as good as mine. Although..."

"Although?"

"The fact that you're here again – and here as you were before, only older – should mean that you have those memories back, that they were refunded to you somehow. This would not only be irregular, but..." His voice trailed off.

"It wouldn't fit with the fact that there's a gap still. That there are things I still don't understand, that I don't remember. Things that are a mystery to me that I probably should remember," Penny offered.

The goat herder nodded.

And it wouldn't explain what Gretchen was doing with them either, Penny thought. *If I paid them to the ferryman, why were they being stored on Earth?*

No. It just didn't fit. There was something important missing.

"Anyway," Napoleon continued, "now that you're back, I'd imagine you're wanting to see Mr. Dante."

"Kip?" Penny said.

Napoleon nodded. "You two were inseparable, after all. I imagine he misses you something fierce."

Misses me? Penny thought. *But... he's been with me.*

Things were not adding up again. She felt a pit in her stomach as something within her warned her that it was probably best to keep this insight to herself. Aloud she said, "I would love to see him."

The faun gave her directions, winding her through three circles of Hell that separated his flock from where Kip could be found. According to him, her old friend was next to a tree of fire on the north end of the River Styx.

Of course, Penny thought. *That was where he left me, wasn't it?*

She wasn't sure how exactly she knew that. It was less a formal memory and more the implication of one, a void where that memory should be, demonstrated by bits and pieces of other things she could remember more clearly that hooked into that empty space.

She thanked Napoleon before departing and making a long sweltering walk across parts of Hell that now seemed so familiar to her, as common as the lines in the palm of her hand, but that she hadn't seen or even thought about for 20 Earthly years.

Everything looked the same. She was the only thing that had changed. It would appear that what everyone said about interplanar time dilation was true. Clearly, only a few weeks had passed on Hell while the Earth had spun and spun.

I Stay Chained to
This Burning Tree of Fire

She saw the tree first, long before she ever saw Kip. It was tall and magnificent, much taller than anything that surrounded it. Hell was like that. Relatively flat, lacking differences in topographical elevation.

The grander estates did have as many as three stories extending into the sky, but no buildings within city or planar limits were taller. Instead, the multistoried homes had lovely basements extending well below ground.

Vegetation in general was sparse throughout Hell. The trees that grew typically didn't make it past the sapling stage, oft burned down during the later multisolar cycles when the great flurry of beasts from the plane's outer limits would rush into the city and ravage the landscape.

But this one tree had made it. It had caught on fire but not burned to the ground. And it was still burning.

It was also a very familiar species, Penny thought. It was a desert willow.

During their time together on Earth, Kip had always met her underneath desert willows. Not always the same tree but always the same species.

In the place where Earthly trees would have delicate fluffy flowers, this tree instead had blaring flames, burning like tiny torches in the sepals.

She saw Kip next. He was sitting and reading a book casually – as he always was when she encountered him on Earth. He was similarly attired, too, fitted in a pinstripe suit with matching pocket square. This time his suit was black with red pinstripes.

Very goth chic, Penny noted, particularly set against the paleness of his bloodless complexion. Although... she noted his skin looked quite a bit rosier than she was accustomed to it being.

He looked more alive than she'd ever seen him.

The other difference was immediately obvious: He was strapped to the tree by a phosphorescent tether that looped upon itself countless times. As she got closer, Penny saw that there were links within this tether.

Kip was chained to the burning tree.

At first, Penny felt a quick jolt of panic. But Kip didn't seem to be that upset about it, however, Penny noted. He hardly had the look of despair you'd expect from a damsel in distress chained to the railroad tracks while a mustachioed villain leered from close by.

Instead, he looked like he was quite comfortable, with the same bearing you'd expect someone to affect while reading on the beach and sunbathing on vacation.

"Ah, little one!" he called out. "It's so wonderful to see you. It's been so long."

"So long?" Penny asked. "How long have I been gone from Earth?"

Kip studied her face. "Of course. No, I mean... it's been so long since I've seen you in Hell. That's all."

"How did you get here?" Penny asked.

"What do you mean, little one?" said Kip.

"How did you get here from Earth?" she pressed.

Kip nodded his head slowly. "It seems I have a lot to explain."

"Please," Penny prompted. "How did you get here?" she repeated.

"Well," Kip said, "I've always been here."

"What?" Penny said.

"I never left," Kip replied. "You went to Earth alone."

Penny frowned. "But you were there on Earth with me. We spoke all the time. You followed me wherever I went."

Kip shook his head. "No, little one, that is not what happened."

"Was it an imposter then? Was I talking to someone pretending to be you?" Penny asked.

"That's not quite right either," Kip said.

"Well, Kip, then what is it?" Penny said. "For a person who said I can ask you anything I want, you're giving me an awful lot of runaround whenever I ask you what are perfectly reasonable questions."

Kip laughed. It was a deep hearty laugh. "Ah, I've always loved your spirit, little one."

"Still not answering my question."

"And I love how you don't let me get away with anything," Kip replied.

Penny crossed her arms.

"And I see that you still do that, too," Kip observed.

"Do what?" Penny asked.

"Crossing your arms," Kip said. "Huffing."

"Kip, you're freaking me out. You're not making sense," Penny said.

Kip nodded. "I'm sorry, little one. How do I explain when I barely understand myself what happened?"

"Start anywhere," Penny said. "Say anything."

"That's good advice," Kip replied, smirking.

"You told me that once," Penny said. "On *Earth*. Where you supposedly have never been."

"Well," Kip said. "Part of me has."

"Part of you?"

Kip nodded. "A projection, a thin slice of my consciousness, my perception. Some people call it an eidolon, and I suppose you could, too, if you wanted to get fancy. But it's not all that complex. You can think of it like a phone call. A video call, actually. I've been here physically the whole time, right here in Hell. We've been in communication, that much is true, but I never left the plane. When Charon sent you to Earth –"

"Charon?" Penny interrupted.

"Charles Huron," Kip confirmed. "The ferryman."

The name was familiar to Penny. Her newly returned memories bloomed, connected to the word, provided a picture. She could see Charon in her mind. It was strange. He looked nothing like he did in her mythology textbooks, which typically provided illustrations of him looking skeletal, akin to the grim reaper or death personified.

This Charon the acquaintance was middle-aged, a little sparse on head hair, and sported an oddly charming little pot belly. He was a sitcom dad. The kind of man you might look past easily in a crowd. There was nothing offensive about his appearance, but he certainly wasn't striking in any sense.

He looked about how you'd expect a city bus driver to look.

"Charon," Penny said. "Yes, I remember him."

Kip smiled. "Yes, good. I presume Gretchen was able to help you out then."

"The memory eater," Penny said, remembering Gretchen's strange infatuation with Kip. She rolled her eyes involuntarily at the thought.

"Yes, Gretchen. I believe that's what she's going by these days," Kip replied.

Penny pondered asking Kip for more information about that, but she couldn't quite stomach hearing more about lovesick Gretchen Mills. "So you didn't come with me to Earth?" she said instead.

Kip shook his head. "I couldn't afford to send both of us."

"Is that why you're chained to this tree?" Penny said. "Is this debtor's prison or something?"

Kip laughed. "No, little one. No, I guess you wouldn't remember that now, would you? Since Gretchen could only return to you what you already knew." He smiled. "And it seems like it's taking a bit for the new memories to integrate with the old ones, even so."

"Whatever," Penny grumbled, feeling uncomfortable. She hated to be the last one to know things.

"I guess that's how it can be when memories are returned. It's kind of like transplanting crops. There's a shock at first to the plant, just the very act of moving it from one place to another. And even after the shock subsides, it can take a while for the plant to put down new roots and to fully integrate into its new home," Kip said.

"You're still not explaining why you're tied to the tree," Penny pointed out.

"Very good, little one," Kip praised her. "I'm here as deposit."

"Deposit on what?" Penny asked.

"Why, on you, of course," Kip said.

"Wait," Penny said. "They have you tied here with magical chains as some kind of... hostage?"

"Well, I guess that's a more colorful way of putting it," Kip said, laughing. "But yes. Essentially. Couldn't have me running off while you were out... Yonder. Couldn't risk you staying lost, unaccounted for. Charon's an industrious sort, but he's not stupid. There's no amount of money in this plane or the next worth invoking the wrath of Harry Stygius. He had to make sure you came back. And the best way to ensure your return was for me to stay fixed here all of this time." Kip closed his book and smiled. "It wasn't so bad most of the time. The storms that came in the late multisolar cycles. The beasts..." He shuddered. "Well, let's just say I'm glad you're home. And your father will be as well of course."

"My father," Penny said, wondering at the sound of it. She knew that it was true. The memory of her father was there in her mind, accessible – although it would be a while yet before it felt like it really belonged to her. Or until the roots grew in, as Kip had put it. "My father," she said again, hoping the sound of it would make it seem more mundane, more natural.

Kip nodded. "He's been awaiting your return, little one. Patiently at first but impatiently lately."

"He just let me run away?" Penny asked.

"Running away is something most Hellions do. You wouldn't be developmentally normal if you didn't take off every now and then. If you didn't push boundaries, try to figure out which rules are laws and which ones are just suggestions. If you didn't do that, you'd be more like your sister," Kip said, frowning. He looked away. "But a lot of things have changed lately, little one. You're needed at home. That's why your father sent for you."

"*He* sent for me?" Penny said.

Kip nodded. "He sent other eidolons. I imagine some of the messengers got mixed up with your ghost friends and spread it like gossip. And eidolons are beings who know how to talk to the living, at least certain members of the living anyway."

"So that's why the dead knew my other name," Penny said.

Kip nodded.

"Okay, Kip," Penny said. "I don't know how to unlock that crap you have on, but let's do it. It's time to go home."

Kip closed his eyes and inhaled deeply. As he did, the glowing chains slunk to the ground. He stood up unfettered.

"I thought you'd never ask, little one," he said.

Penny gawked.

"Little one, I don't think you understand," Kip said. "Here in Hell, you are royalty. Here your word has consequences. You have power you could only dream of on Earth."

Penny shook her head. "This has been the weirdest day ever. I feel like I've woken from one dream to find I'm still asleep and dreaming something else. But I'm not sure which one is the nightmare."

Kip smiled. "Little one, I think that's the best description of plane-shifting that I have ever heard."

The Stygiuses Do Some Soul Searching

The man of the manor was tall and lank with a ruddy complexion. Like most things in Hell, he did not smell of fire and brimstone. No, Harry Stygius smelled like paprika, chile powder, and earthy red pestled heat.

He had a certain gravitas, a presence you didn't soon forget, and he had a way of setting you at ease – instantly –without even trying. He was never someone you put your guard up around, and that was a big part of his power.

Harry Stygius could negotiate, drive a hard bargain, without the other person even knowing he was transacting business. It was easy to make a deal with the devil, without being aware that you were doing so.

That was why he was so perplexed to find himself on the losing end of a power struggle for the first time in his long memory.

"No, no, no," Harry said. "You've got it all wrong. Stephanie's just being dramatic again. I'm a very present husband. And a good father. This... taken for granted, absent husband talk? Well, it's nonsense. It's just claptrap."

"You can say bullshit, Harry," Stephanie said. "I know you can."

Harry bristled. "For such a beautiful woman, the coarsest things come from your mouth."

"You see what I mean?" Stephanie said, rolling her eyes. "He's so critical. Always putting me down."

The couple's counselor seated across from them nodded sagely without making eye contact, scribbling frantically on a legal pad.

"He doesn't even think he has a problem," Stephanie continued. "The only reason he's here in the first place is because I threatened to leave him if he didn't talk to someone with me."

"Cruel, isn't it?" Harry remarked. "That my own wife would say such a thing. Can you imagine? Both of our children are gone – and the way she responds to this is to say she'll leave me, too, unless I do exactly what she says." He looked at the floor. "If my rivals knew I was here, if they knew the victor of victors was getting marital counseling…"

"I dunno," the therapist said. "Hell's more progressive than it used to be. Folks are getting more open-minded all the time about therapy. About soul searching."

Harry scoffed at this notion. "The only soul searching that's acceptable in Hell involves the beasts of Hexasol and the scrappers."

The therapist nodded. He was familiar with the practice. He knew that throngs of seekers often combed the rings looking for anything valuable they could pick up whenever some unfortunate soul got caught in the stampede and involuntarily jumped planes. "Well it used to be that way, and I can see why you feel that way," he validated, "but Harry, Hell is changing. Everyone knows it."

"That's what people say," Harry replied. "I'll believe it when I see it."

"It's been a while since the last Hexasol," Stephanie said.

"Oh, there you go again with all that Hexasol talk. The plane skips one cycle, one measly Hexasol cycle, and everyone thinks Hell is freezing over. Or is about to. Planar cooling is a hoax. These things move in waves," Harry protested.

Stephanie rolled her eyes.

"Anyway, who gives a flying fff—fig about missing Hexasol? It's not like anyone misses the beasts," Harry said.

"No one is saying that skipping Hexasol is a bad thing," the counselor said, still not making eye contact. "All I said is Hell is changing."

"And then Stephanie brought up Hexasol. Like it matters," Harry countered.

"It doesn't?" the therapist challenged him.

"No, of course not. Who cares if Hell freezes over if there's no one here to rule it? Who cares about the sun cycles when we can't find Dem?" Harry said.

"What about Dem?" said Penny, interrupting the therapy session.

"Rhea!" Harry and Stephanie cried in unison. They leaped to their feet and walked towards their daughter.

"I see. When you think about your legacy, how does that make you feel?" the therapist said to empty chairs.

No one answered.

Penny moved in for a hug, and both parents cringed away.

"Oh dear, you have been on Earth for a long time, haven't you?" Stephanie said.

"I'm sorry?" Penny said.

"Hugging isn't a Hellish custom. It's frankly a little bizarre. We preserve physical intimacy for our mates. So hugging a family member is quite perverse," Stephanie explained. "It's like…" she thought for a moment, trying to recall her own time on Earth, long past, and find a suitable parallel. "Hugging is a bit like dry humping."

"Mom!"

"Or grinding. I believe they call it grinding up on someone," Stephanie continued.

"Mom, no!"

"Rubbing up on someone," Stephanie offered. She looked at her husband. "Am I being clear?"

"Crystal," Harry replied, stifling a laugh.

"Oh shit," Stephanie said. "Right. I've violated some Earthly social norm, haven't I? Mothers don't usually talk that way to their daughters on Earth, do they?"

Penny shook her head no.

"Well, we'll figure things out, won't we, Rhea?" Stephanie said in an encouraging tone. It sounded a bit forced to Penny's ears, as though Stephanie were trying to convince herself most of all that it was true.

"Rhea," Penny said. "It's been so long since anyone's called me that."

"Oh?" Harry said. "Did you go by a different name on Earth?"

Penny nodded. "People call me Penny."

"Penny?" Harry scoffed. "That's currency, isn't it? It's like calling yourself Dime or Nickel. Penny? That's absurd."

Penny thought it best not to tell her parents that she was also using the last name Dreadful. Instead, she said, "Well, Rhea wasn't going so well either."

"Really?" Harry said. "It's such a noble name."

"Unless the other kids call you Diarrhea," Penny said.

Her parents broke into laughter. As they did, Penny saw a youthfulness to them she wasn't expecting. They physically appeared to be in their late 40s in Earthen age, but she knew that time dilation meant that they were much, much older. When they laughed, their faces warped into younger versions and neither of them looked older than 20. It was quite eerie and unsettling.

"Princess Diarrhea," Stephanie said, struggling to catch her breath. "Well, I'll be."

"Anyway," Penny said, "what happened to Dem?"

Harry frowned. "She was so depressed when you ran away this last time. I'd never seen her so despondent. She wasn't eating, wasn't sleeping. As you know, she's never been one to even test the rules – behavior basically unheard of in Hellspawn, to be such a goody-two-shoes, but that was our Dem. Oddly, she never ran away from home. But when you didn't come back, she changed."

Stephanie nodded. "One morning we woke up, and she was gone. There was only a note she left, saying she'd gone to find you."

"We've sent search parties to every ring of Hell, every dark corner, every hideout, and no one has been able to find her,"

Harry said. "Charon hasn't seen her. There's no sign that she left the plane."

"She has to be somewhere," Stephanie said. "I know she's somewhere in the city."

"That's why we sent for you," Harry said. "You're her twin sister. We figured if anybody would know where she was, it would be you. That twin-tuition of yours. You two always had that strange link."

"So you want me to find her and bring her home?" Penny said.

"Please," Harry said.

Ah I see, Penny thought. Her heart sank. She had been summoned home for a rescue mission. She was called here to retrieve her sister, the one who actually had value. The child that was useful and wanted. *They were happy to live without me, but when it's her… well, it becomes a family emergency.*

"Okay," Penny said aloud. "Don't worry. I'll find her."

Her parents beamed. "Wonderful, Rhea," Harry said. "You're a good girl. I'm so proud of you."

Penny felt herself smiling in response to her father's approval in spite of herself.

"It's quite strange. When you left here, you were just a little girl. And even though planar time dilation is a known quantity, I must admit it's rather jarring to see it in practice. You're so lovely, Rhea. You look so much like your mother it's uncanny," Harry observed.

"She really does," Stephanie agreed.

Penny shrugged, uncomfortable with the praise.

"Thank you, Rhea," her father said. "I believe in you."

Upon hearing those words, Penny's heart swelled up so large that she had to leave before she embarrassed herself.

Kip waited outside. "How'd it go?" he said.

"They were having couples therapy," Penny said.

"That's very evolved of them. Very new age," Kip said. "But I suppose things are changing in Hell. Everyone says so."

"And they want me to find Dem," Penny said.

"And you agreed?"

Penny nodded. "I'm gonna need your help though, Kip."

"Anything, little one," Kip said.

"I have a feeling I know what happened," Penny said. "I can't explain how, but it's clear to me. Dem and I are very different people of course, but I've always had insight into how she thinks."

"You two are like reverse sides of the same coin," Kip said.

"Anyway, I figure she set off on her own, but she got snatched along the way somewhere. That she's being held against her will. That just leaves one question, and it's a question that I think *you* can answer, Kip."

"And what's that, little one?" Kip said.

"Who has a reason to hurt my father?" Penny asked.

"How long do you have?" Kip replied.

Lord Bubba Beasly

Beasly, Bubba. Penny noted the name on the directory.

"It's a bit strange that he doesn't have his own place, isn't it?" she asked Kip.

"Strange? Strange how?" Kip replied.

"Well, he's a victor, too, isn't he?" Penny said. "Like my father? It seems odd that he'd be living in an apartment."

Kip shook his head. "Not at all." He gestured around him. "This structure is a compound, not an apartment building. The other inhabitants aren't residents *per se*. They're more like employees." He paused. "Or *servants*, I suppose you could say." He cracked a smile. "Although victor staff generally prefers the term *employees*."

Kip poked a finger at the other name plaques below Lord Beasly's.

Emp 1. Emp 2... Emp 45.

"Ah," Penny said, feeling foolish for not noticing that herself, that these other units were marked by employee numbers, not traditional names. "I see."

Kip pressed the buzzer. The front door flew open almost instantly. A short lumpy figure in a bellhop's uniform craned his wrinkled face into view.

Though this doorman scowled, Penny found his elongated pointy ears rather adorable.

"Oh, it's you, Kipper Dante. What the fuck do you want today?" Pointy Ears muttered.

"Why to speak to the lord of the manor of course," Kip said, his voice mellifluous and calm.

"WhY tO sPeAk To ThE lOrD oF tHe MaNoR oF cOuRsE," the doorman parroted in a whiny high voice, scrunching up his face. "Fuck you, Dante," he said and moved to slam the door.

Kip stuck one knee next to the door frame to prevent this.

"Hey!" Pointy Ears cried and then rattled off six different vulgar insults in three different Hellish dialects.

"I'm not alone today," Kip said. He swung the door open a bit wider to reveal Penny.

"Ahh… Mrs. Stephanie Stygius. I am so honored," the doorman said. The words came out of his mouth robotically, lacking any sort of sincerity. It reminded Penny of the apology that comes from a person who doesn't regret the act itself but is sorry that they got caught.

"Sir," Penny said, giggling. She supposed it could come in handy, being mistaken for her mother.

Kip shot an approving glance her way. *The resemblance really was uncanny, wasn't it?* Kip thought. It would get even worse when Dem came of age – whatever millennium that eventually happened. All three of the Stygius women would be nearly indiscernible. The plan was to have Dem become Harry's successor on the day that the lord finally left the plane, but Kip found himself thinking about a Hell ruled by a triumvirate of strong-willed women of spring.

It was something most of Hell would consider a perversion – a downright travesty. But to Kip? It sounded pretty grand.

"This way, my lady," the doorman grumbled. To Kip, he added, "I guess you can come, too, you nerf herder."

"I see you're still watching foreign films," Kip observed.

"Stuff it, you clown," Pointy Ears warned him.

Kip waggled his eyebrows at Penny, who suppressed a giggle.

They followed the disgruntled doorman into a gilded elevator. The car had engravings on its walls that reminded Penny for all the world of Hieronymus Bosch's triptych *The Garden of Earthly Delights*, except redone with a more bold, even psychedelic color scheme.

"The art in here is lovely," Penny said.

The doorman grunted in response. "Beasly's got money coming out of his ass," he explained.

After a long ride to the top, the elevator doors opened, revealing a surprisingly corporate neutral-toned executive office.

Sitting behind a rather conservative mahogany desk was an athletically built man sporting a crewcut and wearing a nice slate gray business suit.

The only unusual thing about him was that his skin was royal blue.

"Stephanie, how the blazes are ya?" he called boisterously. He rose from his desk, walked over to her, and shook her hand.

Penny searched her mind. Was this okay by Hellish standards? Or was this like hugging someone?

This is like copping a feel, the answer came to her from newly integrated memories. She pulled away from the handshake. "Lord Beasly," she scolded him. "I don't believe my *husband* would appreciate such a gesture."

Bubba Beasly scowled petulantly. "Well, Harry's not *here*, is he?" He frowned. "Why did you come then, if not to consummate what we both know is in our hearts?"

"What are you talking about, Beasly?" Penny snapped in a voice that surprised her. It wasn't her usual way of talking at all and reminded her powerfully of her mother's tone and cadence. Somehow, her subconscious was providing useful information to help her cope with this strange setting. *This must be those roots of memory Kip was talking about coming in. Good timing.*

"Oh Stephanie, don't play dumb," Beasly said, licking his bluish lips in a way that was probably meant to be seductive but just made him look hungry. "I've seen how you look at me at the society balls. You undress me with your eyes. I can see right through you."

"If you really believe that, Beasly, then you need to get your eyes checked," Penny snapped. Her tone was authoritative, but a bolt of anxiety coursed through her.

"It's a good thing you brought your henchman with you," Beasly said. "I have half a mind to…" He stopped himself.

"Half a mind to what?" Penny pressed him, her heart pounding in her ears. "Kidnap him like you kidnapped my daughter. Lock me away with her?"

"Careful, Mrs. Stygius," Beasly warned. "That's a very nasty accusation. You have no proof."

"Or do I?" Penny challenged him. She felt adrenaline rush through her as she bluffed.

"Get the fuck out of my office, you whore," Beasly said.

"Okay, Lady Stygius, I think we've socialized enough for the day," Kip intervened. "I do believe the lady was finished with you anyway, Lord Beasly."

"Hardly," Beasly countered.

Pointy Ears gleefully escorted them into the elevator and outside, giggling to himself all the while. Such a pleasure to see low lives like the Stygiuses get their just desserts. He didn't cease his maniacal giggling until after he'd slammed the door in their stupid faces.

"One down," Penny said to Kip.

"One to go," he replied nodding.

"Lead the way," she said.

"Sure thing," Kip said. "Little one," he said after they had walked a little way.

"Yes, Kip?"

"Where did you ever learn to act like that?" Kip asked. "I would have sworn I were standing next to Stephanie Stygius."

Penny considered the question. "I have a lot of experience pretending to be something I'm not."

Kip grinned.

"So where are we heading next?" Penny prompted him.

"To see Lucien Farr," Kip replied.

"Wait a second," Penny said. "Beasly, Bubba? Lucien Farr?"

Kip nodded. "Yes."

"Kip, those names are ridiculous," Penny said.

"Ridiculous?"

"They sound like Beelzebub and Lucifer," Penny said. "You know... other names for the devil."

"Well of course they do," Kip said.

"What do you mean 'of course they do'?" Penny snapped. "Do victors just go around naming themselves after nicknames for the devil? That's silly."

"Ah," Kip said. "Pardon my saying so, but you have that exactly backward, little one."

"Backward?"

Kip nodded. "The victors aren't named according to Earthly conventions. The reason those are nicknames for 'the devil' on Earth is because of the victors."

"I don't follow," Penny replied.

Kip smirked. "I'm sorry, little one, I don't mean any disrespect, but it's amazing to me how much Hellish culture you've missed because you've been away."

Penny frowned. "I know you don't mean to be rude, but it would really help me if you'd explain."

"Certainly," Kip said. "I'm no expert on Earth of course. I used to live there, and as you know, I've visited there in a limited capacity as an eidolon the past 20 or so Earthly years, but as best I can tell, most of what is known there about Hell came from some very suspect sources."

"Suspect sources?" Penny said.

"Yes," Kip said. "Hellish tabloids basically."

"Tabloids?" Penny said, laughing.

Kip nodded. "Bizarre but true. I'm sure you know by now, but the information that gets spread around is typically the most entertaining or selfishly aggrandizing version of events, not necessarily the most accurate."

"Oh yeah," Penny said. "That's caused a lot of problems on Earth, too, especially recently."

"It's the same in Hell. And the same with interplanar news," Kip explained. "So yes, what folks on Earth know about Hell is what was printed in our most popular tabloids, much of which then got added to various mythological texts in your world as though it were the word of the divine."

"Wild," Penny said, grinning.

"The most popular tabloid journalists all use pseudonyms for the victors and their families, to shield them from libel laws. However, they keep them incredibly easy to guess. Your mother Stephanie is called Persephone. Harry is—"

"No, lemme guess," Penny interjected. "Hades?"

"Very good, little one," Kip said. "Precisely."

"And Lucien Farr and Bubba Beasly are Lucifer and Beelzebub?" Penny said.

"Yes," Kip said.

"But… on Earth, those are all treated interchangeably as names for the same being – Lucifer, Beelzebub, Hades," Penny said.

"Yes," Kip said. "And that irks the ever-loving crap out of Beasly and Farr, let me tell you, that Earth gives Harry all the credit for everything they do." He screwed his face up and did a passable impression of Lord Beasly, "That's brand dilution, that's what that is!"

"No wonder they're so mad at my father," Penny said. "It has to be infuriating to be constantly mixed up with your competition."

"Ah, little one," Kip said. "Maybe I was wrong about you. Maybe you're savvier when it comes to Hellish culture than I gave you credit for."

Lord Lucien Farr

Lord Lucien Farr's face was bubbling, Penny noted. It was quite a sight to behold, how the black and red marbled visage flowed and moved like it was the threshold between lava and magma, that liminal space where molten rock is breaking up through the earth's crust via an angry volcanic eruption.

His face was angry, agitated, and couldn't quite make up its mind what exactly it was or wanted to be.

It ill suited Lord Farr, who was far from explosive and instead seemed rather pensive and reticent to speak, if anything.

Still, Penny thought, such individuals could have fury below the surface. Passive-aggression could lie in wait. One never knew.

She kept expecting Lord Farr's face to succumb to gravity and slough off onto the floor of his lushly carpeted receiving room, scorching the fibers irrevocably. However, it didn't. Instead, his face remained a closed system, one resistant to gravity, and while his skin bubbled and spat, the contents of said face stayed more or less in the general facial region, rather than flowing uninhibited as lava would.

"Have you considered consulting Lord Beasly about this matter?" Lord Farr said coolly.

"We just came from there," Penny replied.

"Did you?" Lord Farr challenged.

Penny nodded.

"Funny that," said Lord Farr.

Penny cocked her head quizzically.

"I heard from Lord Beasly. He told me that Mr. Dante visited him, but Lord Beasly said that he brought Stephanie Stygius with him." He curled one long blistered red and black finger under his chin, popping an active bubble in the process. "Pardon me, my lady, but you're Rhea Stygius."

Penny felt a wave of panic shoot through her. She didn't know what to say. She looked to Kip for assistance.

"I suppose you're wondering how I know," Lord Farr continued. "You might fool a simpleton like Bubba Beasly, but you'll have to do better with more sophisticated victors." He grinned, revealing a mouth full of marbled red and black pointy teeth that looked to Penny like obsidian daggers. "But I don't suppose you'd know that, seeing as at this point you're more Earthling than Hellion." He shrugged. "Pity. You were such a firebrand when you left. Earth has changed you, cooled you." He frowned. "Diminished you. I guess travel isn't *always* broadening."

Kip clenched his fists.

"If you're so sophisticated," Penny ventured, "then why don't you know where Dem is?"

Lord Farr rolled his roiling marbled eyes. "I didn't say that. I just asked if you'd consulted Lord Beasly."

"Then you do know," Penny said.

"Do I?" Lord Farr asked, his voice graduating into a tinny laugh.

Penny closed her eyes and concentrated. She could feel Dem, could almost see her if she focused. She wasn't close, but she wasn't far away either.

Penny opened her eyes. "You might," she said.

"Oh dear, is that the best you can do?" Lord Farr said, laughing. "I heard you were a detective on Earth. One would think you'd be a little better at investigation."

"H-h-how do you know about that?" Penny stammered.

Lord Farr smiled. "There are ways of getting information across the planes if you have enough resources." He gestured around him to the grandness of his current surroundings. "I might just have a few resources."

It was a sobering thought for Penny, the idea that information about her could have been trickling back to Hell this entire time. Meanwhile, she'd been completely in the dark about where she came from. Until recently, her family in Hell had made no effort to contact her. It made her feel rather vulnerable – like all this time she had existed behind one-way glass, fully visible to those in the underworld while not being able to look back at them.

Even if it had been by her own design, the inability to look back, it had the effect of making her feel like a museum exhibit rather than a person with her own agency. Yes, she had done it to herself, but it didn't feel good.

"Oh come now," Lord Farr said. "You're so much prettier when you smile, Rhea."

Penny scowled harder on purpose.

"Ah yes, there's the Stygian spirit," Farr said. "Your sister will be happy to see you. She's been a real pain in my ass."

Penny gasped at this confession. "Then you know where she is?"

Farr nodded. "Of course I do," he replied. "You said it yourself: I'm sophisticated."

"Then you have to take us there," Penny insisted.

"Of course," Farr replied. He snapped his fingers. Penny spun around just in time to see one of Farr's employees plunging a syringe into Kip's back. She felt a pinch in her own back that told her the rest of the story.

She felt her body slump to the ground but couldn't do anything to stop it.

Her vision went gray.

PSYCHIC INFERNO

It flashed across Viv's vision so quickly that at first she didn't recognize it as one of her visions. The image more had the quality of phosphenes, those splotches of light that spring up on your eyeballs when pressure is applied to them, perhaps when you rub your eyes too hard.

Her whole world dissolved in a flash of light that not only rendered her blind but made her head throb. She blinked reflexively at the sensation, hoping that blinking would clear her field of vision, but the light lingered. It was on its own schedule. It would dissipate when it was good and ready.

In this case, that was approximately 10 seconds, during which time the entire world seemed to stand still and hold its breath.

Then the light began to recede, bit by bit, until the picture became clear.

Before Viv stood a man, or at least a being in the approximate shape of a man, because she realized uncomfortably as she studied his face that the features weren't quite right. There was a little something around the eyes, Viv thought. Something that was both familiar and unsettling at once. She felt simultaneously as though she knew him and had always known him – and also that he couldn't quite be real.

"You don't need to know my name," the being said.

"A lot of people ask you that, don't they?" Viv said.

He nodded. "That's because people are terrible at asking questions. They stick to familiar paths, questions that they've heard others ask thousands of times before, instead of asking what they want to know. Or questions whose answers would help them. It's like they're speaking lines from a play rather than actually living."

"Even psychics?" Viv said.

He nodded. "You're really not that different from... what do you call them?" He thought for a moment before a look crossed his face that indicated he'd snatched the word from the air. "Normals."

"Try telling the normals that," Viv said.

"Change," the being said. "Change Patterson."

Ah, Viv thought. *There is something familiar about him, after all.* She hadn't met this figure personally before now, but she'd heard of him. He'd visited Penny during a former case, delivering one of those "warnings" that are veiled threats.

Of course, telling Penny not to do something was the surest way to get her to do it. His scaring her away from pursuing the investigation had been a doomed errand from the start.

Not that it mattered that they hadn't met before, Viv thought, as rumor had it Change was a shapeshifter – or claimed to be. In all likelihood, he appeared very different now than when Penny had first seen him. He looked nothing like Penny had described him at the very least. When Penny had seen him, he'd been impersonating one of the dead that frequently communicated with her. And as he stood before her now, he seemed very much flesh and blood – if a little... artificial around the eyes.

"You must have trouble doing eyes," Viv said aloud.

Change winced. "Could you tell?"

Viv nodded. "They aren't quite right." She thought about it for a moment. "They look less like eyes but more like someone's idea of what eyes should look like." She nodded at this, before adding, "They look like what someone would draw if they had never seen eyes, but someone described them in words."

Change shook his head sadly. "Eyes are harder to replicate than you'd think. I keep working on it, but I can never quite get it. I thought I had... I mean... they still looked janky to me. Like something was off about them, but I thought maybe I'd been looking at them too long, staring too deeply into the problem. That can happen, you know. You can focus on a problem so long that no solution will ever look adequate."

"Kind of like how you can say a word so many times it starts to sound like nonsense?" Viv asked.

Change nodded. "Semantic satiation. Exactly like semantic satiation."

"Showoff," Viv said.

Change raised an eyebrow.

"You've been holding on to that phrase forever, just looking for an opportunity to say it and look smart," Viv said.

"Really? I can change my form at will, and my vocabulary is what impresses you?" Change frowned, fidgeting.

"I'm not impressed with your vocabulary. You just think I should be," Viv said. "And anyway, you can't do eyes, so what does your form-taking prowess matter? Why would I be impressed with your shapeshifting when it's clearly second-rate?"

Change nodded solemnly. "You're right. I can't do eyes. I can't argue with that."

"Well, don't give up," Viv said. "It'd be worth your time to learn"

"You think so?"

She nodded. "The eyes are really important as a visual focal point. They're what makes a person look alive. If you can get those down, well, there's no stopping you then, is there?"

Change brightened at this thought. They both stood in silence for a few moments as he savored the idea.

"Are you here to threaten me?" Viv said suddenly, and as she did, even she was surprised at the venom that crept into her tone.

"Not at all," Change said. "But I can see your view of me is rather one-dimensional."

"You did threaten Penny," Viv said.

"No, I didn't threaten Penny. I warned her," Change corrected.

"I see that Mr. Semantic Satiation is a fan of semantics."

Change sighed. "Look, Viv, I had a job to do then. That's all it was, whatever you want to call it. And I have a different job to do now."

"And that is?"

"I'm here to help you," Change said.

"And how are you going to do that?" Viv challenged him.

"Like this," Change said, before snapping his fingers. He burst into flame. Viv noted that there was no heat emanating off this flame though, and while the flames licked all over his entire body, there was no attendant smell of burning flesh that one would expect.

Viv knew at once this was a visual effect in which he had spontaneously combusted and was being consumed by the flame. No more dangerous than a pyrotechnic display. It was a mere illusion, albeit a convincing one.

Change's body visually burned before her, immolating and reducing quickly to almost nothing in mere moments. After the flame finished with Change, there was nothing left but a pile of ashes.

Viv stepped forward to look into the ashes and see if something had been left there, a part of him that hadn't burned, or perhaps something he had been carrying on his person. As she bent over to examine the remains, a swift wind hit her – and *that* did feel real, slapping against her skin – causing ashes and cinders to fly up into her eyes.

The cinders smacked her painfully but fell to the ground. The ashes, however, were fine enough to partially stick.

Getting the particulate in her eyes smarted. She rubbed both pupils vigorously with her hands, trying to get the irritant grit out but only succeeded in blotting her eyes over in phosphenes. Each bright blotch partly overlapped another. The effect was like a luminous bingo card, one in which the owner was not only making bingo in multiple directions but close to securing a win under blackout rules.

Great, she thought. *I keep swinging back and forth from one blindness to another. From light to ash back to light.*

However, the phosphenes mercifully receded as her eyes teared up and washed out the ash, and she noted that the pile of debris on the ground before her had begun to stir. Feathers of fire jutted up from the ground. They grew like the stalk of a plant being viewed in time-lapse photography. Quickly after the wings were unearthed, up flew a bird made entirely of flame.

It hovered in mid-air, a bright mass of red, orange, and yellow. The bird looked like a sunset might if you got it good and angry.

"Okay, jackass," Viv snapped at the shimmering avian form towering over her. "I get it. You're the mighty phoenix. Well played." She looked for the telltale sign of the shapeshifter's strangely rendered eyes but found the bird's face was too bright to focus on any one detail long enough to discern that much nuance.

The phoenix flapped its mighty wings, causing another great wind. Viv found her eyes drawn to the wings, which were indeed roaring with long tendrils of flames.

The flames moved within themselves. She realized suddenly that they were acting as a kind of screen and that there was an entire motion picture underway in them, shimmering. A picture within a picture.

Rapt, Viv watched.

She could see the fires being set. There were two arsonists actually. A woman and a man. They turned towards the camera – towards her, and she could see their faces clearly.

And in that moment, she realized she'd met them before.

The great fiery bird cried out. It flapped its massive wings, causing another wind that moved ash towards Viv's face. She clamped her hands on both of her ears to block out the cry and shut her eyes to guard them against the flying ash.

When she opened her eyes again, the bird was gone. Amarynth was standing next to her with a concerned look on her face.

"Do you have medication? Something I should get you?" the Connections Agent asked her.

Viv shook her head slowly.

"You were here, but it was like you were... gone," Amarynth explained. "I know you have spells where you aren't quite right sometimes, but I wish you would have warned me what they were like. Or told me what to do beforehand."

"I can take care of myself," Viv replied gruffly.

Amarynth studied her face. "You know now," she said. "You know who set the fires."

"I do," Viv replied, "although I'm not sure how to find them." She screwed up her face. "But I know who would know...and that's enough. Before you ask, no camera crew. I want to do this part on our own."

"Wasn't going to ask," Amarynth said.

"Good," Viv replied. "C'mon."

A huge smile crept onto Amarynth's face. "Then we're almost done."

"Almost?" Viv asked.

"You'll see," Amarynth replied.

"I'm afraid something has gone terribly wrong," Augustus Cross said.

He was as stunned to see his daughter as she was to see him.

"I'm not doing it!" Karen screamed. "I'm not marrying my own fucking father."

The emotions that burst from her and her father were a sharp departure from the numbing tedium of the courses she'd taken at the Mentus Center.

"Of course not," Augustus said. "And when I find who is responsible for this mishap, they will certainly pay."

He cast a menacing gaze around the hotel room, which Karen could now see was virtually identical to the one she'd woken up in next door. Shabby. Nondescript.

"Wait," Karen said. "What are you doing marrying *anyone*? Did something happen to Celia?" Karen felt a wave of nausea bubble through her as she spoke her stepmother's name. She had never been a fan of the woman, not simply because she'd so abruptly stepped into Karen's mother's place the moment she had taken off, but also because she seemed less like a proper wife to her father and more like a devotee, a groupie.

The level of adulation her stepmother Celia showed Karen's father wasn't healthy. And it certainly didn't help to keep his massive ego in check, especially ever since he'd founded his cult. The Grounded Temple. The whole thing was a joke, especially the name – for there was nothing grounded about Augustus Cross.

"No, no, nothing happened to *Sissy*," her father said, emphasizing the ridiculous nickname he used for the woman. "*Sissy* is quite fine."

"Hello, Karen," a voice called from across the hotel room.

It was Celia. Sissy. Whatever.

Karen frowned and ignored her.

"So you're marrying women half your age now while your wife looks on," Karen summarized. "Great. You know, Dad, if you were trying to look like a creepy cult leader, I'd say you're doing an awfully good job."

"You're so small-minded sometimes, Karen," her father said. "So irrational."

"Irrational?" Karen said.

"Governed by your emotions. Your base instincts," her father replied. "Kind of remarkable since you graduated from the program. You went through all of it, but you never really *learned* now, did you?"

"Wait, the Mentus Center..." Karen said, not wanting to finish the sentence, already knowing what it meant.

"Yes, it's a training program for the Grounded Temple," Augustus finished. "We not only get a lot of new recruits, but we get ones who graduate ready to serve the Temple. We owe a lot to Dr. Mentus. I don't know where we'd be without him."

"Oh, I bet you gave him four wives or something."

"A dozen," her father said. "Most of them work at the center. Well, the ones who aren't busy making recruits the old-fashioned way."

Karen scowled. "Dad, all of that is so damn gross."

"You only say that because you're small-minded. Always swept away by your baser instincts. Your fear. If you could only become unencumbered, then you'd see things clearly. Then you'd understand," her father said.

Karen did a quick feels check. She felt only irritation coming from her father. Everyone else around them – Celia, the officiant, and a few witnesses – seemed amused, except...

Marilou. She was astonishingly unreadable. Which was sort of refreshing and puzzling all at once.

"Well, whatever the case, it's nice to have you back home," her father said.

"Nice for you maybe," Karen grumbled.

"I can see we have a lot of work *still* left to do on your attitude," her father said. "You've been a very expensive problem, Karen."

"Good," Karen replied.

"I have work to do, figuring out how this little mix-up happened and holding my people accountable. In the meantime, your stepmother will take you back to our home," Augustus said.

Our home? Karen thought. That was a rich thing to call a place she had never been, a place where she was expected to live with people she hadn't seen for years and who had never really accepted or respected her. Karen considered making a break for it, but sizing up all the individuals around her, she suspected she'd get rounded up and caught rather easily.

And besides, she was tired. She could use a meal, a good night's sleep, and a shower. She could always escape later.

Eventually, there would be an opportunity.

Karen moved towards Celia.

"No," her father said.

"You said to go with my stepmother," Karen replied.

"Not me, dearie. I'll be going with Gus," Celia said. "Your other stepmother."

"Hi," Marilou said.

Karen's eyes flared wide.

Viv knocked on the door with her full force.

"Careful, Viv, we're pursuing a lead, not leading a SWAT team into the premises," Amarynth said.

Viv shot her a dirty look.

"Are you sure you want to do this?" Amarynth asked her.

"Why wouldn't I?" Viv countered.

"Well, I could see if you wanted to let me do it or get a team together or something. With what happened with your mother on the last case, it would make sense if you weren't comfortable following up this lead," Amarynth said. She felt foolish as soon as she said it though. She knew that mentioning Viv's mother would do nothing to deter Viv and only anger her. Amarynth felt her muscles tense, dreading Viv's inevitable tongue lashing.

"Am," Viv said. "I get where you're coming from. But you should shut up."

Amarynth relaxed. It wasn't exactly a pleasant thing for Viv to say but not too bad, considering.

The door opened. Viv's sister Love stood there. She was wrapped in a silk bathrobe. Her hair was a little mussed, and while there was makeup on her face, it was clear by the smeared state of it that there was also makeup somewhere else. Love managed to look semi-presentable, even a little glamorous, but rough. "Viv? What in the world? You should have called."

"Who is it, darlin'?" a deep voice called from out of sight.

"Just a moment, sugar," Love called behind her. She swiveled back to Viv. "I have a gentleman caller at the moment. Maybe you could come back?"

"Love, why did you answer the damn door if you were shagging some guy?" Viv said.

"Well, you knocked so damn loud," Love said. "Anyway, I thought you were the delivery boy. We get quite the appetite worked up when we're having one of our... get-togethers."

Viv rolled her eyes.

"It's not my fault you have no social life," Love continued.

"We can come back," Amarynth said.

Love peeked around Viv and saw the Connections Agent. "Oh!" Love said, her eyes widening. "I didn't know *you* were here. Miss Watson. Oh my goodness. I am *so* sorry." Love physically pushed Viv out of the way to get a better line of sight on Amarynth.

Love batted her eyelashes. "Please come in and sit down in my parlor. I'll be just a moment..." She threw a glance back over her shoulder, before finishing, "...tying up some loose ends."

"Or cutting me loose is more like," the deep voice boomed from the distant room.

Love threw up her hands in the air. "Sound carries so terribly in this house. At least property values are good." With that, she skittered off to take care of her ongoing "business," leaving the door open behind her.

Viv and Amarynth stepped into the parlor. *It happened again*, Am noted. *Someone else trusting me to close a door.* What would polite society be without trust? She wondered. Or whatever kind of society that Love was emulating – because polite wasn't on the shortlist of how Amarynth would choose to describe Love.

"Well, hullo, ladies," the booming voice said as its owner stepped into the room. Of course. It was Alexander Baker, the ever-substantial party guest. And half-dressed, too.

Viv hung her head in disgust. Love really was set on replacing her mother, wasn't she? But Viv couldn't let that distract her. No, she had a job to do. She set aside her distaste that Mr. Baker was at her sister's house... paying a social call. Viv involuntarily shuddered at the thought, before steeling herself. It had thrown her off guard, as she knew that Love would be able to connect her to the Bakers, but she hadn't suspected her sister to be carousing in bed with one of the arsonists.

You could call it a lucky break if it weren't so unsettling. *Poor Liz*, Viv thought, before reminding herself that Mrs. Baker had also been involved. No doubt about it.

"Why did you and Liz set the fires, Mr. Baker?" Viv said.

Mr. Baker startled, flustered. "Why that's... I mean..."

"You're not going to lie to a couple of psychic detectives, are you, Mr. Baker?" Amarynth challenged him.

Mr. Baker sighed. "How did you know?"

"We're PsyOps. We know everything," Amarynth said, with resoluteness in her voice that Viv wasn't at all used to hearing coming from the normally dazed and frazzled Connections Agent.

Amarynth turned to Viv. "I've been waiting to say that for a while," she explained.

Viv rolled her eyes. "Everything will go a lot more smoothly if you come with us back to headquarters," she said to Mr. Baker. "I'm sure the State will show mercy, so long as you explain why you did it. I'm sure you had a good reason?"

It was a trap of course. But a lot of the time, traps actually worked, Viv found. Ignorance of the law was no defense – and it also gave the law an upper hand in situations like these. If Karen were here, she'd no doubt lecture Viv about this dishonest approach, but Karen wasn't here now, was she?

Alexander Baker shook his head. "No, ma'am, I am not going anywhere with you. Not without my lawyer."

Viv frowned. He was smarter than he seemed.

"Now if you'll excuse me," he continued, "I think I'll be calling him right about now." As he did, he walked towards Viv and Amarynth, causing them to take a step back. He repeated the process several times, effectively herding them towards the door.

"Does that mean we don't have time for a second round?" Love called from another room.

Viv scoffed. "Fair enough, Mr. Baker," she said, as she and Amarynth stepped outside onto the stoop. "Just keep in mind that there are other ways at the same information. And if it comes up pointing towards you, you're gonna wish you cooperated with PsyOps."

"I'm willing to take my chances," Mr. Baker replied, slamming the door in their faces.

"What now? Where to?" Viv said to Amarynth.

"The Baker Residence, of course," Amarynth said. She closed her eyes and spoke the address aloud.

"How do you do that?" Viv asked her.

"Do what?"

"How do you just come up with addresses out of nowhere? You can't explain anything important, but random addresses you have locked down," Viv said.

Amarynth shrugged. "I guess you could say," she ventured, "that I have Connections."

Viv groaned as they set off for their next destination.

"Wake up, Rhea. You, too, Kip. I don't like this game you're playing."

Penny did her best to open her eyes. She couldn't remember her eyelids ever feeling this heavy, but she managed.

It took a few moments to orient herself to her surroundings. Her eyeballs throbbed. The room swam. Everything was a haze.

But her eyeballs pulsed a few times, and as they did they worked optical magic, bringing the picture into focus in a way that reminded Penny of that precise point in science class when the slide under the microscope snaps into focus because you've managed to finally get the knobs adjusted into the correct figuration.

Beside her, Kip groaned and stirred.

A child stood before her, with her hands thrust defiantly on both hips. She had a beautiful, kind, and sunny face and long blond hair that shone under the fluorescent bulbs that studded the ceiling of the room they were in. There were no windows and only a single door that had a menacing sign that indicated it was electrified and that no one should even think about touching it. "Oh good, you're finally awake. I knew you had to be pretending to sleep. Next time add some fake snoring. It's more convincing that way."

Penny gazed at her in wonderment. "Dem?"

"Duh," Dem replied. "Who else would I be? A past version of you traveling through time to warn you about something? Get real, Rhea. Time only travels one way. How would you get home? Everyone knows you can't swim against the current."

"It's so good to see you, Dem," Penny said. And she meant it. After all these years of traveling from one place to another, of only sometimes being included and rarely accepted, it was a great relief to see her twin sister again. Being around Dem felt very much like being at home – even if planar time dilation had made them look different.

Perhaps Hell isn't my home, Penny thought. *Maybe my sister is.*

She noted that she hadn't felt this particular resonance when she stepped into the dwelling that was her childhood home. And while being around her parents had been pleasant enough, they didn't set her at ease the same way either.

The closest she'd gotten to this feeling was being around Kip. And even that was much lower in intensity than the calm that she felt wash over her.

"What are you looking at?" Dem said, snapping her from her thoughts.

"You," Penny admitted.

"Do I have a booger on my face?" Dem asked, swatting at her nostrils.

"No," Penny replied. "You're perfect." Because her sister was.

"You're acting weird, Rhea," Dem said. "What did they do to you on Earth?"

Penny shook her head. "Nothing. I did everything to myself."

"Alright," Dem said. "Suit yourself. Don't tell me."

Penny laughed. "Well, I'll tell you anything you want to know, but maybe we should get out of here first."

Kip groaned some more and rubbed his head.

"HEY SLEEPY HEAD!" Dem yelled straight into his face.

"Yes, Princess?" Kip grumbled.

"We're having an ops meeting here. Care to join us?" Dem said, this time not quite yelling but at a volume louder and in a sterner tone than was strictly necessary.

Kip opened his eyes and nodded weakly.

"Escaping's no big deal anyway," Dem said.

"Really?" Penny said. "If that's the case, then why are we locked in here?"

"Well, I'm not exactly sure why *you're* locked in here. Probably did something stupid, I'd imagine, like harassing the other victors," Dem began.

Penny bit her tongue.

"But I'm only locked in here because I want to be," Dem finished.

"What do you mean you're locked in here because you want to be?" Penny said.

"I was playing hide and seek, silly," Dem explained.

"Hide and seek?"

Dem nodded. "I went off and hid just like you."

"Just like me?"

"Geez, Rhea, do you need to clean out your ears or something? Yes, just like you. You ran off to Earth and hid, knowing that I couldn't follow you because I have to stay here and be ready to rule Hell whenever Dad bites the big one. Not cool by the way. It's cheating to leave the plane when you hide. You're a cheater."

Penny's mouth hung open wide. It never ceased to amaze her how easy it was for major miscommunications to occur. Our intentions were so obvious to us, weren't they? But other people had to guess at them. And they often guessed wrong, while never knowing just how far off the mark they were.

"Hey, you're not arguing, so I guess that's as good as admitting it. You're a cheater," Dem said.

Penny shook her head in disbelief.

"Anyway," Dem continued. "I figured if you were going to be a butthead and cheat that I'd just start a new game, one I actually had a chance of winning. So I got myself 'kidnapped' and decided I'd wait it out until you came and found me."

She drew dramatic air quotes with her fingers when she said "kidnapped."

"You got yourself kidnapped because you wanted me to come back and find you?" Penny said.

"Duh," Dem replied. "I swear, Rhea, sometimes you're such a little dumbass."

She reminds me so much of Viv, Penny thought idly. *Rough around the edges, cutting sometimes. But sweet, underneath it all.*

Then another thought hit her: *Is that why it was so easy to fall in love with Viv in the first place? Did she remind me of my twin?* It was an uncomfortable thought.

"Anyway," Dem continued, "it wasn't too hard so don't feel bad. I just waltzed up to Lord Farr, jumped on his foot a few times, and said he wasn't half the victor my daddy was, and presto change-o, they locked me up here. No big deal. I could probably get kidnapped again no problem."

Penny giggled. "I suppose you're right. The only question remains... how did we get un-kidnapped?"

"Oh, that's not too hard either," Dem said, proudly. "You really have forgotten a lot since you were on Earth, haven't you?"

"It certainly feels like that way," Penny admitted.

"Well, c'mon," Dem said. "I'll show you."

Dem led Penny and a groggy Kip to the back wall. As Dem pressed one of her tiny palms to the stones, they began to shimmer and then melt away, creating a small hole that straw yellow Monosolar light shone through.

Dem nodded at Penny. "C'mon, Rhea," she said. "It goes faster if you do it, too."

Penny cast a nervous glance back at Kip.

He nodded at her. "As I said before, little one, you have power here you could only dream of on Earth."

And though it felt surreal, Penny placed her hand next to Dem's on the stone wall. She closed her eyes and concentrated, feeling a mysterious heat course down her arm, out through her palm, and onto the stones. She smelled smoke and felt warmth but no pain, and finally, she felt nothing at all. She opened her eyes to find that together they had burned a sizable hole to the outside.

After the deed was done, Penny examined her hands and noted that they looked the same as before. They weren't on fire or burnt or red.

"See, you butthead? You were overthinking things. Again," Dem said.

Penny smiled at her twin sister, so small but technically older, at least here, the one plane where their age difference really mattered. She took her sister's tiny hand in her own and together they stepped through the hole they'd created and back outside into the open air of Hell.

Liz Baker lay prone on her belly, feeling very much like a lizard sunning on a rock on a hot day. She'd blended in with the wallpaper yet again at Love's party, eclipsed by the bigger personalities that had dominated the evening – her boisterous husband Alex, dramatic and scantily clad hostess Love Lee, Love's sister Viv the PsyOps agent, and that

Watson woman with the frizzy hair who was getting the hog's share of the attention.

"Liz, you stupid lizard. You're Betty. What were you doing trying to be Liz?"

The damn AC was out again, but she couldn't be bothered to call anyone about it.

After all, Alex should be fixing it. And he would be, if he were here actually participating in their marriage like he'd agreed he would, instead of gallivanting off... wherever.

He wasn't alone. That much Betty knew for sure.

She'd been feeling for years like she was trying to swim through rapids. Trying to make their marriage work on her own. Surely if she were just... different somehow... he would finally be satisfied with her. He would pay attention to her. Spend time with her.

As it was, she felt more than a little pathetic chasing him around, vying for his affection.

Still, all the magazines said the same thing: If she were a good wife, he would only have eyes for her. So there had to be something wrong with her. If only she could figure out what it was, then she could live the life she'd dreamt of so many times as a little girl.

Sometimes a thought crept into her head, treacherous and unbidden: Was the problem that he was a bad husband? Was he naturally a liar? Unfaithful?

She'd heard of other couples who had agreements – where they could both see other people and it didn't mean anything was wrong with their marriage. Betty had always thought an open marriage would be a difficult adjustment for her, but

after everything she'd been through with Alex, it wouldn't be
so bad.

But when she brought it up with him, he'd dismissed the idea
out of hand.

"Is it because you can't stand the thought of my seeing other
men?" she'd asked a little hopefully. She didn't have many
other indicators that Alex cared for her, so even a little
indirect validation via jealousy, no matter how maladaptive
that validation, would be a welcome change.

"Oh no, sugar," Alex had said, laughing. "No man's gonna
want you. It'll just depress you sitting home alone every night
while I'm out on the town."

But I'm doing that now, Betty had thought, feeling her throat
swell and tears well up in her eyes. She'd just nodded meekly.

To her, it seemed like the thrill of deceiving her was half the
draw for Alexander anyway. It was a major part of his kink.

I could have it a lot worse, Betty reminded herself regularly.
And she tried again now, stretched out prone on the bed,
sweating in the overheated house. But it wasn't working.

Everyone around her had such low standards for men
that it was impossible to distinguish between romantic
incompatibility and the normal cost of being with a man.
Was he a bad man, or was this all that men had to offer?

She'd heard it said that if you can't handle a few flames, then
you don't deserve to be warmed by another person's heat.
That was the price of being with someone special, wasn't it?
You might find yourself uncomfortable at times. Scorched
even, by their brilliance.

She'd thought he was special and that she was supposed to suffer for him. It was dawning on her more and more that she'd had it mixed up all along. She was the special one. And now she'd made a terrible mistake.

She was so depressed that she didn't even move when she heard someone coming into the house. *I must have left the back door open*, she thought. *Maybe I'll luck out and they'll murder me after they finish robbing me.*

She couldn't muster up a single iota of fear as she closed her eyes and waited for everything to end.

"My God it's hot in here," Viv said, as she and Amarynth stepped into the Baker Residence. They'd lucked out. The back door had been left unlocked.

"It often is," Amarynth had said when Viv had discovered they had a way inside and announced that the door was open.

Viv pondered asking Amarynth how she knew this but decided she didn't care. Maybe the Connections Agent was a cat burglar in her off-hours. One never knew.

Sure, Viv thought. *Amarynth lives a double life.* She giggled, as they walked through the kitchen into the main living area. Somehow, the thought struck her as funny. The Connections Agent lacked the finesse, the nuance, for that.

No, Viv thought, tripping over an expensive area rug in the Bakers' living room, *what you see is what you get with Amarynth.*

This is it, Amarynth was thinking. *This is where it all happens.* She had seen this series of events coming long in advance, and as it was playing out now, she was struck with a profound feeling of déjà vu.

"You must keep going, Am," the voice inside her head said.

"I know," Amarynth replied.

"Did you say something?" Viv called to her. She was bent over rifling through a hulking rolltop desk.

"Nothing important," Amarynth called back.

"It's time, Am," the voice inside her head said.

Nodding, Amarynth climbed the stairs. Viv plodded along behind her, nipping at her heels.

"Upstairs?" Viv said. "You think what we're looking for is upstairs?"

"No," Amarynth said. "I know it is."

As Amarynth walked by the front bedroom, she saw Betty Baker lying on the bed facedown. Betty's face was on a pillow that by the look of it had been stained by the woman's tears.

At first glance, Betty appeared so motionless, she could very well be dead, but at just that moment, she let out a deep sigh that shook her whole body.

"Hey Betty," Amarynth called to her.

"Go away," Betty said.

"I will," Amarynth said, "but first I'd like to search your back bedroom if that's okay."

"Do what you want," Betty said. "I'm done with everything. I'm done with it all. I'm just done."

"So to be crystal clear," Amarynth reiterated, "we have your permission to search the premises?"

"Yes," Betty said. She turned onto her side and curled up into the fetal position. Her face was so sweaty it had turned a pale pink.

"You get that?" Amarynth said to Viv. At times like these, it was normally quite handy to be accompanied by an eideticist, who could function as a living camera. None of this was going to be normal, but Amarynth felt compelled to act like it would be.

Viv tapped her head. "Every second. Sealed in here."

"Fantastic," Amarynth said, but her heart sank as she did.

They opened the door to the room at the end of the hallway.

The walls were covered with vibrant abstract murals. All of flame. Erotic figures could be seen throughout these flames, invariably curvy women, their heads bent back in ecstasy.

A large black leather bed was pushed against the back wall, sporting an excellent restraint system. An oversized dog cage was in a far corner. It was large enough to not only have enough room for a full-sized adult to stand up in it but also a small chemical toilet and two metal bowls. From the look of the cage, which hadn't been cleaned for quite some time, someone had lived there for a while.

"It's humiliating, isn't it?" a weak voice came from behind them.

Betty.

"Well, I don't know about that," Viv said. "Everyone's got their kinks. We don't judge."

Betty shook her head. "It's one thing if it's consensual. If it's something everyone is into. But if you're pushed..." She looked at her feet.

"You were trying to please him, weren't you?" Amarynth said, phrasing it as a question instead of a statement, trying to be gentle although she already knew the answer.

"I tried everything," Betty said, with a heaviness that indicated that what she said was true.

"You did the best you could, Betty," Amarynth said.

"The fires were part of it, you know," Betty said. "That was the only time he'd touch me. The only time he'd be with me. He'd get so worked up after we set them... he'd basically attack me, pinning me to the bed. He was rough then. It wasn't how I wanted it even then. But it was better than nothing. It was better than feeling invisible." She stopped, stared off in the distance. "I was ready to set the world on fire if it meant he'd actually see me."

"Why those buildings though?" Viv said.

"You're asking me if there was some significance?" Betty said.

Viv nodded. "It's all taken into account when it comes to your trial and sentencing. The State will want to know your motive."

Betty sighed. "It'll probably all come out anyway. I'm not proud of it... but... they were my friends."

"Your friends?" Amarynth said.

"Other women I'd met through the Temple," Betty said. "That's the Grounded Temple," she explained. "It's a church group."

"We're familiar," Viv said, glad that Karen wasn't there. She'd quickly correct Betty, tell her that the religion was a cult. And some things were better left unsaid, especially when they were well on their way to a full, detailed confession.

"I haven't been a member of the Temple long. It's not their fault. I'm nobody there, too. I just joined because I was lonely," Betty said. "I hoped I'd make friends, but now that's probably out of the question." She looked a little stricken at that last thought.

"Had the women you targeted wronged you? Had they slept with your husband?" Viv said, pressing onward for a motive.

"No," Betty said. "They were all women I admired."

"Then why did you set their businesses on fire?" Amarynth asked.

"Because I was jealous of them," Betty said.

Ah, there it was. Viv mentally checked off a box for the motive. *Jealousy.*

"Thank you, Mrs. Baker, we really appreciate your cooperation. It's stifling in here, and the State would love to get this firmly on the record, so if you wouldn't mind coming with us back to PsyOps, that would be wonderful," Viv said.

"We'd hate for you to get heatstroke in here," Amarynth added.

"Well, alright," Betty said. "I think that would be fine."

As they walked her down the stairs and toward the front door, Viv recommended an HVAC repair service.

"Our boss Martin has this brother, kind of a jack of all trades. His rates are crazy cheap. He could do it for you while we're talking to you, and by the time you get home, the house will be cool for you," Viv said to her mentally adding, *if you get to return home*, knowing that an arrest could be made at PsyOps and that Betty would likely be held awaiting trial.

It was one of those traps again, the duplicity that bothered her deeply, one that she sometimes had trouble maintaining, even though it was her job to do so.

"Oh, could you?" Betty said. "That would be great."

But as the three women exited the house, they ran headlong into Alexander Baker and his lawyer.

"And just where do you think you're taking my wife?" Mr. Baker huffed.

"To PsyOps of course," Viv said. "She's let us in on everything, Mr. Baker. Step aside."

"You're not taking my client's wife anywhere without me," Mr. Baker's lawyer interjected.

"You're not representing Mrs. Baker," Amarynth snapped back.

"But my client's interests and Mrs. Baker's are... intertwined," the lawyer argued. "I have a right to be involved in the process."

"Whatever," Viv said. "If you want to waste your time, knock yourself out. I'll drive extra slow so you can follow."

"Y-y-you're just going to PsyOps, aren't you?" the lawyer stammered.

"Sure," Viv said. "But I've known plenty of lawyers who couldn't find their way out of a paper bag. Not taking any chances with you."

The lawyer frowned as he ducked into his car with Mr. Baker in tow.

"The trouble with you," Marilou said to Karen, "is that you keep calling your father's religion a 'cult.'"

"Nothing wrong with telling it like it is," Karen shot back. She was slouching in her seat as Marilou drove them to her father's house, wherever it was. It occurred to Karen as they passed by unfamiliar surroundings that she had no clue where her father even lived these days.

Probably in some gauchely extravagant mansion financed by his followers. All this shit he spewed about being grounded... Pah. He probably was living the high life. Karen wouldn't put it past him.

"Yes, there is," Marilou said. "Calling it a cult is exactly the wrong thing you should be doing if you want to stop them."

"Them?" Karen replied. A curious word choice, not us but *them*. Marilou's emotional state gave it away even more. "Why, Mrs. Marilou Cross, I do believe you're a defector."

Marilou's lips blossomed into a smirking smile. "It isn't easy rigging a bunk assignment. The Mentus Center has their tech locked down pretty damn tight."

Karen laughed. "But you managed, didn't you?"

Marilou nodded. "Sorry about being so high-strung in the beginning. I'm not much of an actress. I tend to overshoot. Not on stage of course. On stage, I always get the opposite criticism... that I need to project more, make bigger facial expressions." She shook her head at the memory. "I think there are some of us who aren't built for any stage, not a theatrical one, not for movies, not even for real-life roles. We just don't get to be natural anywhere." She shrugged. "So I went for obnoxious roomie. It's a hard role to screw up."

"Where are we going?" Karen asked.

"North of Skinner," Marilou replied. "At the edge of the sprawl, right where the bus line picks up. I'd drive you back home, but I don't want to risk anyone in your neighborhood seeing me."

"You embarrassed to be hanging out with me or something?" Karen joked.

Marilou laughed. "No, you dumbass."

They both laughed together for a bit, in that peculiar way that people laugh when they've become close enough to insult one another and not take offense.

"Seriously though, I'm not done doing what I need to do. I'm going back in," Marilou continued.

"Wait, you're going to go and live with my father?"

"Yup," Marilou said.

"As his wife?"

"Yup."

Karen shuddered. "That's so gross."

"Well, he's got, like, 30 wives now so I should be okay," Marilou said. "I don't think I'll even have to spend the night with him if I play my cards right. I'll just blend in, get lost in the crowd. See what I can do about changing... the schedule... if I have to."

"There's a schedule?" Karen said.

"Yeah, it's super ridiculous," Marilou said. "Like something a teenage boy dreamt up. It's physical though, not electronic. He keeps a whiteboard outside of his bedroom. Names get put up, and the lucky wife gets to accompany him for a night of… whatever."

Karen shuddered.

"I know, I know," Marilou said. "I'm just glad the dumb shit uses dry erase markers."

"Why does that always happen?" Karen said.

"Why does what always happen?"

"Why do these arrogant assholes always leave such easy ways to screw them over? It would be so easy to lock something like that down tight. To come up with a system that's harder to mess with," Karen said.

"You just explained it," Marilou said.

"I did?"

Marilou nodded. "They're arrogant assholes. They don't safeguard against getting screwed with because they don't think anyone will try to mess with them." She put on her turn signal. "The crazy part is that a lot of times, they're right. It's really easy to get people to a place where they don't even think to fight back. Where they just assume it's impossible to win, so they don't even try."

"Where they just sit there, and no matter what happens to them, they don't react," Karen said. "Like Level 4."

"Precisely," Marilou responded. "My friend, I do believe we just spent the summer at Learned Helplessness Camp."

Karen laughed. "The craziest part is that the training actually worked. I feel better than I have in a very long time. My mind is so clear."

"Wow," Marilou said, "next thing I know you'll be doing a testimonial for the Floor 1 promotional video."

"Never." Karen scrunched up her nose at that thought. "So you never explained why," she said, "Not really, anyway. What's so bad about calling them a cult?"

"Ah," Marilou said. "That part's easy. It's us and them language. Ingroup and outgroup. Calling them a cult frames the whole issue in a way that actually makes it *easier* for them to recruit, not harder. Cultists are crazies. They've lost their minds – unlike the rest of polite society. But the thing is... while cultists do end up doing crazy things, they don't start out that way. Followers are normal people, usually people who are lost and looking for meaning in a life that has a shortage of it– which is hardly rare and hardly a crime, having an existential crisis. See, no one thinks they're capable of joining a cult. But they would admit they're capable of joining a church or a self-improvement program or whatever. And that's what they join. Not a cult. That's how it happens, how they get sucked in. People guard themselves against cults, but their barriers are down when it comes to other groups that are essentially the same thing, once you get past the marketing. Or at least could lead to the same thing once you're invested."

"So if we talk about cults, if we call them cults, we not only alienate the people in these groups and make it less likely that they'll break from the group – even if they have their doubts – but we're also preparing people to only guard against groups that are labeled a way that no group will ever be labeled," Karen summarized.

"Yes," Marilou said. "I guess it's not surprising that you understand me so well after everything we've been through."

"Not at all," Karen replied.

Marilou pulled up to the bus stop. "Do you know the bus routes home from here?" she asked Karen.

"Sorta," Karen replied. "I can figure it out anyway."

Marilou pressed several dollars' worth of bus fare into Karen's hand. "Until we meet again, my dear friend."

"And your stepdaughter," Karen said.

"Ugh," Marilou said. "Don't remind me."

Typology of Memory

Properly speaking, a person's eidetic memory is their short-term visual memory. Pretty much everyone, intuitive or normal, has some form of eidetic memory. It's what allows you to briefly see something in your mind's eye soon after you look away from the object or close your eyes.

Research has revealed that eidetic memory stems primarily from the posterior parietal cortex in the brain. In most people, the actual eidetic image is present only for a few seconds, at which point it dissipates completely and any relevant information is encoded into short-term memory. Sometimes nothing is encoded, and once the image fades, to our minds it is as though we never saw it.

In rare instances, even a normal might find that they have a particularly long-lasting eidetic memory effect. This is sometimes colloquially known as "having a photographic memory." Instead of the image dissipating quickly, they can recall it for a much longer period of time.

Pure photographic memory is exceedingly rare in non-intuitive populations. Even those with arguably photographic memories are subjected to more decay than we would associate with photographs, with the most persistent photographic memory-based images lasting perhaps a few months at most.

However, there are intuitives called eideticists who possess the power of pure photographic memory, gifted with eidetic memories that are perfect and never seem to fade. Indeed, some eideticists complain miserably of not being able to forget unpleasant experiences; the best they can do is simply move quickly past them as they are recalling other memories close to that period. The psychic population is still quite young yet, with the Psychic Phenomenon emerging only in the past three decades. However, as the first eideticists are aging, a common complaint is the length of time it takes them to pull up specific memories as their overall eidetic archive increases.

To date, no eideticist has simultaneously possessed expressive telepathic powers, so for the most part their photographic memories stay locked within them. However, with the aid of expressive and receptive telepaths and a skilled thoughtographer, it has become possible in recent years to retrieve memories archived within an eideticist.

Eideticists are relatively rare among the psychic population. However, thoughtographers are even far less common. As of this writing, there are only a handful of known thoughtographers. They largely work in the employ of the Psychic State, used for mnemonic subpoenas on high-profile cases.

There's some dispute among taxonomists about the classification of thoughtographers. Some prominent subject matter experts advocate that thoughtography belongs in its own category, however small their population might be. Others contend that thoughtography is essentially a specialized form of expressive telepathy, one that manifests the thoughts of others not in transmissible cognitive form but more concrete, tangible forms, most commonly on either still or moving film. At present, the State is working with its most skilled thoughtographer to attempt digital transmission, but efforts up until now have proven futile.

Naysayers of the digital thoughtography program state that it might be a bit too ambitious to move from abstraction to abstraction and that it would be best for society if thoughtographers just stick with what they're good at – etching visual memory upon physical forms. They argue that the greater good would be better served by utilizing every thoughtographer actively in the public interest rather than sacrificing any of them for experimental programs that are unnecessary and may never pan out.

Time will tell whether the State's gamble on digital will pay off.

What is for sure is that the number of eideticists and their ratio to the relative number of thoughtographers is quite reminiscent of the number of photo developing centers to the number of shutterbugs. Or, rather, the ratio as it was in the predigital age, when you had to bring in your film to have it developed commercially, unless you were a whiz with a functioning darkroom (something that was out of the reach of most amateur photographers).

This seeming dependency is quite an apt comparison, as eideticists are very much like the film negatives and camera and the thoughtographer very much like the developing process that turns them into photographs.

This balance has led some taxonomists to wonder if there's order among the chaos of emerging and/or newly discovered typology.

from Insecta Psychica: Towards an Intuitive Taxonomy by Cloche Macomber

"Are you ready, Detective Lee?" the thoughtographer said.

"Ready as I'll ever be," Viv replied.

"I never understood why people say that," the thoughtographer replied.

Viv frowned. "It's just something people say. It doesn't have to mean anything more than that."

"I suppose," the thoughtographer replied. "But it's kind of a sad thought if you really think about it."

"Good thing I don't," Viv clipped.

The thoughtographer sighed.

"Okay, okay," Viv said. "No need to pout about it. You have something you want to tell me. Might as well out with it. The session will last twice as long if you're distracted... and I'm already dreading how I'm going to feel afterward. The last time I did one of these procedures, I felt like I'd been run over for about three days. So spill it."

"Well, just think about it," the thoughtographer said.

Viv waited for her to finish.

"If that's really true, if this is as ready as you'll ever be, wouldn't that mean you've peaked? That you've reached your superlative level of readiness. It's a sad thought if you really focus on it," the thoughtographer explained.

"Well, I guess it kind of depends on what it is. Seems like it depends on what you're ready for. If it's something big and important to you, sure, I guess it's kind of sad to be at your peak, to not have anything to look forward to. But if it's routine..." Viv let her voice trail off.

"Like a thoughtography procedure," the thoughtographer offered.

"Like a thoughtography procedure," Viv confirmed. "If it's something relatively low stakes, well then who cares if you'll ever be more or less ready? Might as well just go for it."

The thoughtographer smiled. "That's a lovely thought."

Viv smiled back.

"I bet your thoughts are beautiful," the thoughtographer said.

"Only one way to find out," Viv replied, leaning back in the chair.

When Penny, Kip, and Dem arrived back at the Stygius Estate, they received a hero's welcome. Precisely one hero's welcome though, and seeing as though there were three of them, this was less than enough to go around.

Dem was promptly bathed and redressed. A party was scheduled to celebrate her homecoming. Harry Stygius gruffly badgered a tiny servant into sprinting all over the Ninth Circle bearing the invitations.

It wasn't that Penny had expected to be treated like a princess – although that was allegedly what she was. But she had expected more than to be virtually ignored while the household spun in frenzied circles around her sister's return.

Even Kip was taken aback by this turn of events. "I am not sure exactly what to do either, little one," he reassured her as they stood in the front room, listening to activity that did not involve them ripple throughout the house. He had expected to awkwardly wait – that was a large part of what any servant of the estate did, after all.

But it confused him as to why Harry and Stephanie had barely addressed Penny at all. They were too busy dealing with their eldest daughter, it seemed, to even notice their younger one. It didn't seem fair that she was expected to awkwardly wait as well.

"I'm beginning to understand why I left in the first place," Penny said.

Kip didn't respond.

After a while, Penny's feet began to ache from standing. "Let's go sit down," Penny said.

"I'm not supposed to do that without permission," Kip replied.

"Well, I'm a princess, aren't I? And I'm giving you permission," Penny replied.

Kip shrugged and followed her over to the soft chairs in the parlor. As they settled down, a servant – one of the kitchen staff, judging by her pristine white apron – clucked in disapproval and ran off to parts unseen.

"They'll be with us in a moment," Kip predicted.

Penny cocked her head. "Really?"

"Oh yes," Kip said. He leaned forward and smiled. "We've committed a *faux pas*."

"There are *faux pas* in Hell?" Penny said.

"Of course there are," Kip said. "How else would people find enough ways to look down on other people?"

Penny laughed.

"That's something I've always adored about you, little one," Kip said.

"What is?"

"That you can find the way that things are so funny," Kip replied.

"Well, if I don't laugh, I cry. And I look beastly when I cry."

"So do we all," Kip replied.

As predicted, Stephanie appeared in the parlor, a flurry of pastel-colored fabric. "Rhea! Did you need something?"

"I was just sitting in the living room of my own home," Penny replied.

Stephanie considered this and frowned. "Right," she said. "Well, there's a party to get ready for," she said. "You do remember where your old room is, don't you?"

Penny nodded. "I think so."

"There should be clothes in the closet. You can bathe in your bathroom," Stephanie said. "You mustn't dally. Dem's party is a very important affair."

More important than your youngest child's return from abroad apparently, Penny thought bitterly. "Yes, mother," she said aloud. She felt peculiar as she did it, as she feigned compliance while seething with resentment. Passive-aggression wasn't common in Hell. It was an Earthly custom, one that she'd become quite practiced at during her time away from home.

A normal Hellion would push back. Spar. Give her mother a piece of her mind.

Penny knew that from her old memories, which were seeding deeper into her consciousness with each passing minute.

But she didn't feel like fighting. There was something about the entire situation that was making her want to slink through it without putting up a fight. For it to be over as quickly as possible.

It was not very Hellish of her. But it was how she felt.

She climbed the stairs and walked down the hall to her old bedroom. Kip followed her up until the door.

"I'll be out here if you need anything, Princess," Kip said. He'd almost said "little one," as was his normal habit, but at the last moment, he thought he'd upgrade her title. She clearly needed it. As he lingered in the hall behind the closed door, he thought how strange it was that she didn't have any ladies-in-waiting in her bedroom with her, helping her prepare.

It was all a bit unsettling.

True, the Stygiuses had always understaffed their youngest daughter relative to her older sister Dem. They'd never made any show that the two sisters were equal and demonstrated clear favoritism to Dem in just about every way, which of course included the number of attendants they assigned her.

But this was a bit lopsided even for them. It was worse than things had been before Penny had left for Earth. What did it mean?

Penny opened the large wooden doors of her impossibly huge closet only to discover that while all the garments contained within were quite lovely indeed – they were all sized for a seven-year-old girl.

Ah, she thought. *Of course. I haven't been gone all that long to them, have I?*

"Kip!" she called.

"Yes, Princess," he said through the door.

"Come in. I need some help," Penny said.

Kip couldn't quite make out what she said, so he cracked the door an inch and called in, "May I come in?"

"Yes, please," Penny called back. "I'm decent."

Kip walked over to the open closet.

"Do you see a problem, Kip?" Penny said.

"Well, if you were looking for a scarf to wear to the party, then you're set," Kip joked.

"It's not funny!" Penny protested, before cracking up. "Well, I guess it kind of is."

"Not to worry," Kip replied. "I'm on top of things. Wait here."

He left the room and walked down a series of hallways until he reached the room in which the lady of the manor kept her overflow wardrobe, the outfits she hadn't worn for ages but couldn't bring herself to discard. After a cursory search, he selected a gown he thought would look lovely on Penny. It was simple perhaps – a cocktail dress with spaghetti straps. But the empire waist and A-line skirt would flatter Penny's curves – and the cascading teal and sapphire layers would make her look like the ocean when she moved. He remembered that. Stephanie had only worn it once herself before relegating it to overflow saying the watery effect was a bit whimsical for Hell, but she, too, had looked like the sea had grown legs and fled its bed for dry land.

He was sure Penny would look exquisite and precious... well, as precious as water in Hell.

He retrieved the garment and walked into the hallway, where he was spotted by another passing servant, this time a housekeeper. This housekeeper shook her head openly at him and hurried off.

Great, Kip thought. *Busted.*

And sure enough, as he approached the door to Penny's bed-chamber, he was intercepted by Stephanie.

"And just what do you think *you* are doing, Kipper Dante?" she snapped at him.

"I'm getting your daughter something to wear to her sister's party," Kip explained.

"That is *my* dress," Stephanie said.

"That you haven't worn in ages," Kip said.

"Kipper Dante, Rhea has plenty to wear in her closet," Stephanie said.

"Plenty for a *little girl* to wear," Kip said. "As you can plainly see, she's grown a lot since she left. Her clothes don't fit her anymore."

"Well," Stephanie said. "It seems like she should have thought about that before she ran off to a place like Earth, doesn't it?"

Kip wasn't sure what to say to that. The response stunned him.

Stephanie took full advantage of his silence. "You two put us in a terrible position, you know, when you helped Rhea run off. Do you know how *humiliating* it was for Harry to have his younger daughter abscond? And to such a seedy place like Earth? He had enough to deal with already. The other victors *already* gossiped about him before any of this happened. If it weren't for the Styx's approval of him, he would have lost his station ages ago."

They gossiped about you mostly, Kip thought but knew better than to say.

"We can't afford another scandal," Stephanie continued. "What in Hell am I supposed to do with a messed-up daughter who has been corrupted by Earth? Send her to a special school? Feed her to the beasts? She stinks like Earth. She's damaged. I certainly can't just put one of my dresses on her and send her to the party and act like any of this is normal."

"I don't see why not," Kip replied.

"Well, that's why you're a servant," Stephanie replied. "If you understood how things actually worked, maybe you would have made something of yourself in Hell by now. How long have you been here again?"

Kip didn't answer. He wasn't proud of the truth.

"Anyway, you can have that ugly bunch of rags if you want. But you're not bringing the family embarrassment to Dem's party," Stephanie said.

"Yes, ma'am," Kip said. "May I ask one question?"

"Fine," Stephanie said.

"Why did you call her home if you weren't going to welcome her when she got here?"

"She had a job to do," Stephanie replied. "And now that it's done, we'd rather she go away, frankly. It's just a matter of figuring out the best way to tell her so that she doesn't embarrass us any further."

"I see," Kip said, feeling quite sad indeed.

"Now, if you'll excuse me, I have to get ready for Dem's party," Stephanie said, before rushing away.

Kip froze in place as she disappeared. He didn't know how to explain any of this to Penny. It was an awful reality, one he was certain would hurt her.

He looked at the door, which was slightly ajar. Swinging it open, he realized he didn't have to tell her. Penny was sitting on the bed crying.

She had heard every word her mother said.

"I just want to say goodbye to Dem first," Penny said. "And then this family embarrassment is leaving."

"I know it's been a rough year," Martin said, "but I can tell you I never expected this."

"Expected what?" Viv prompted.

Amarynth knew, and so she kept quiet.

"This," Martin said. He set a VHS tape and a typed report onto his desk. Both the plastic brick and the sheaf of papers were labeled the same way.

> THOUGHTOGRAPHIC ANALYSIS. REPORTING EID – – LEE, VIV. BAKER ARREST.

"Read the report," Martin told Viv.

Viv frowned.

"Go on," he urged her.

Viv picked up the report. It was a summary of the accompanying videotape, as was the standard in all investigations of this type. The text wasn't terribly long – a little shy of three single-spaced pages and a covering title page, housed in a plastic protective covering.

Shorter than most college essay assignments, Viv noted grimly.

Viv flipped open the booklet and took quick mental photographs of each page, before handing it to Amarynth.

Amarynth already knew what it said but pretended to read it out of politeness while Viv closed her eyes and reviewed the content she'd glanced over.

"That's bullshit!" Viv exploded.

"Is it?" Martin said.

"That's not how it happened at all," Viv protested.

"That's what your memory says happened," Martin said, "so I'm a little confused why you're arguing with it."

Martin shook his head and looked out his office "window" at the artificial vista. Did the businessmen who worked in those palaces up in the sky have to deal with the things he did? Did they go home to unhappy wives who mocked them for associating with tueys?

The stigma was hard enough most days. The pay for a PsyOps supervisor wasn't terrible – far better than a psychic detective salary –but it wasn't great either, something his wife reminded him every time she saw one of their peers sporting something expensive on social media.

"I get it," Martin had said. "You have FOMO."

"FOMO?" his wife had replied.

"Fear of Missing Out," Martin had explained.

At that point, she'd shaken her head. "No, I don't have Fear of Missing Out. I *am* missing out."

It was not fear, she'd insisted, but frustration with what her husband's ideals were doing to their family.

Martin felt the same frustration course through him as he turned from his pseudo-skyline and studied Viv's face for signs of discernible deception. There were none.

"Viv," he said gently, "something's not right. I don't know why you'd lie to me. I've never suspected that any of you lied to me before, but this is not making sense."

"Well, let's make it make sense," Viv said, an edge of desperation entering her voice.

Martin shrugged. "Have it your way. Hit that light, will ya?" he said, gesturing at Amarynth, who flicked the switch, darkening the office. He picked up the tape and slid it into a compartment in his desk. He pressed a few buttons, and a raggedy screen unfolded itself on the back wall of the office. A light shone, projecting the images from the tape.

It reminded Viv of the rickety elementary school contraptions of her youth. The quality of the video was poor, marred with black flecks and the occasional phantom line. But the scene in question played out and was quite visible.

Up to a certain point, everything was as it had really played out. Viv and Amarynth entered the Baker residence and performed a cursory search of the first floor before Amarynth had decided to go upstairs, with Viv following her.

But on this tape – as the report also indicated – Amarynth spotted Betty Baker lying in the first bedroom but did not stop to ask her permission to check the back bedroom. The confession was also absent.

In this version of events, Amarynth was visible noting *something* in the front bedroom, almost certainly Betty, and then Amarynth searched the back room without anyone's permission and Amarynth arrested Betty on the spot without speaking to her or reading her rights.

In this version, Viv was passive. Less of a detective and more of a camera.

"But this is bullshit!" Viv cried. "Amarynth *did* ask Betty. Mrs. Baker gave us permission to search. She confessed." Viv shook her head in frustration. "And we didn't arrest her. She came willingly with us to the station."

"It's okay, Viv," Amarynth said. "You don't have to protect me."

Viv spun around, blinking at Amarynth in disbelief. "Protect you? Why would I do that? I don't even *like* you. I'm just telling Martin what happened."

"Whatever you need to do, Martin, I understand," Amarynth said.

"This is crazy," Viv said, storming out of the office.

Martin stopped the tape. The screen retracted.

Amarynth sighed, flicking the light switch, flooding the room with fluorescent light. It had all come to pass. She would accept the blame for the discrepancy between the thoughtography report and what had actually happened. Was it the truth? Of course not. But it was a better route than the alternative: Telling the truth.

If anyone knew what had really happened, why the thoughtography audit didn't match what they'd initially told Martin, Viv's career would be over. What use did

PsyOps have for an eideticist whose memory engrams were corrupted? Even if it were only a temporary condition secondary to medication changes – as this incident was – it would cast such doubt on Viv's one special career skill that she would be of little use to the State.

It wasn't something that anyone talked about openly, but psychics had been fired – and sometimes disposed of – for less.

It had been an easy choice for Amarynth to make, to take the blame.

And as Amarynth stood there waiting for Martin's reaction, she hoped he would be evenhanded with her. He usually was, but past actions were no guarantee for future behavior. And as clearly as she saw the moment she was currently living through, what came next was shrouded in mystery.

"I can't believe it, Am," Martin said.

"I'm sorry," Amarynth said, hanging her head. Even though she was being dishonest, it was a genuine apology, albeit for something else. She did feel remorse at that moment, for lying to Martin, even though it was the right thing to do. She needed to protect Viv.

 "No," Martin said. "That's not what I meant. I literally can't believe it. I can't believe you'd do something like that."

Amarynth shrugged. She had never been a good liar – and certainly not a comfortable one. Her head was spinning with the amount she'd already done. She'd far exceeded her limit.

Martin sighed. "You're suspended," he said. "Pending further notice."

Amarynth nodded. "A fair punishment," she said.

"Without pay," Martin added.

"I understand," Amarynth said. She felt a silent relief that she wasn't dependent on her PsyOps salary the way her coworkers were. A silent relief that, yes, she was secretly one of *those* Watsons. It made the punishment far more manageable.

"Geez, Am, aren't you going to put up more of a fight?" Martin pushed her.

"Would it make any difference?" Amarynth asked.

Martin thought about this. "No. You've really screwed up this time. Even without the legal complications of what you've done, I'll be lucky to not have the president on my ass. I'm still not sure what I'm going to tell Regina Withers, how I'm going to explain that even though her crew followed you around all this time, they've ended up with so little footage." He shook his head. "It's a mess."

"What's going to happen to the team?" Amarynth asked.

"The team? You mean when they stop running around everywhere and actually report back to work?" Martin said.

Amarynth nodded.

"I guess we'll see," Martin said. "It all depends."

"On?"

"Geez, you're prying awfully hard for someone who was just suspended," Martin said.

"I care about them," Amarynth admitted.

"Wow," Martin said.

"What?"

"After the way they've treated you. Especially Viv..." He looked out his "window."

Amarynth shrugged. "I care about them," she repeated.

"If Viv can manage to finish this case on her own, then I'll think about reinstating the team. Without you, of course. But it all depends on what Viv does. And if Karen and Penny ever return from vacation," Martin said.

"Thank you, Martin," Amarynth said. "You know how to reach me." She left his office.

Martin rose after she was gone, pressing his palms on his desk. "I don't think anyone really knows how to reach you, Amarynth."

"I'm going on another trip," Penny said to her tiny older sister. "But it's not hide-and-seek. I'm not leaving so that you'll come to find me. I just have to go."

"Will you come back?" Dem said.

"I hope so," Penny said. "Maybe."

"Why maybe?"

Penny struggled not to cry. The last thing she wanted to do was break down in front of her sister. It wasn't the way Penny wanted Dem to remember her, as a sobbing mess with a red face, as a woman who had been rejected and was fleeing the plane with her proverbial tail between her legs.

No, she wanted Dem to think of her twin sister as an adventurer.

"Well," Penny said. "Mom thinks that Earth changed me, and maybe it has."

"Changed you so much that you can't live here in Hell with me anymore?" Dem asked.

Penny nodded. "I'll be honest with you. I'm not sure when I'll be able to come back. But life is long – especially here in Hell – so I don't want to say never."

"But it could be never?" Dem prompted.

Penny hesitated. She nodded. "It could be."

Dem considered this, as her ladies-in-waiting powdered her tiny face and stuck an array of bows into her coiffed blonde hair. "I understand," she said finally.

"I will come back if I can," Penny said.

"I know," Dem said. "I know you better than you give me credit for, butthead."

Penny smiled.

"I think Mom is wrong by the way," Dem continued. "But you know how she is."

Penny nodded. "I do."

"Always so worried about other people being embarrassing when she's really the embarrassing one," Dem said.

One of her ladies-in-waiting gasped.

"What?" Dem said to the servant. "I'm the future ruler of Hell. There's no sense messing around pretending to be something I'm not."

"That's my department," Penny said sadly.

"Hey," Dem said. "You're being a butthead again. You can't pretend to be something you're not. It's actually impossible."

"Oh yeah?"

"Yeah," Dem said. "You're a little bit of everything, Rhea. So you're never really faking. You're just bringing out a different side of yourself, that's all."

Penny felt a smile creep onto her face.

"You're still a butthead though," Dem continued. They both laughed.

Neither of them said goodbye, which made it the best kind of parting. Penny had always preferred those kinds of goodbye conversations, she thought as she and Kip walked back to the Styx to find Charon the ferryman. She had always preferred goodbyes where the word was never said but instead implied. Those conversations also seemed to include a lot of other unspoken understandings, which pointed at an intimacy that could easily endure partings and reunions, as many times as they happened.

It made leaving so much easier knowing that you shared a lot with someone else that would last even when you were apart.

"Rhea Stygius!" Charon cried out as Penny and Kip approached his craft.

"In the flesh," Penny said.

"In the rapturous flesh, you mean," Charon replied.

Penny blushed uncomfortably at this unnecessary upgrade. "Um..."

"I-I-I mean... you look lovely, Princess," Charon tried again. "You really do."

"Just like my mother, people say," Penny said. This time the idea gave her a small pit in her stomach. It was tough knowing that she so closely physically resembled the woman who had rejected her. When she had thought she was an orphan, she hadn't quite understood Viv's plight regarding her strained relationship with her own mother. Nor had she quite grasped the complex feelings that Karen must have about the mother who drove off one day and abandoned her family. Karen rarely spoke of it of course – and never at any length – but Penny could always tell it hurt her.

She imagined it felt a lot like this new pain, the pain of being rejected by the woman who had given you life and whose biology you shared.

"Nah," Charon said. "You don't look like Stephanie Stygius at all. You're way prettier. There's something... braver about you." He stopped and searched for a word. "Feistier! That's it."

And though Penny knew it was probably just another come-on, she smiled anyway. It did feel good to hear. "Thanks, Charon."

"Don't mention it," he said. "No, literally don't mention it. Don't want to be getting in trouble with Lord Stygius, y'know."

"I won't," Penny said. "Actually, I was thinking of leaving Hell for a while. That's why I'm here."

"Ah," Charon said. "Plane-hopping again, are we?"

Penny nodded. "With any luck."

"Well, luck doesn't pay your passage, Rhea," Charon said. "You know how it is. Penny for your thoughts, a dollar for your memories. You rode free once, and that was only because of the hard bargain your friend Kip drove. I'm not cutting you the same deal this time."

"A bargain?" Penny said. "What bargain?" she asked Kip.

Kip sighed. "Leaving me here as collateral. Owing Charon here a big favor, a favor of his choosing."

"It's true," Charon said. "You still owe me one, Kip."

"I haven't forgotten," Kip replied.

"Are you sure we can't strike another deal?" Penny said. "Are you sure there's nothing you want?"

Charon studied her. He moved his eyes slowly up and down her body. "Oh, there's a lot that I want, little lady. I can tell you that. I'm just sure it's nothing you're willing to give me. And there would be half of Hell to pay if I took it without your say-so."

The ferryman clearly wanted her. The last thing she wanted to do was bed down with him, but maybe she didn't have to, Penny thought. This was her chance. She saw another angle, a way to gain passage without bedding him.

"Okay," Penny said. "I think I have an idea. Something that will work for both of us, so we can both get what we want – and *need*." She trailed her pointer finger down the midline of his chest. Penny hated to give him false hope, but she figured that the negotiation would go much more smoothly if he were a little distracted by the possibilities.

Charon shivered with pleasure.

"I know you want me in a carnal way," she said.

"I do," Charon admitted.

"I'll do you one better," Penny said.

"Oh?"

"If you grant me passage back to Earth, I will not only mate with you when I return to Hell, but I will marry you when I get back here. I will be your bride," Penny said.

Charon's eyes widened.

"Is it a deal?" Penny said.

"That's... amazing. That would be wonderful," Charon said. He studied Penny's body even more overtly, gazed at her beautiful face. His thoughts began to float away to what a royal marriage could mean for him. He'd be a victor himself, wouldn't he then? Lowly Charles Huron, Hell's lonely transit worker, His Royal Highness. Married to a Princess of Hell.

Talk about upward mobility! A rarity in Hell, to be sure.

"I said, is it a deal?" Penny asked.

"Of course it's a deal," Charon said. "And it's an amazing deal." He caught himself in his whimsy before he went completely mad with the idea, and he continued, "Of course there will be provisions, stipulations."

Penny bristled. "Of course," she said, feeling rather suspicious.

"I will need your hair," Charon said.

"My hair?" Penny said. "Why my hair?"

"A number of reasons," Charon said. "Some of them sentimental, I admit. But practically speaking, it will allow me to make sure it's you when you return. It may sound odd, but Earth has a way of changing a person, and I want to make sure I recognize you."

"And that I can't return without you knowing," Penny added.

"Sure, if you want to put it that way," Charon replied.

"There are also charms that you could summon with her hair," Kip offered. "Rituals that involve the subject's hair."

"Yeah, that's true, too," Charon said. "That's not why I'm taking your hair, but that's true."

"What kinds of rituals?" Penny asked.

"All sorts," Charon said. "Although you generally have to be here in Hell for me to perform them."

"Seduction rituals, blessings, and curses," Kip said. "If you give Charon your hair, you're basically giving him power over you."

"But only on this plane," Charon said. "I can't, say, call you back here to Hell with your hair."

Penny frowned. It seemed a steep price to pay, but what choice did she really have? She wasn't exactly welcome here. If she never returned to Hell, it hardly mattered what Charon could do to her later. "Fine," she said. "Done."

Charon grinned. He pulled a pair of long scissors out of a small box on his boat that Penny had previously assumed was a first aid kit and snipped Penny's hair. It wasn't a good pixie cut, by any means, but when he was done, her hair was certainly a lot shorter. He caught the cut hair in his hands before it fell to the ground and twisted it into a coil that he then tucked back into the same box he'd retrieved the scissors from.

"And the other thing I will ask will be the same as before, a living deposit," Charon continued.

"Kip as your hostage?" Penny said. She turned to face Kip.

"You really have a way of making everything sound terrible," Charon replied. "When you're my wife, we'll have to do something about that." He giggled to himself at the thought.

"Kip, I can't make this bargain. I can't leave you chained here again," Penny said.

"I don't see why not, little one," Kip replied.

"Because it's your sacrifice he's asking for, not mine!" Penny cried.

Kip nodded. "Perhaps," he said, "but it's one that I'll gladly make for you."

Penny shook her head. "It's too much. It's too selfish."

"Little one," Kip said, "I have never known you to be selfish. Brave, yes. Impulsive, yes. Perhaps a bit reckless. But selfish? Never."

"Well, what do you call a person who leaves their friend imprisoned so they can go off and live their life?" Penny asked.

Kip smiled.

"What?" Penny said.

"We had this conversation the first time, too."

"We did?" Penny said.

Kip nodded. "Although you called me more names the first time. You're considerably gentler this time around. Less crass. I much prefer it."

"How did we resolve things the first time?" Penny asked.

"The way I'm about to resolve them now," Kip replied. He turned to Charon. "Charles Huron," he said to the ferryman, "you have yourself a deal."

At that moment, the chains appeared. "Away with you," Charon commanded. Kip nodded and turned to walk to the burning tree.

"You know where to find me, little one," Kip called back over his shoulder.

"Yeah, yeah, yeah, bon voyage and all that crap," Charon summarized. "C'mon, Rhea, we'll get you back to Earth."

Sighing, Penny climbed onto his boat.

"Nice of you to show up," Martin said.

"Whatever. Don't make a big deal," Viv grumbled.

Martin studied her. "You're very lucky we've built up a working relationship. And you're very lucky that you have that to fall back on."

Martin paused for effect.

"And you're very lucky that Betty Baker is digging her own grave legally," he finished.

"Oh?" Viv said.

"They've had to transfer her. She's been setting small fires at the jail," Martin explained.

"Setting fires at the jail? How is she managing to do that? Is she slipping through the bars?" Viv asked. "She's a tiny woman, but that's still pretty impressive."

Martin looked at her quizzically. "I thought you knew."

"Knew what?" Viv said.

"Betty Baker is an intuitive. A pyrokineticist. "

Pyrokinesis

Before the rise of the Psychic Phenomenon, there were many anecdotal reports of pyrokinetic events. In some of these incidents, individuals were reported to have spontaneously combusted. Other reports emerged as well of objects set aflame by individuals after those in question gazed at those objects intensely. However, these reports were largely presumed to be hoaxes.

To date, conclusive evidence that pyrokinesis exists as a reliable phenomenon has been extremely lacking.

In the past few decades, a small number of cases have emerged, however, that seem to fit the theoretical profile. The reader is cautioned that what follows is in the realm of speculative taxonomy, lacking the requisite rigor our agency strives to enact.

As we have begun to come up with varied methods of testing for the presence of psychic powers, we have unearthed incidents that cannot be explained any other way.

It should be noted that the difficulty of scientifically operationalizing what precisely it means to be "psychic" has confounded intuitive taxonomy's efforts to catalog the range of intuitive behavior and potential.

The current running explanation is that psychic powers stem from quanta. But in what field? That's the question other scientists – primarily physicists – are hard at work answering. Without going too far afield of this volume's mission, the intuitive phenomenon is linked to an unclassified field or a combination of fields that are beyond the current Standard Model. This has caused a great stir in the scientific community with the first potential "new physics" in many decades.

The initial experiments to track down a physical explanation for the Psychic Phenomenon did in fact discover electromagnetic effects. That was originally thought to be the extent of the disturbance. However, when future study tried to replicate such effects by producing electromagnetic patterns similar to the ones that had been detected, nothing happened. Therefore they concluded such EM effects were likely the fallout of the true disturbance, one beyond our current abilities to detect.

"In other words," one lead scientist told this author off the record, "we found the ashes and thought we'd found the fire."

These psychic "ashes" are posited to result from the decay of a theoretical particle dubbed a "psyon."

While the resultant decay patterns are not proof-positive of psychic activity, they are quite intimately correlated with it – to the point where any sensible theoretician would have trouble ignoring it.

In lay practice, detection of these decay effects is dubbed psyon detection (despite the inability of direct detection). Current detection ability is often imprecise but good enough to confirm the presence of intuitives or psychic activity in situations where suspected practitioners are noncompliant with more routine testing, such as the Comprehensive Perceptive Battery or any of the specialist modules that have arisen from the hard work of taxonomists and psychometricians.

Since the implementation of this practice, several pyrokinetic events have been investigated, and in more than half of the cases, psyon byproducts were found, suggesting that there may very well be something to this notion that certain individuals possess the ability to excite atoms to the point at which they burst into flame simply by focusing their attention in the desired direction.

We look forward to further research in this area and endeavor to understand the pyrokinetic phenomenon on an even deeper level going forward, aided appreciably by the efforts of the Black Square Program.

Although controversial, Black Square's ability to circumvent ethical protections offers a level of analytical expediency that evades most modern research inquiries, especially those that directly involve human beings.

*from Insecta Psychica: Towards an Intuitive
Taxonomy by Cloche Macomber*

"She's refusing to take a Comprehensive Perceptive Battery. Well, to be more precise, she set the testing materials on fire. But they've managed to confirm it anyway. They brought in the psyon testers. The ashes were rife with psyons. It's not the best evidence we could have for proving that she's an intuitive in court, but coupled with the video we have of her staring at things and those same objects catching on fire a few moments later... well, it's a pretty good case."

"So she'll be put directly into the Black Square Program then?" Viv asked. That was what they did with the most dangerous psychic citizens, the ones whose powers were considered an imminent threat to society. Black Square status was an intuitive's worst nightmare. It meant permanent imprisonment and typically being subjected indefinitely to dampening fields that suppressed psychic powers, a process that often involved great discomfort at the levels the psychic detainment centers used.

"Yes," Martin said. "Without a doubt, she's Black Square now."

Viv felt a tightness in her chest. Betty Baker had probably been hiding her powers for years, doing her best to escape detection by the Psychic State, and now because of a man who didn't deserve her, she was going down.

Maybe that was the other reason it seemed like she was trying so hard to be invisible, Viv thought. *Maybe it wasn't just because of that husband of hers.*

"What's going to happen to Mr. Baker?" Viv asked.

Martin shrugged. "I guess we'll see at trial. If that hotshot lawyer has anything to say about it, they're going to pin everything on Betty." He shook his head slowly. "With the right jury, he might have a shot. The man was married to a closet pyrokineticist all these years. With the right spin…"

"And enough psychophobia," Viv offered.

Martin winced. "I hate to admit it, but you're probably right. Anti-psychic sentiment isn't going to help the State put him away."

"Well, so long as they try," Viv said.

Martin winced again.

"What?" Viv said.

"Hm?" Martin said.

"You made a face," Viv said.

"Jesus," Martin said, "have you been taking lessons from Karen or something? Doing a home correspondence course in empathy?"

"Stop trying to change the subject, Martin," Viv said. "Out with it. I know there's something you're not telling me."

He sighed. "Well, there's a lot of pressure coming from the big guns to make a deal with Mr. Baker. We'll see what happens, but there's a good chance that this never makes it to trial. That he ends up doing probation or something."

Viv's irises turned a swirling combination of sunset colors. "That's bullshit," she said. "That bastard deserves to burn."

"You won't get any argument from me," Martin said. "The way the law shakes out isn't always fair though."

"Color me naïve," Viv snapped, "but I sorta assumed that justice was supposed to be just."

"You're many things, Detective Lee," Martin said, "but naïve isn't one of them."

Viv smiled at this.

"Go home and get some rest," Martin told her. "You've been working hard. Even though this turned into a bit of a shitshow, you did your best. And even if the State doesn't really get it, well... I do. I get it. I'm going to see what I can do to keep the team together."

"Thanks, Martin," Viv said.

"The minute Penny and Karen get back, you give me a call, okay? With Amarynth out of commission, our hands are really tied. You're a good detective, but I can't exactly send you out there without backup," Martin said.

Especially because we don't arm our agents properly, a tiny voice crept into his head. It was something Martin had been fighting for, among his peers. It was ridiculous that PsyOps sent intuitives out without any sort of physical protection. The normal detectives who worked for Skinner PD all had guns, billy clubs, and tasers.

But every time Martin had tried to bring it up, the fact that they should be arming their psychic agents, he'd been laughed at by the other supervisors and their department heads. Intuitive labor was cheap and plentiful. Psychics were a dime a dozen. Guns, now *they* were a commodity.

Better to risk the life of a tuey – which to his peers couldn't be put to a more productive purpose than preserving law and order – than to sink a bunch of unnecessary funds into protective equipment that was more valuable than the lives it was protecting.

The conflict really bothered Martin. The callousness of his peers wasn't something he felt he could convey well to the team – although he suspected they already knew on some level, having been subjected to microaggressions constantly since the day they'd received their psychic designations. He disagreed totally with this outlook, with viewing intuitive life as next to worthless, but what could he do?

He was just one man, who was struggling to survive himself. He had people to answer to, he told himself. His hands were tied.

Viv grinned. "Thank you, Martin. I will keep in touch," she said, before half-skipping out the door.

After she left, he felt very tired... and guilty?

The guilt was a curious sensation and one that surprised him. It was true that he couldn't do everything he wanted to for his PsyOps agents. That he felt wrong sending them out with less protection than normal detectives. And their salary was a joke.

But he always did his best. He was always fighting for his team.

He spent his energies focusing on the things he could affect. He'd worked very hard to get them a work vehicle. True, it was a hunk of junk, but Viv appreciated the effort and clearly adored the ole beater. He also noted with great pride he was going to bat for them once again. He was going to get Viv and the rest of the team reinstated... even though half of them were off who knew where, and the fourth was on involuntary suspension.

It was more than his peers would do. Martin knew that for damn sure. His peers would have them thrown off the team, thrown them to the wolves. And then they'd replace them with fresh psychics picked from the new crop. Just more fodder for the fire, easily consumed by the State. His peers wouldn't even give it a second thought.

So why did he feel guilty then? It didn't make sense. His conscience nagged at him, even so.

Maybe, Martin thought, it would be better to be all good or all bad. Or even just convinced you were. This business of knowing you were somewhere in between really irked him.

Sailing across the Styx had a hypnotic effect, Penny observed. It had never seemed that wide when she stared at it from the inner edge. It had always seemed like a quick journey to the other side, to where Hell the city ended and Hell the outer plane began.

But now that she was actually a passenger, it seemed to be taking forever. The sky graduated to a dim orange as the second sun, Disol, began to rise.

At this rate, we'll be stranded out here on the water when the beasts start raging. Penny found herself wondering if there were beasts that would come from below in the Styx, too. Angry sea monsters that would capsize the boat.

That would be just the way life worked sometimes, wouldn't it? She'd be sitting here with this ugly ass haircut, stuck on a tiny boat with someone who couldn't wait to wife her up, miserable enough – and then a freaking leviathan would pop up, and she'd get pulled to the depths and drown.

She knew sulking didn't make things any better, but she couldn't help herself. It was hard to muster up an "attitude of gratitude" given the situation she was in.

She was thinking of sea monsters when her eyelids began to feel heavy, and sleep took her. But in her dreams, it was not a leviathan that met her – but another serpent. It was a ball python coiled agreeably next to a clutch of eggs.

"It's rather extraordinary," a phantom voice commented. "She hasn't had any contact with a male member of the species for over 15 years, and she's done it. She's reproduced."

"Is this unusual?" another unidentified voice asked.

Penny tried to turn towards the dream voices and look at them, but she couldn't tear her eyes away from the clutch.

The python's eyes met hers. *Do not look away from the children*, it hissed. *We must protect them. No matter what happens, you must protect the children.*

"A little," the first voice said. "Parthenogenesis has been seen in other pythons before, but it's not exactly common. And it's usually the larger species, like the reticulated python. Ball pythons usually don't live this long either."

"So you're saying," the second voice replied, "that this is the zoo version of a miracle."

"Hey, you're the one saying it, not me, buddy," the first voice replied. "But I'm thinking we better call the press about this anyway."

Don't look away from the children, the python hissed again. *No matter what happens, protect the children.*

At that moment, Penny woke from the dream to find herself back on the bed that she had laid on previously in the

Warrens of Persephone. There was no sign of Gretchen, although the spot next to her was rumpled in a way that suggested that the memory eater had been there not too long ago.

As Penny rose from the bed, Gretchen appeared, confirming her suspicions. "Ah, you're back." Gretchen stopped in place, studying Penny's face. "And you're... glowing!"

"What?" Penny said, feeling uncomfortable.

"You look different," Gretchen replied. "Oh my God, I know what it is," she said. "Rhea Stygius, you're pregnant!"

"Holy crap, Gretchen, what the Hell is wrong with you?" Penny said.

"Oh?" Gretchen said. "I'm sorry... I just... oh dear. I didn't mean any offense. I'm not saying you're fat or anything."

"You're not making it any better," Penny warned.

"Forget I said anything," Gretchen said.

"Thank you," Penny replied. But as she said it, she knew that she wouldn't be able to forget.

"So how was Hell anyway?" Gretchen asked.

"It was... okay," Penny said.

"Such a wordsmith," Gretchen replied.

"Look, I'm exhausted. I've been gone for... how long have I been gone for?"

"A month," Gretchen said.

"I've been gone for a month. I've gone to Hell and back... literally. The last thing I want to do right now is to have a session about how I spent my summer vacation. Especially not with you," Penny said.

"Fine," Gretchen said. "Completely fair. I'll see you out."

They walked to the front door in silence. As Penny moved to leave, Gretchen said, "Just remember, Rhea, if you need me, you know where to find me."

"I'm sure I won't!" Penny shot back, stomping away.

Gretchen closed the door. "I wouldn't be so sure about that," she said.

Penny was relieved to find that her key still worked in the lock of the little house on Bell. Still, she had to fiddle with her key a bit more than normal, flustered by everything she'd been through in the last few weeks, and a sleepy Viv met her at the door, spurred down there by all the commotion.

"What the Hell did you do to your hair?" Viv said.

"I love you, too," Penny shot back.

"I mean… it's not so bad," Viv said. "It's just a little uneven."

"I felt like a change," Penny replied.

"Clearly," Viv said.

Penny frowned.

"Hey, don't be like that," Viv said.

"Like what?"

"Don't be hard. Don't be unforgiving. That's not you. And that's not us," Viv said.

And just like that, Penny did feel something within her appreciably soften. Viv could be brash herself, but she really did have a way of coaxing out her softness. Still, Penny wasn't quite sure what to say, so she said nothing.

Finally, Viv said, "Did you find what you were looking for?"

Penny nodded.

"Then that's good enough for me," Viv replied. "Welcome home. I'm happy you're here. Come in, have a seat. I'll make us some tea. I want to fill you in on the case Amarynth and I solved while you and Karen were gone."

"Karen left, too?" Penny said.

"Oh yes," Viv replied. "It's just been me and Am."

Penny stifled a giggle at the idea of Viv and Am working together. "That had to be something to see."

"You have no idea," Viv said. She led Penny into the living room. Started the water boiling.

They sat down and caught up for a bit before Viv brought Penny a cup of tea.

"Wait," Penny said, a strange and sudden fear gripping her. "Does this have caffeine in it?"

"No," Viv said. "Why?" It was an odd question. Normally Penny was fine with drinking caffeine any time, day or night.

"No reason," Penny replied. *Damn that Gretchen Mills. Getting under my skin. Making me paranoid.*

After Viv had finished filling her in on the arsons, the thoughtography audit, and Amarynth's suspension, Penny expected to be grilled about her trip next. But the inquiry never came.

"Aren't you going to ask me about my trip?" Penny prompted.

Viv shrugged. "I figure if you want to tell me about it, you will. You've always been like that, you know. You keep some secrets from me but never out of malice. You have a good sense of when it's better to share things with other people and when it's better to hide them. I trust you."

"I trust you, too," Penny said and smiled because it was true.

Viv's trust in her made Penny feel much more at ease when she crept off again later. She had a specialized item in hand she'd bartered for among the neighbors, dodging intrusive questions all the while.

"What do you need *that* for?" her neighbor had asked. "I thought tueys weren't allowed to have kids. You're sterilized, aren't you?"

"Of course I am. Don't be daft," Penny had shot back. "I need it for a friend."

"You're a better friend than I am," her neighbor had said, handing over the pregnancy test.

She ran to the desert willow now in the botanical gardens. Kip was there, waiting as always. He was in a familiar form now, his eidolon version that lacked the warmth and rosiness of his Hellish self. He put down his book and met her gaze.

"Kip, I don't know how this happened," Penny said, showing him the test. The display showed two identical lines. Pregnant.

"Well, little one, it seems like you were quite busy in Hell," Kip joked.

"Kip! It's not funny!" she protested. "I need to know the truth."

"What truth is that, little one?" Kip said. "Are you wondering if you're pregnant? Because you clearly are."

"No," Penny said. "I need to know how it happened." She hesitated. "And who the father is."

"Well, what do you think, little one?" Kip prompted her.

"I've given it some thought," Penny said. "And there are a few different possibilities. One is that Gretchen Mills was able to impregnate me... somehow. There was a ritual to even get to Hell that involved a bed. Maybe the ritual got me pregnant. It sounds strange, but honestly, none of the explanations are exactly normal. This shouldn't be possible. And she did seem to know I was pregnant, even before I did."

Kip nodded. "That *is* suspicious. What else?"

"Well, I don't know what was in those syringes that Lord Farr's goons got us with. For all I know, that's why I'm pregnant now. He could have injected me with something that's causing this. Although it does leave the question of why he'd do that, and also I don't imagine you're pregnant, are you?"

Kip shook his head. "No, I'm not pregnant."

"So really that just leaves Charon. I fell asleep on the voyage home. Maybe he took advantage of me when I was sleeping. Hell knows he wanted to," Penny said.

"Hmm," Kip said. "I suppose it's a possibility..."

"But you don't think that's what happened," Penny said.

"No," Kip replied. "You remember what Charon said. He'd have half of Hell to pay if he bedded you without your consent. Even during an interplanar exodus, I doubt Charon would risk it. Not only is he generally a man of his word, but he's also a coward. And I trust his cowardice more than I trust most people's word – and especially more than I trust his."

Penny sighed. "Then what else could it be?"

"Well, there's one more explanation, little one," Kip offered.

"Which is?" Penny prompted.

"It's going to sound stranger to you than the rest of the possibilities since you're more Earthling than Hellion now, but it's the one that makes the most sense to me."

"Seriously, Kip, spill it. I need to know," Penny replied.

"You got atmospherically pregnant," Kip said.

"I'm sorry," Penny said. "What?"

Kip grinned. "Hell is such a fertile place that most reproduction happens incidentally. Beings do engage in physical love that's very similar to how sex happens on Earth, but they don't do it to mate. Sex is simply for pleasure in Hell. Reproduction happens atmospherically."

"So if you walk around in Hell for long enough, there's a chance you'll end up pregnant," Penny said.

"Essentially yes," Kip replied. "If the Styx wills it."

"Oh great," Penny said. "So the Styx knocked me up."

"Sometimes a father is wrapped up into the genetic code of offspring but not always. And yes, when you come of age, you can spontaneously become pregnant," Kip said. "I'm sorry no one ever gave you the birds and bees talk in Hell, little one, but parthenogenesis isn't a miracle there. It's how Hellish babies are made. I would imagine an Earthly sterilization procedure doesn't guard against it."

She thought again of her dream of the python. *Parthenogenesis.* The word rang like a semantic echo.

"There's no way to be sure, of course," Kip concluded. "But it's what I would assume happened."

"Great," Penny said. "I'm the virgin Mary. Wonderful."

Kip laughed.

"I have no idea how I'm going to tell Viv about this," Penny admitted.

"You'll know how when it's time," Kip said.

"You're not just saying that, are you?" Penny challenged him.

Kip shook his head. "No, little one, I believe in you." He smiled. "If I didn't, I wouldn't be chained to this tree now, would I?"

Penny returned to the house to find a giant commotion underway.

Karen had returned. She looked bedraggled, her favorite hoodie in desperate need of a wash. But Viv beamed at her with an intensity that showed that she didn't care how rumpled Karen looked.

"Karen!" Penny said, scooping her shorter partner up into a hug. It felt good to see her, to hold her.

"It's so good to be home," Karen said. "Viv tells me you found what you were looking for."

Penny nodded. "I did. Did you?"

Karen's eyes darted evasively. "Ah, I don't want to get into all of that. It's a long story."

"I have time," Penny said.

"Penny," Viv said sternly, "you of all people should understand that sometimes people need to have their secrets. When Karen wants to tell us what happened, she will."

"Thank you, Viv," Karen replied.

Penny turned from them, embarrassed. It was probably psychosomatic, but she felt the newfound weight of her pregnancy pull on her. She would have to tell them eventually but when? *Not now, not now*, something within her told her. *You will know when.*

"Oh Penny, don't worry," Karen said. "I'm not mad."

Penny turned around. "Oh," she said. "Oh good."

"Anyway," Karen said. "I'm not sure it's much of a good story anyway. I found a free mental health program. Took some classes. I've been working on myself."

"I can tell," Viv said. There was something new about Karen. And Penny, too. They both seemed changed from their trips. It was something like confidence but not quite. Viv couldn't quite place it, but she could sense it was there.

I wonder if this is what Amarynth feels like when she sees connections, Viv thought, before rejecting the idea. There was no way she was thinking like Amarynth. It had been a nice gesture for Am to professionally throw herself on the grenade, so to speak, but at the end of the day, they had nothing in common. That much Viv knew for sure.

Now that her partners were both back, Viv knew what she must do.

Viv dialed Martin's phone number at PsyOps with a flourish, feeling triumphant. "Hey Martin, the team's back together," she said into the receiver.

"That's fantastic news," Martin replied. He hesitated for a moment, creating awkward dead air on the line.

"You still there?" Viv asked.

"Yeah," Martin said. His voice sounded a little off. Very unlike him.

"What's wrong?" Viv said.

"Well, it's nothing wrong so much as... I have other news to give you, and I'm not sure how you're going to take it," Martin said.

"Okay, Martin, you're really freaking me out," Viv said. "And yes, I'm sitting down before you ask. People always ask that. 'Are you sitting down?' Like sitting down renders you emotionally invulnerable or something."

"I think it's so you don't hurt yourself if you pass out," Martin said.

"I know why they say it," Viv snapped. "I just think it's dumb."

Martin didn't respond.

"Out with it," Viv said. "Waiting is worse than any news you could give me."

Martin sighed one of his famously long sighs. "Okay, so with Amarynth on suspension, I was doing some work on her file, and it came up that we didn't have a bioprint on her. No blood typing. No DNA. Nothing."

"Well, that's weird, isn't it?" Viv said. "You registered all three of us when we started working for PsyOps."

"Yeah," Martin said. "That's standard procedure. Not sure why, but somehow Am slipped through the cracks."

"Typical," Viv said. "None of the normal rules seem to apply to her. I guess this wouldn't be any different."

"Anyway," Martin continued, "we got a sample, and when they put her into the database, it came up as questionable."

"Questionable how?" Viv said.

"She shared a lot of key indicators with another agent. It set off a bunch of red flags," Martin said.

"Oh my God, she's a fraud, isn't she? She stole someone's identity. I knew there was something off about her," Viv said.

"No," Martin said. He paused for what felt like an eternity. "I don't know how to tell you this, Viv, so I'm just going to say it. Amarynth is your half-sister. You have the same father."

Viv dropped the phone on the floor.

"You okay, Viv?" Karen said. Viv stared straight ahead, her gaze fixed as it always was whenever she had one of her visions.

Penny scooped the cell phone off the floor. "She's gonna have to call you back, Martin."

When Martin heard the call cut out, he knew what he had to do next. He dialed the number.

"Hey Amarynth," he said.

"Martin," she replied.

Once he had told her, she simply said, "I see. Thank you for telling me."

"You don't sound surprised," Martin said.

"I'm never surprised," Amarynth replied. She breathed the agitation in and breathed it back out. "I've love to be surprised just once."

About the Author

Page Turner is the award-winning author of four books. With a professional background in psychological research and organizational behavioral consulting, Page is best described as a "total nerd." She's been cited as a relationship expert in a variety of media publications including *The Huffington Post*, *Glamour*, *Self*, and *Bustle*.

She clearly can't see the future because she didn't see any of that coming.

Due to her incurable wanderlust, she has lived many places, but these days she calls Dallas home.